GREY'S ANATOMY

Overheard at the Emerald City Bar

GREY'S ANATOMY

Overheard at the Emerald City Bar

NEW YORK

Copyright © 2006 Touchstone Television

Overheard at the Emerald City Bar written by Chris Van Dusen

All rights reserved. No part of this book may be used or reproduced
in any manner whatsoever without the written permission of the Publisher.
Printed in the United States of America. For information
address Hyperion, 77 West 66th Street, New York, New York 10023-6298.

Library of Congress Cataloging-in-Publication Data

ISBN: 1-4013-0882-1

Hyperion books are available for special promotions and premiums.
For details contact Michael Rentas, Assistant Director,
Inventory Operations, Hyperion, 77 West 66th Street, 12th floor,
New York, New York 10023, or call 212-456-0133.

FIRST EDITION

10 9 8 7 6 5 4 3 2 1

GREY'S ANATOMY

Overheard at the Emerald City Bar

Welcome to Emerald City

There's a part of Seattle Grace Hospital where doctors don't use antibiotics or scalpels to save lives. They don't use penicillin. They use tequila. And the lives they're saving are their own. It's called the Emerald City Bar. Okay, so technically, my bar isn't actually part of Seattle Grace. But, you'd never know it from all the doctors who are constantly walking though my door.

Allow me to introduce myself. I'm Joe, owner and chief mixologist of the Emerald City Bar. It's the place right across the street from Seattle Grace. You know, the place where people meet to talk with the people they like . . . and learn to live with the people they don't.

When I decided to open a bar, I scoured Seattle for the perfect location. Capitol Hill had one too many bars already. Belltown was crowded and chock full of tourists. University District was out, too—my bar was *not* going to be a college hangout. No. The perfect place for the Emerald City Bar was directly across the street from Seattle Grace.

Something told me that a bar within walking distance of a place where people work hard would no doubt attract people who play hard. Maybe it was my keen business sense. Or maybe it was because I knew the training programs up at the hospital drove people to drink. Hey, I like to be there for my friends in need.

Interns, nurses, residents, attendings—heck, even patients—all make their liver rounds here in the bar. Some more than others. And by some, I'm talking about the interns. Particularly those first-years. Dude, the first year interns are *always* here. But, I must admit, they make for some quality entertainment.

Now, if you think about it, being a bartender is a lot like being an intern. Okay, not really. But, the job of serving drinks *can* sometimes be a matter of life and death. Seriously. *You* try going a little light on the tequila in an intern's margarita—you'll see what I mean. Those interns come into my bar after long, exhausting days of saving lives and, well, trying to make the least number of errors as possible. Because if those guys make a mistake, somebody ends up dead. Talk about pressure. When they ask for a margarita, *my* life depends on making a good one. And by good, I mean strong.

Of course, there's more to my job than just serving, stirring, straining, and shaking. There's also blending and mixing. Oh, and listening. Ah yes, the listening. I listen to the things that people are afraid to tell their spouses, their shrinks, their mothers. I listen to people at their most vulnerable. All night, I listen. Who's having sex in the on-call room? Which doctor is doing which nurse (or nurses)? Who can't escape their fate as "007"? Who's the slut? The jackass? The slutty jackass? I *listen*. I listen to all the gossip, hear all the rumors, and learn all the secrets.

Here in the Emerald City Bar, I hear about *everything* that happens across the street in that big, shiny, gossipy hospital. And if I don't hear it directly from people in my bar, then I hear it from my best friend, Nurse Debbie. She's the queen of all that goes forward in the name of gossip. I love her.

Okay.

I'm going to stop right here and take this moment to be honest with you. Who the hell am I fooling? Dude. I'm at my breaking point! A man can only take so much! I mean, I think I'm starting to internalize everybody else's problems and that's just really, really not good.

I need to spread the gossip. I need to unleash the rumors. I need to let go of the secrets. I'm sorry, but I *have* to tell someone about Dr. Taylor's drinking problem. I *have* to stop thinking about Nurse Taryn, Nurse Kristi, and Dr. Johnson getting down and dirty in the on-call room last Saturday night when they should have been checking on the patient in room 3214 because that patient WAS CODING!!!!

Okay, wow. See? I feel *so* much better . . . Which . . . brings me to my blog. I decided to create this blog because I can't afford a therapist. I mean, the Emerald City Bar does well, but I think I may be just a little too generous when it comes to letting people keep their running tabs open. This blog is therapy. For me. It keeps me sane. It keeps me healthy. It lets me get everything I hear out of my system and keeps me normal. Really. Mixing drinks would be kinda hard if my hands were in a straitjacket, don't ya think?

This blog is a place for me to get a lot of things off my chest. It's exactly what I need after listening to everybody else's problems. Besides, blogging is fun. I find great pleasure in just letting it all out. No matter who's out there to read it. Okay, I know people tell you that it's not very wise to mix business with pleasure. But when your office chair is a barstool, it's kind of hard not to . . .

ALL ABOUT JOE

NAME:	Joe
AGE:	33
OCCUPATION:	Owner and Chief Mixologist, The Emerald City Bar
HOMETOWN:	Duvall, WA (just outside of Seattle)
FAVORITE DRINK:	Irish Car Bomb
LEAST FAVORITE DRINK:	Low-carb beer
FAVORITE FOOD:	Spicy buffalo wings
LEAST FAVORITE FOOD:	Still thinking about this one.
HOBBIES AND INTERESTS:	Listening to other people's problems, keeping the peace, breaking up fights

over games of pool and darts, babysitting drunk employees of Seattle Grace, controlling the flow of alcohol as well as the remote. I also enjoy movies, television, exercising (in small doses), and just about any outdoor activity.

ABOUT ME: Brilliance pending.

Instant Message Conversation

JoeKnowsBest—logged on at 3:12 a.m.

JoeKnowsBest:	Tell me ur still up.
DebbieDoesGossip:	Of course I am. U know I can't sleep tonight. Way too excited about tomorrow!
JoeKnowsBest:	As you should be . . . Just met two of the newbies.
DebbieDoesGossip:	Great. The night before their first shift? Means I'll have HUNGOVER newbies to deal with tomorrow.
JoeKnowsBest:	Yup. They came in after you all left.
DebbieDoesGossip:	LOL. Some of them needed even more to drink after the intern mixer? Bad sign.
JoeKnowsBest:	Crazy, right? They have no idea.
DebbieDoesGossip:	They never do.
JoeKnowsBest:	All lively and awake. All united by their fear of "The Nazi."
DebbieDoesGossip:	I love it when they see Bailey for the first time.

JoeKnowsBest:	Hehe. Oh—ur gonna love Alex.
DebbieDoesGossip:	Who's that?
JoeKnowsBest:	Slutty frat jackass.
DebbieDoesGossip:	LOL. Can't wait.
JoeKnowsBest:	Promise you'll message me the first time you make him give some dude a rectal.
DebbieDoesGossip:	Promise.
JoeKnowsBest:	OK, I'm off to blog.
DebbieDoesGossip:	Night, Joe.

JoeKnowsBest—logged off at 3:23 a.m.

Summertime

In case you've ever wondered why somebody warned you to stay clear of hospitals during the summer months, I'm going to tell you why: interns. You see, the summer is when new batches of interns begin to invade hospitals across the nation. Yesterday, these kids were doodling in their notebooks while a teacher explained the difference between veins and arteries. Today, they're checking your pulse and taking your blood pressure, all while eagerly awaiting a chance to slice your head open and catch a glimpse of your brain.

Kinda scary, right?

Well, maybe for those of you about to check into a hospital, but not so much for me. I actually *like* when the little tykes start their internships. Probably because I find great pleasure in hearing about all of the stories and scandals that take place at the hospital up the street: Seattle Grace. The summertime may mark the start of higher hospital mortality rates, but it also signals the beginning of a whole new season of good, old-fashioned, dirty, he-said-she-said gossip. And, well, that gossip is what keeps me in business. Really—What better place is there to talk about all of that hospital gossip than the bar around the corner?

Well, folks, come tomorrow morning, a whole new crop of interns will be running amok up at the hospital. And I can already tell that they're going to be a rowdy group, sure to create and participate in lots of drama. Nice. Just the kind I like . . .

Now, I'm used to seeing only familiar faces in my bar the night before a new group of interns begin their first 48-hour shift. There'll be Nurse Debbie and her friends in one corner, a resident or two over there, an attending over here. Never (and I seriously mean *never*) has a first-year intern decided to get totally plastered the night before her first day at Seattle Grace. Until now.

That's right—a cute little blonde named Meredith walked in tonight and took a seat at the bar. She was already pretty tipsy when she got there. Apparently, Meredith had just left Seattle Grace's annual first-year intern mixer. That's when I stopped pouring the shot of tequila she had just ordered. What?? This girl was an *intern*?? About to start work *tomorrow*?? Why on earth was she in my bar asking for shots of tequila *tonight* of all nights??

Maybe Meredith didn't understand the concept of a 48-hour shift. Maybe she hadn't heard about Dr. Bailey, and why they call her "The Nazi." Maybe Meredith didn't care that, the very next morning, she was going to be pushed to her breaking point. Or maybe she did . . . And that's why she was in front of me, demanding those tequila shots. That had to have been it. It was at that point when I decided, yeah, I really like this girl.

Dudes were staring at Meredith the whole night. But only one really got her attention. Some guy in a red shirt with really great . . . hair. I have to admit, he was pretty charming, whoever he was. Ordered a double scotch, single malt. One moment, Meredith and this guy were laughing. And next thing I knew, they were gone. Wonder where those two went. Any guesses?

Later on, *another* first-year came into the bar. This one's name was Alex. Just picture an overgrown frat boy from Iowa and, well, that's Alex. I must admit, the dude entertained me. He was pretty funny—kept flirting with all the nurses. Yeah, a real ladies' man. Alex had me start a tab—which, by the way, he never closed. I think the bastard went home with some nurse he kept eyeballing the whole night. It's all good, though. I have a feeling I'm going to be seeing Alex around here a lot.

But seriously . . . These guys clearly have no idea what's in store for them. Because let me tell you, if they did, they certainly wouldn't have been pounding drinks until the wee hours of the morning. It's sad, really. Amusing—but so, so sad. If the two first-years I met tonight are any indication of how the other newbies are, then this year is going to provide some pretty memorable stories. And you know what? I can't wait! Ah, the summertime. It's just the beginning . . .

48 Hours Later

What's crazier than seeing first year interns in my bar the night before they start their first 48-hour shift? That would be seeing them in my bar the night *after* their first 48-hour shift. You'd think that after two long, grueling days of running labs, administering rectal exams, and SAVING LIVES, the Emerald City Bar wouldn't be your next pit stop. Well, not so for *one* first-year: Alex Karev.

Alex was the flirty frat fool I told you about earlier. And what'd I say—I *knew* I'd be seeing Alex in here a lot. I just didn't expect to see him again so soon. I mean, his shift ends and, like clockwork, he's downing a beer. Alex is a trooper—you gotta love him for that.

Between everything that Alex and Nurse Debbie told me, I think I got a pretty good sense of what's happening up at Seattle Grace. It turns out that the hospital has a new "007"—you know, "License to Kill." Some poor guy named George O'Malley. Well, *somebody* had to be the first one to almost kill a patient. This year, that would be George. You know, I think I'll buy him a drink whenever he decides to come to the Emerald City Bar (and you *know* he's going to come to the Emerald City Bar—*every* intern comes to the Emerald City Bar).

Alex, along with a lot of other people tonight, kept talking about some intern named Izzie. Apparently, she's an ex–lingerie model who had a slight change of heart and decided to become a doctor. Ha! Can you believe that? Oh man, I *have* to meet this one. Izzie Stevens. Traded her sexy Bethany Whisper underwear for a pair of shiny blue Seattle Grace scrubs. Now, that's a new one.

I asked Alex if he happened to run into the other intern I saw in here the night before the big first day . . . Meredith. Well, as it turns out, Alex refers to her as "Nurse Grey." Yeah, he thinks the nickname is a lot funnier than I do. Now that I think about it, something tells me that Alex isn't exactly liked at the hospital. I mean, the guy's a jackass. And I don't feel bad for saying that, because I call him a jackass to his face. He doesn't care.

So, it turns out that Meredith's last name is Grey . . . As in Ellis Grey . . . As in some fancy surgical method named after Ellis Grey. Yep. It's all starting to become clear. Meredith. That cute little blonde girl who was in here two nights ago? Totally bummed about having a famous surgeon as a mother. After all, that's a hell of a lot to live up to. The girl's definitely got some big shoes to fill. And it terrifies her—that's why she was in here the night before her first shift, throwing back shot after shot of tequila. Trust me on this one—I'm a bartender. Along with my flawless ability to pour just the right amount of alcohol into a drink, I come complete with a finely honed sixth sense about people and their issues.

You know, I hope I get to see more of Meredith. Hey, any girl who gets drunk, goes home with a stranger (no matter how charming he is), and then survives 48 nonstop hours of Dr. Bailey's tender loving care is definitely worthy of my friendship. Oh, and Alex better get his sneaky ass back in here to pay his tab. What, does he think I don't notice when he leaves without paying? Jackass.

Words to Live By . . . in German

In college, I minored in German. Don't ask me why. And please don't ask me to speak it. There's a German proverb that goes like this: "Dienst ist Dienst und Schnaps ist Schnaps." Literally, it means: "Work is work and schnapps is schnapps." All right, so I remember it because of the schnapps liquor shout-out—Hey, I'm a bartender, what do you expect? Anyways, I'm sure you've heard of the proverb's English equivalent: "Don't mix business with pleasure."

Now, there's a very good explanation for taking this moment to talk about business and pleasure and proverbs and schnapps . . . all in German, mind you. It's because of one specific customer I had in the bar tonight. He's been to the Emerald City Bar just once, and I remember him for two reasons. One, he ordered a double scotch, single malt, again. And two, HE WAS THE DUDE THAT TOOK MEREDITH HOME LAST WEEK.

Yes—Much of the German language, I forget. But, red-shirt-wearing, great-hair-having, double-scotch-single-malt-ordering customers THAT TAKE HOME FIRST-YEAR INTERNS? I remember every last one of them. And to make it all a little bit juicier—are you ready for this? This dude is an attending up at Seattle Grace. Yes, the same hospital where Meredith works. Yes, that makes him her boss!

It turns out that his name is Dr. Derek Shepherd—emphasis on the whole "Dr." part. At first, he wasn't very talkative. I could tell that something was definitely on his mind. Yeah, maybe the whole attending screwing an intern thing, who knows? But he loosened up a little bit after he finished his drink and ordered another.

Apparently, Dr. Shepherd just moved across the country from New York City. Left a private practice of some sort. One of the first things he asked me about was whether I knew Dr. Preston Burke. Ah, Dr. Burke. He's the surgeon that's all business and no pleasure. I mean, Dr. Burke hasn't really been in the bar too much. Nurse Debbie tells me that he's very focused—on taking

Chief Webber's place when he retires. So that's what I told Dr. Shepherd. I guess it didn't sit too well with him, because he got a little uncomfortable. He just sorta smiled. It couldn't have pissed him off too much because he left a really big tip!

Okay, seriously, the whole mixing business with pleasure thing? It should be avoided at all costs. It's dangerous. It's silly. And, in the end, it will *always* bite you in the ass. Unless you're a bartender. Lucky for me, business and pleasure go hand in hand. But if you happen to be a first year intern about to start the most difficult surgical training program this side of the Mississippi, then you might want to keep the two separate and avoid sleeping with your boss. I'm just sayin' . . .

I wonder what it's like up at the hospital between Meredith and Dr. Shepherd. Was it just a one-night stand? It had to have been. Do people know? Wow, an intern screwing an attending is really, really not good. Man, I wish I remembered how to say "Bad news travels fast" in German. Because that's what happens up at Seattle Grace. Up there, bad news can travel faster than an STD among sexually frustrated, workaholic doctors. Just trust me on that one.

Instant Message Conversation

JoeKnowsBest—logged on at 1:12 a.m.

JoeKnowsBest:	Sooooo . . . Notice anything funny about Meredith Grey and Dr. Shepherd yet?
DebbieDoesGossip:	OK, random. What are you talking about?
JoeKnowsBest:	They had sex the other night.
JoeKnowsBest:	Hello?
JoeKnowsBest:	Deb, u there?
DebbieDoesGossip:	Shepherd's an attending.

JoeKnowsBest:	Yup.
DebbieDoesGossip:	Grey's a first-year intern.
JoeKnowsBest:	Uh huh . . .
DebbieDoesGossip:	So, the notion of them having sex the other night is crazy.
JoeKnowsBest:	Very crazy. But also very true.
DebbieDoesGossip:	Who's your source?
JoeKnowsBest:	ME! I'm my own source! I saw it when—
DebbieDoesGossip:	You saw them having sex? Really, Joe, do you think—
JoeKnowsBest:	NO, I didn't see them having sex. I told you that Meredith was in the bar a few nights ago. She left with some dude in a red shirt. That dude in a red shirt was Dr. Shepherd. He was just here! And *that's* what I saw. Jeez, it's all in my blog, aren't you still reading it???
DebbieDoesGossip:	Slow down. R u SURE it was Dr. Shepherd?
JoeKnowsBest:	OF COURSE I'M SURE. OK, it's last call, I gotta run. You need to learn to trust me.
DebbieDoesGossip:	Never trust a gossip ☺

JoeKnowsBest—logged off at 1:45 a.m.

Three's a Crowd

Tonight was a good night. Nobody stiffed me on tips. Nobody made too big of a mess. I didn't have to kick the frat boys out because of their drunken stupidity. And, most importantly,

I finally met a few interns I've been dying to meet: 007 and Dr. Model. Yes, George and Izzie. They didn't even have to introduce themselves. As soon as I saw them, I knew *exactly* who they were—thanks to Nurse Debbie and her highly accurate descriptions.

I had just finished making a vodka tonic when I looked up and saw a friendly-looking guy across the bar. He was leaning over a table, talking to some nurse. Okay, maybe he wasn't really talking to her. It actually looked more like a really long, rambling stumble of run-on sentence after run-on sentence. Clearly, he was still in "I need to make friends and be nice to everybody at school" mode. Ah, this was George O'Malley.

Lucky for George, a tall, blonde girl soon came to his rescue. She pulled him away from the table and took him up to the bar. I soon noticed that every single guy in the bar turned his head to check this girl out. She was really attractive. The kind of girl you'd expect to see grace the pages of those Bethany Whisper catalogues. Yes, Izzie Stevens.

I told 007 his first drink was on the house. Then I had to promise I'd never call him 007 again. It turns out that Izzie isn't too fond of the whole "Dr. Model" moniker, either. I get it. Anyways, George and Izzie are *a lot* of fun. They each did an Irish Car Bomb within minutes of taking their seats! Good people, I can already tell.

They came to Emerald City tonight to celebrate their new digs . . . Apparently, they're moving in with Meredith. *Three's Company* all over again (I loved that show). I hope Meredith has a big place. I really can't imagine working *and* living with the same people—especially people you just met. I mean, you don't know their habits. You don't know their quirks. You don't know whether they like to have loud, inconsiderate, bed-and-wall-rattling sex until four in the morning every single night for 36 consecutive nights (which reminds me of my college roommate, but hey, that's an entirely different blog entry).

Everybody needs their space. Especially from co-workers. I couldn't imagine living with somebody I work with every day.

Let's see, I could never live with Stan, the guy who delivers all of the Emerald City Bar's alcohol. Or even Carl, my cook—although his buffalo wings *are* the best in Seattle. And, oh man, I could *never, ever,* share a bathroom, let alone a house, with D.J.—one of my regulars who literally lives off of Carl's buffalo wings. Okay, now I'm really happy I've got my own place.

Meredith, Izzie, and George are bound to have some problems. Izzie was already talking about redecorating. George was talking about cleaning. And it didn't take long for them to start whining about the sizes of their rooms. I thought a full-blown argument was about to erupt, so I quickly offered them some more shots. But they didn't hear me. They just kept arguing. Roommates are great, aren't they?

When a leather jacket–clad chick slammed her motorcycle helmet down on my bar, Izzie and George went silent. The heated discussion about the square footage of their new rooms quickly died. The chick was Cristina (again, I immediately knew who it was thanks to Nurse Debbie). Let me tell you, Cristina is a real sweet little kitten of love, joy, and happiness. She's the competitive one—challenged O'Malley to a game of darts as soon as she kicked his ass in a little tequila-shot contest. I think I might love her.

No surprise, Cristina beat George in the darts game. I think they set a new record—fastest darts game ever. George left with Izzie pretty quickly after that. I think he was a little embarrassed. Poor George.

So, Cristina can't believe Meredith let Izzie and O'Malley move into her house, either. We talked for a little while—both of us think the whole roommate thing is a pretty terrible idea. I found out that Meredith's house actually belongs to her mother (you know, the famous one who's traveling).

Oh—you should have seen Cristina's face when some dude rolled up and asked to buy her a drink. I think it was a Psych intern. He was annoying and didn't want to stop talking. Until Cristina told him she was having a one-on-one conversation with me, Joe the Bartender, and, well, three's a crowd. Then she mentioned some woman up at Seattle Grace who bit off a guy's penis. Nice. That shut the dude up. I'll tell you again—I think I might love Cristina.

Competition

Every year, there's a day when hordes of drunken bike messengers decide to race each other across the traffic-filled streets of downtown Seattle, heading straight for the Dead Baby Bar, all for free shots of tequila. It's an insane, no-holds-barred, underground competition held by a bar with a pretty ridiculous (read: stupid) name—hey, the owner and I don't really get along too well . . .

If you're ever in Seattle on "Dead Baby Bike Race Day," you better look both ways before crossing any street. Because, let me tell you, these fools will come out of nowhere. They won't try to dodge you—you have to try to dodge *them*. Last year, my friend Eric was walking down 4th Street on his way to work. He was about to cross the street when, in an instant, he suddenly found himself right in the middle of the race. The next thing Eric saw was a flying bike tire coming directly toward his head. He ducked, but he couldn't avoid the flying bike messenger that quickly followed. Yeah. Eric woke up at Seattle Grace with a pretty bad head injury. We never found out what happened to the messenger.

I'm sure Seattle Grace was inundated with all sorts of bloodied fools today. I didn't even hear from Nurse Debbie—and when I don't hear from Nurse Debbie, I *know* times must be rough up there. She was probably busy sewing legs, arms, and fingers back together. Dealing with guys that had bicycle spokes coming out of their chests. Dudes with serious tire marks and burns across their faces. I'm telling you, this bike race is no joke.

Everybody's favorite intern came into the bar tonight: Alex Karev. Or rather, "Evil Spawn," as he's called around the hospital.

By the way, whoever came up with that one can drink for free—it's seriously the perfect nickname (of course, that's coming from a place of love). I noticed that Alex was even more cocky than usual. I'm used to seeing him flirt with the nurses, talk a big game, and just generally do the evil spawn things that evil spawns do, but tonight he was on a whole different level. To top it off, he actually *paid* for his drinks. And my man *never* pays for his drinks!

Alex kept walking around, telling people to smell him. As in, put your nose up to his body and take one big, long whiff. I politely declined the invitation, but demanded to know his deal. Apparently, he had just assisted in open-heart surgery. The thrill of seeing a live, beating heart made his own beat a little faster. Good for him. Yes, Alex was still in his happy, shiny place . . . flirting, talking, asking people to smell him and *finally* paying for his beer.

Later on (but still pretty early), I sent Alex off in a cab to the Dead Baby Bar. Hey, he wanted to go! To tell you the truth, after the whole "smell me" game, I was sick of dealing with him and his antics. I guess Alex didn't get enough blood, guts, and glory at the hospital, so he wanted to go and see the intoxicated carnage that us Seattleites are used to witnessing on Dead Baby Bike Race Day.

Of course, part of me wanted Alex to go and check out the poorly named Dead Baby Bar for my own selfish reasons. I, just like everybody else, like to keep up with my competition. Now, I mentioned earlier that I'm not exactly B.F.F.'s with Larry, owner of the Dead Baby Bar. This is because Larry is a moron.

Here's a little backstory. Larry and I grew up in the same small town of Duvall, about half an hour northeast of Seattle. It's the kind of town where everybody knows one another (or, at the very least, has heard about one another). Ever since we were little kids, there's been some kind of competition between Larry and me . . . And, of course, our mothers.

When we were three, it was who brought home the superior finger painting from preschool. When we were nine, it was who could assemble his Lego castle the fastest. Seriously. I remember our moms standing over us with a stopwatch. When we got to high school, it was a matter of who had a date to the prom first. Then, upon graduation, it was who got into a better college. Well, we both went to U-Dub. And, after both becoming tired of monotonous 9-to-5 jobs, we opened up bars—across town from each other. At that point, it turned into who was going to be more successful. *That* competition has continued ever since. Yeah, it's been an ongoing contest between Larry and me—and, you guessed it, our mothers—for our entire lives.

So, about ten years ago, Larry and his boys came up with the brilliant idea of having the Dead Baby Bike Race. The way I see it, this race is just an attempt to make his bar (you know, the one with the unfortunate name) more popular . . . all at the expense of others. Yeah. Let's have dozens of guys (and even some girls) hurl their bodies across the streets of Seattle in the name of drinking at Larry's bar. What'd I tell you—he's a moron, right? If I sound bitter, well, I guess I sorta am—he actually beat me in that one Lego castle–building contest!! Hey, I just like a little reassurance that the Emerald City Bar is, in fact, the best bar in town, that's all. That's why Alex went over to the Dead Baby Bar tonight—to tell me that Larry's drinks are watered down and the atmosphere sucks . . .

You know, whether it's inebriated bike messengers racing for free tequila, first-year interns fighting for the best surgical cases, or bar owners struggling to attract more customers—we all compete. And we all want to win, right? I mean, it feels good to win. A little friendly competition never hurt anyone, anyway. Well, unless you compete in things like the Dead Baby Bike Race.

It's All Fun and Games . . .

A lot of you probably think that my job is all fun and games. Maybe that's because my job consists of catering to people who want to do just that—to have fun and, well, to play games. Yes, I have an endless supply of alcohol. Yes, there's always a great tune coming out of the jukebox. Yes, there's a pool table. And a dartboard. And yes, I have a lot of fun serving drinks to all of my friends. Hey, I enjoy bartending! But, like any job, there are definitely moments in the bar when time just seems to stand still . . .

These are the nights that seem to go on forever. When there's only a few people in the bar, ordering the same drink, over and over and over . . . When there's nobody having any fun. When there's nobody playing any games. Well, my friends, tonight happened to be one of those nights.

It was an unbelievably slow night. The exact kind of night that warrants a little solo bartender game I like to call "Pick His Poison." Here's how you play: First, you wait for someone to come into your bar. Hopefully, someone does come into your bar. Then, as the customer approaches, you size him up. That means you look at his clothes. His shoes (the shoes are extremely important). You see if he's wearing a watch. What kind of watch? You notice his hair. His teeth. The way he walks. Okay, no, you're not about to ask him on a date—you're trying to gather all of the minute details about this customer so that you can "Pick His Poison." Fine, maybe I'm getting a little carried away. All you're doing is guessing what drink he's going to order. So it might not seem like a lot of fun to a lot of you. But, like I said, it was a slow night.

I started off doing pretty well for myself. One guy (I'm pretty sure it was that Psych intern, Raj) came in with a buddy. Well, Raj was in the middle of telling some lame joke about nurses. So, I picked a Malibu and Pineapple. And I was correct! Lame drinks for lame folks, right? His friend was wearing one of those cheesy message T-shirts that said, "Come back in a couple of beers." Dude, message T-shirts are as played out as ordering a margarita *without* the salt. So that's exactly what I picked for this cornball. And, what do you know, I was two for two!

A few hours later, after having accurately picked two Rum and Diet Cokes for two sorority girls in matching U-Dub sweatshirts, my man George came in. He looked a little troubled. Even walked up to the bar with his head down. I knew that picking this one was going to be a little trickier.

Now, George has been in my bar a few times. He's one of my rare customers who's constantly changing his drink order. One night, George was spinning himself on a barstool while throwing back shots of tequila. Another night, he was drinking beer over by the dartboard. There was even a night when George asked for a little more rum in his piña colada. Ah yes, I remember making fun of him for ordering that drink. He said it had something to do with escapism. He wanted to imagine being on a tropical island. Surrounded by lots of really pretty women. And yes, they were all drinking piña coladas. George is funny.

Anyways, I figured that because he looked so down, George was in the mood to escape . . . You know, I thought he wanted to be on that tropical island with all the pretty women and piña coladas. So, yeah, that's what I picked . . .

So, I asked George what he wanted to drink. He told me to pick for him. Okay, I love it when this happens—when my customers unknowingly play "Pick His Poison" right along with me! It's like I get bonus points or something. Back to my story. I made George a piña colada and I set it down right in front of him. He sort of stared at it and then looked up at me. I swear to you, in that moment, I thought he was going to cry. George got angry. Really angry. He got all flustered and really red in the face and then tried to say something but ended up slurring all of his words together. He was angry George—but the kind of angry that only George can do.

The dude went off on me! He said my piña colada was an insult to his masculinity and that I was as bad as Izzie and Meredith. Then he kept shouting, "I am not their sister! I am not their sister!" Apparently, George has been having a really hard time with his roommates. They want him to buy tampons! And George can't buy tampons because George is a man (his words). I apologized and told him that I wasn't trying to offend him by sliding a piña colada his way. I tried to make it up to him by pouring a double scotch, single malt. That didn't do any good. George took one sip and immediately spit it out all over my bar. Dude! He was so embarrassed. He bolted soon after. Ah, poor George. Well, at least it was a slow night. It would've been a lot worse if the bar was crowded. Man, if Nurse Debbie was here, the whole hospital would have heard about George's little mishap by noon tomorrow. Who knew a simple little game of "Pick His Poison" would have such disastrous results?

. . . Until Somebody Finds a Picture of You in Your Underwear and Tapes it Up All Over Seattle Grace

Izzie Stevens wasn't just a model. She was a Bethany Whisper model. And now she's a Bethany Whisper model turned doctor. How hot is that? I mean, if you're into that sort of thing. I saw a xeroxed copy of Izzie's ad in the bar tonight, courtesy of that jackass of an intern, Alex Karev. Thanks to him, the entire hospital now knows exactly what's underneath Izzie's pretty blue scrubs.

You can see Izzie's ad for yourself if you have any of this month's national magazines. She's lying across a couch, showing off more than just a pair of skimpy underwear. Alex posted the ad all around Seattle Grace today. He even wanted to put some copies in the bar. But I told him I didn't want anything to do with his sick, twisted little joke. Personally, I think Alex likes Izzie. You know, in the kind of way a little boy pulls a little girl's hair on the playground at recess. Yeah. He's definitely got some growing up to do.

Surprisingly, Miss Bethany Whisper herself came into the bar tonight with George. I guess they're over their little fight about Izzie being a woman who needs tampons and George being a man who won't buy them. George ordered two margaritas. I almost mentioned the whole piña colada incident from a few nights ago, but I held my tongue . . .

Although she would beg to differ, Izzie's even more stunning in person than in some airbrushed magazine spread. And man, she is seriously *pissed* at Alex. I'm talking about an "I wouldn't help you even if you were lying in a ditch on the side of a deserted road" kind of pissed. It's actually pretty great. Apparently, *nobody* likes Evil Spawn Alex. And, after hearing Izzie and George's anti-Alex rant, I'm not so sure I like Alex anymore, either. My love for the dude is seriously fading fast.

Izzie had a rough day, to say the least. Even one of her patients got a look at her Bethany Whisper ad and refused to have her as his doctor. But after another margarita, Izzie seemed to cheer up a bit. She started talking about her boyfriend, Hank. Apparently, he's some hotshot hockey player who's coming to town next week. Izzie doesn't get to see Hank very much because he's always traveling. She was going on and on about the guy, pretty much telling me every detail about their relationship. Intimate details. Too-much-information details. It was weird—almost like Izzie was trying to convince herself that she still liked the guy.

I told Izzie that I'd like to meet this Hank guy. You know, just to make sure he's a decent fellow. That's when she came up with the idea of having a little get-together at their house. Just a few friends—a meet-the-boyfriend kind of thing. We set it for next weekend. I'll bring over a few bottles of liquor and plenty of tequila. It'll be fun.

George noticed Izzie getting a little tipsy and passed me his credit card to close out their tab. You know, George is a really great friend. He's good people. He deserves a good woman in his life. I think I shall start a campaign. A "Get George Laid" campaign. Hey, it's been a little while for my man and the dude is in serious need of some action. So, if you happen to know of a cute, smart single woman in the Seattle area, tell her to come to the Emerald City Bar. I'll be more than happy to introduce her to my man George.

Instant Message Conversation

JoeKnowsBest—logged on at 2:14 p.m.

JoeKnowsBest:	U ready 2 party?
DebbieDoesGossip:	Four infected wounds.
DebbieDoesGossip:	Two groin abscesses.
DebbieDoesGossip:	Two debridements.
DebbieDoesGossip:	Oh, and a case of explosive diarrhea.
DebbieDoesGossip:	I've got my own party going on right here . . .
JoeKnowsBest:	Well aren't you just a bundle of sunshine and joy this afternoon. So, are you going?
DebbieDoesGossip:	Where?
JoeKnowsBest:	To the party!
DebbieDoesGossip:	What party?
JoeKnowsBest:	Ummm . . .
DebbieDoesGossip:	Who's having a party?
DebbieDoesGossip:	Joe?
DebbieDoesGossip:	U there?
DebbieDoesGossip:	Joe? What party?

JoeKnowsBest—logged off at 2:22 p.m.

Party Time

As soon as I graduated from college—many, many years ago—I was convinced that my partying days were over. Long gone were the endless nights of shotgunning beers up at the Sigma Nu house. Taking shot after shot of vodka and tequila even though I had a final exam the next morning? Not anymore. The drinking, the drugs—now all things of the past. It was like I suddenly became an adult. With responsibility. And a job. Okay, I opened up a bar and started bartending, but that's still a job nonetheless.

Sadly, since graduation, I never stepped foot inside another raging frat party ever again. That is, until tonight. Meredith's house (well, Meredith's famous mother's house) was turned into one of the wildest, craziest frat-house parties I've ever had the pleasure of attending. And I loved every minute of it!

The music was loud. The liquor was flowing. The people were drunk. And when I say drunk, I mean the "dancing on tables while swinging your sweater above your head like a helicopter" kind of drunk. I arrived a little late after closing down the bar. As soon as I walked in, Cristina handed me a shot of Jäger. Let me tell you, I am not someone who'll ever turn down a shot of Jäger. One shot of that herbal concoction leads to ten. I can't get enough.

Man, Cristina was wasted. She kept making fun of George because he had apparently spent half the night making Jell-O shots. I noticed that George kept offering them to people, but nobody seemed to want to take them. Poor George. I grabbed one of his watermelon shots and tossed it down my throat—just to make him happy, of course. You know, I don't think he ever let the Jell-O set properly. They were all pretty watery. Anyway, he smiled, hugged me, and then proceeded to call me his best friend. Obviously, Cristina wasn't the only one who was wasted.

Dr. Bailey looked amazing. She went all out. I mean, she got her hair done, a manicure, *and* a pedicure. Even wore a dress. I'm talkin' her Saturday-night's best. I really love Dr. Bailey. I think the bourbon she was drinking the whole night allowed her to let her guard down. I actually caught her laughing and cracking jokes a couple times. At one point, she even made fun of herself after telling O'Malley to get her another glass of bourbon—"Now. Now, now, now!" You know, if you're ever able to crack Dr. Bailey's tough outer shell, you'll see that she's definitely got some softness underneath.

Alex wasn't there. To tell you the truth, I don't think he was ever invited. But that's no surprise. However, Izzie never showed up, either. Can you believe that? Alex is one thing. I mean, the dude is hated by the entire hospital. But Izzie? I would have expected her at her own party. I heard people saying that she was stuck at the hospital. Dude, that sucks. She couldn't even go to her own party because of her job. At least my job *is* my party. It has to be frustrating for these interns who can't seem to have a life outside the hospital. Oh, and I missed Izzie's boyfriend, Hank, too. All George could say was that he was really, really tall.

I only saw Meredith for about three minutes. Then she disappeared. I didn't even get a chance to talk to her! She looked pretty drunk, though. What's funny is that everybody kept talking about some mistake she made at the hospital today. She, like, poked a heart or something. And tomorrow morning, she faces the Chief. Yeah, she was definitely drinking her problems away tonight. But that's what tequila is there for, right?

George seemed pretty upset that Meredith left without saying good-bye to anyone. One minute, he said he saw Meredith walking around with a half-empty bottle of tequila. The next minute, she was gone. I suggested that maybe Meredith went somewhere to sober up. George shook his head and then went to go look for her. Now that I think about it, I hope Meredith is fully functional in the morning. It sounds like this mistake she made has put her career on the line. Hopefully, Chief Webber won't smell the tequila on her breath . . .

I left at about 3 a.m. All in all, I'd say it was a pretty good party. Brought me back to my days of being on the receiving ends of beer bongs and ice luges. Ah, those are some good memories. Memories of yesteryear and, well, now . . . memories of last night.

Couple of the Year

Ladies and gentlemen, we have ourselves a winner. The Couple of the Year Award goes to . . . Dr. Derek Shepherd and Meredith Grey. That's right, it's official. As it turns out, brain surgery isn't McDreamy's only talent and rounds aren't the only thing Meredith's been doing up at the hospital.

Apparently, Nurse Debbie saw Meredith and Derek stumble out of a parked car after the big party last night. Now, you don't climb out of a foggy-windowed, parked car with your clothes falling off of your body unless you just had sex in said parked car. Right? Right. Man, these interns are something else this year!

But wait. It gets better. Meredith and Derek were actually spotted by none other than . . . Dr. Bailey! I know! These two were caught right in the middle of their little horny high-schooler "hey, let's have sex in a parked car" fiasco. This, folks, is the stuff that's going to go down word for word, moment by moment, in the annals of Seattle Grace Hospital history.

Man, I wish I could have seen the look on Dr. Bailey's face when she saw her first-year intern getting all hot and heavy with an attending. Classic! Let me tell you, ever since I saw these two leave my bar together a couple weeks ago (the night before Meredith's first shift, mind you), I've had a sneaking suspicion about them. I'm happy Nurse Debbie confirmed my suspicions today.

I wonder if Meredith ran into Dr. Bailey today at work. Or if Dr. Bailey is going to say anything to Dr. Shepherd. Wait, what am I talking about? Of course Dr. Bailey is going to say something to Dr. Shepherd. This is Bailey we're talking about here. Yeah, I bet she'll have plenty of sweet words for McSteamy. Even if he is technically her boss.

You know, I have another sneaking suspicion: Things are about to get really, really interesting.

Liver Rounds

Alex decided to do his liver rounds tonight with that cute red-headed nurse, Olivia. I've seen them in the bar together before. And Nurse Debbie did say she caught them in a supply closet together once. So, I assume they're more than just drinking buddies. Obviously, Olivia doesn't care that Alex is despised by more than half the hospital. Poor girl. I guess she'll learn the hard way . . .

Not too long after Alex and Olivia left, George came into the bar. Again, looking troubled and a little down. I noticed that he was walking a little strange, almost like a hunchback. When he ordered a piña colada, I knew that George must've been having a pretty rough day.

Apparently, George spent 12 hours holding back a 65-pound tumor on a woman in surgery today. Man, 65 pounds?! My 7-year-old nephew weighs 65 pounds. My childhood dog, Rusty (may he rest in peace), weighed 65 pounds. What? He liked to eat. I can't imagine someone letting a tumor get that big before going to see a doctor. George said the woman just put it off for as long as she could. He asked me if I had ever put anything off. I tried to think. And the only thing I could come up with was one time when I waited until the last possible minute to order more beer for the bar. But seriously, that's nothing compared to waiting until the last possible minute to pay my doctor a visit because of a 65-POUND TUMOR PROTRUDING FROM MY STOMACH.

Anyways. After a couple more drinks, I found out what George has been procrastinating about. It turns out that my man has a big schoolyard crush on Meredith. I must say—I almost slipped! I almost told him about Meredith and McDreamy. But then again, I'm a trained professional. I know better than that.

It seems that George has liked Meredith since day one . . . Ever since he met her at the first-year intern mixer. He even remembers what Meredith was wearing. And of course, George remembers Meredith forgetting his name. Tonight at home,

George brought two cold beers up to Meredith's room. The only problem was . . . Meredith wasn't there! All George saw was an empty bed. He told me he didn't know what that meant. Well, I do. It means that McDreamy's patients aren't the only ones getting their temperatures taken tonight. Of course, I didn't exactly say *that*. Dude, I hope something good happens to George sometime in the near future. Lately I've been feeling really bad for the kid. Oh, and by the way, the "Get George Laid" campaign is still in full effect . . .

I called George a cab. On his way out, he bumped into one of Nurse Debbie's old flames—Dr. Taylor. Hey, even anesthesiologists make liver rounds, too, you know. Deb dated Dr. Taylor for a couple months. He's one of the best anesthesiologists in the state. Too bad he's a cheating, slimeball jerk who totally messed with one of my best friend's minds. The dude plays games! This is what Deb tells me, that's all I'm sayin'. Anyway, between you and me, whenever Taylor comes in for his bourbon, I usually give him the cheap stuff. He doesn't deserve any better.

All right, I've got to get some sleep . . . Been feeling pretty sluggish lately. Another set of liver rounds tomorrow night!

My Head Hurts

Things got a little messy at the bar tonight. I had to break up *two* fights! I'm tired. I have a headache. Needless to say, this is going to be a short post . . .

First, I was making a Tequila Sunrise when, all of a sudden, I heard the highly unpleasant sound of glass breaking. Now, let me tell you, glass breaking is never a good sound to hear. I looked up and—what do you know—two guys that I'd never seen in the bar before were going at it by the pool table. Fights always seem to happen by the pool table. I jumped in the middle of them and, after taking a blow to the head with a pool stick, managed to separate the hooligans.

Later, there was a girl-fight right in the middle of the bar. Over some guy—girl-fights always seem to happen over some guy. Anyway. Lots of hair was pulled. Lipstick smeared. And trashy skirts ripped. Usually, I don't mind a good fingernail-clawing, high-pitched-shrieking girl-fight. Hey, they're pretty entertaining. But tonight, I just wasn't in the mood.

So, I hear that Cristina is sick with the flu. Good to know I'm not the only one who's been feeling like crap lately. What's funny is that Cristina is *still* practicing medicine! Talk about motivation. I don't know about you, but if I was Cristina's patient, I wouldn't feel too comfortable knowing that my doctor might be sicker than me. I just hope she doesn't throw up on anybody . . .

Speaking of which, I almost threw up in my mouth a little bit tonight when I heard the details of Meredith and McDreamy's marathon sexcapades. Yeah. Izzie and George stopped by on their way home with plenty of stories. Stories that included reenactments of loud, pleasurable moans. Courtesy of George. I guess Meredith couldn't keep her McSecret any longer. After all, it was only a matter of time before her roommates found out. Now it's only a matter of time before the whole hospital finds out . . .

Man, I feel like my head is about to explode. Another migraine. I bet it was that damn pool stick I took right between the eyes. Good night.

See George Get a Date

Okay, you can stop sending your girlfriends to my bar in hopes of setting them up with my boy George. By the way, thanks to all three of you who actually did that. Ladies, I'm sorry, but George now seems to be taken. Yes, the "Get George Laid" campaign is now officially over!

George called me from the hospital about an hour ago and told me all about some chick he's taking out on a date tonight. Apparently, he has his eyes set on—who else—a hot nurse. He asked if I had any ideas about what he should do on his date. Dude, it's past 11 o'clock. You'd think he'd have a plan by now. I mean, it's sorta late for dinner and a movie. The Volunteer Park Conservatory is already closed. And it's really not very safe to walk around Kerry Park at this hour.

I told George that he should just ask the psychic who's currently up at the hospital. Yeah, I heard that dude is really freaking out the whole staff. I'm sure *he* would know which spot would allow for George and his date's stars to perfectly align. Now, there's a thought.

Anyway, I suggested that George bring his date by the Emerald City Bar later. He sounded really nervous. Said he hadn't been on a date in a really, really long time. Aw, come on, George doesn't need to worry about a thing. All my man needs to do is bring his date to my bar and I'll make sure they have a good time.

You know, the Emerald City Bar *has* proved to be fertile starting ground for a number of high-profile, match-made-in-heaven relationships. Where do you think Nurse Debbie met Dr. Taylor? They were inseparable for quite a while. Until Deb noticed that every single encounter with Taylor seemed to be complemented with his flask of whisky.

Well, what about Alex and that one nurse? Nah, he dropped her the next day. Hmmm. Oh! Of course—there was Meredith and Dr. Shepherd. Yes, Meredith first laid her eyes on Mc-Dreamy when she sat right over there on barstool number three just a few weeks ago. Ever since, it's been nothing but . . . well . . . secretly meeting in elevators, hiding from Dr. Bailey, and pissing off all of their friends.

Okay, so maybe those aren't the *best* examples of my bar being an ideal jumping-off point for relationships. Maybe George and his date will be the couple that breaks this seemingly neverending string of ill-fated relationships that begin right here in the Emerald City Bar. Who knows? Man, I just can't wait to see George in action tonight. This should be good.

Instant Message Conversation

JoeKnowsBest—logged on at 12:15 a.m.

JoeKnowsBest:	OMG
DebbieDoesGossip:	What? Tell me you didn't run out of tequila again.
JoeKnowsBest:	My friend Tony just came into the bar.
DebbieDoesGossip:	And Tony coming into your bar is important because . . .
JoeKnowsBest:	Because he came in with a friend he's trying to set me up with.
DebbieDoesGossip:	Ugh. I hate it when Tyler does that to me.
JoeKnowsBest:	Deb, for this one little moment, could you try to not make this all about you?
DebbieDoesGossip:	OK—why are you freaking out?
JoeKnowsBest:	Tony's friend's name is Walter. As in Walter. As in someone with a "W." Didn't the psychic tell you I'd meet someone with a "W"?
DebbieDoesGossip:	OMG
JoeKnowsBest:	Exactly. You need to get that psychic's contact information. I have lots to ask him.
DebbieDoesGossip:	But . . . that's confidential.

JoeKnowsBest:	Come on, don't u wanna know when the love of your life is going to show up? You don't want to be wearing projectile vomit–stained scrubs when he does, do you?
DebbieDoesGossip:	It'd just be nice to know that he is, in fact, going to show up. I'll look through the patient files.
JoeKnowsBest:	Oh man—you didn't tell me George was getting Alex's sloppy seconds with his date tonight.
DebbieDoesGossip:	LOL. Olivia?
JoeKnowsBest:	They're in here right now. Doing shots.
DebbieDoesGossip:	I wonder if O'Malley knows about his date's shady past with Dr. Evil Spawn.
JoeKnowsBest:	Why would he? He's not psychic.

JoeKnowsBest—logged off at 12:33 a.m.

See George Get Syphilis

I guess it really is true: At a hospital, the only thing that can spread faster than disease is gossip. And let me tell you, there's plenty of both going around at Seattle Grace today . . .

For starters, there seems to be an outbreak up there. A syphilis outbreak. I hear that three interns, four residents, and six nurses have all got the syph. Sounds like one big happy, diseased family. Call me crazy, but I thought doctors knew the dangers of having unprotected sex. I mean, they're DOCTORS. Isn't there a course they have to take on that sorta stuff before they start OPERATING on you? I just hope I don't need to check into Seattle Grace anytime soon. Watch. Knowing my luck, I'll need to go in because of a little headache and come out with a solid case of VD.

They're calling George "Syph Boy." HAHA. I'm sorry, you can't help but laugh. Come on, you know you want to. Anyway, George is one of the interns who was diagnosed a couple hours ago. I've said it before, I'll say it again: Poor George. The kid probably had his first date in years the other night and he ends up getting a whole lot more than a good-night kiss. Why doesn't anything good ever happen to George? What, did he run over some children in his past life? Kill his parents? Please. Somebody give me a reason why George always ends up getting shafted. Otherwise, it's just plain sad.

Okay, so I *knew* Olivia was no good. Seriously. That skank! I knew the moment I saw that little redheaded hoochie in here a few weeks ago. You know, when she was dating (or, rather, doing) Alex. Wait. Does that mean . . . Gross. Dr. Evil Spawn is diseased, too. That means Alex is probably the one who actually gave George the syph. Now that's just nasty.

A bunch of people are in the bar right now, talking about the present downfall of Seattle Grace. First the syph, then the Chief of Surgery going blind (the two are totally unrelated, by the way). Supposedly, Chief Webber has been acting very strange lately. He's been bumping into carts and rubbing his eyes way too often. Nurse Debbie told me he even dropped some big, fancy surgical instrument while operating not too long ago. Remind me to stay clear of Seattle Grace for a little while.

This is just not good. Not good for George. Not good for the Chief. Not good. But . . . And you knew there was going to be a "but" . . . There *is* something good going on with me right now. Yeah, *me*. Joe the Bartender.

I have a date! This weekend. *His* name is Walter. Strange, right? No, not the fact that the best bartender of the best bar in Seattle happens to be gay. I'm talking about the fact that the psychic from the hospital saw that this was about to happen. He saw someone with a "W." At least, that's what Nurse Debbie told me. Crazy!

My friend Tony introduced us. It's really no big deal. Walter and I decided that dinner this Saturday night would be best. You know, no pressure . . . Just a nice little get-to-know-you-outside-of-my-bar kind of thing. I'm pretty excited. See. Joe gets a date, too. And no—Joe does not get syphilis.

Breaking News

Usually, I blog after work. I come home from a long day of mixing drinks, sit down in front of my computer, and just blog away. Sometimes, when times are slow, I blog directly from the bar. I take advantage of every opportunity that allows me to come to you live from the Emerald City Bar. Well, at this exact moment, I'm not at home. And, times are *definitely* not slow. No. I've decided to blog from a little corner in the backroom of my bar, directly between a stack of beer boxes and broken barstools, because I have big, big news: Derek is married.

Yes, you read correctly. McDouchebag, McAsshat, McAdulterous-Lying-Son-of-a-Bitch is married! McDreamy is dead to me. Okay, maybe I'm overreacting. Maybe there's an explanation for this. Wait a second. There's no explanation. How can anyone explain that he has a wife he forgot to mention?

Well, I guess that's the end of that. Nothin' like the old wife comin' to town to kill the connection. It'd be kinda hard to have a real, fulfilling relationship with somebody that has a wife he's been hiding for a couple months. I mean, you'd think the romance would quickly fizzle after that. Right?

Man, Meredith is sitting out at the bar right now. Her head is in her hands. Shot glasses that once held tequila are lined up in front of her. She looks, well, she looks like she just found out her boyfriend has a wife. She's calling for me. She needs another shot. Gotta run. Damn! McMarried?!

Breaking News—Part Two

I'm back. Had to grab some aspirin—my head is killing me. Since I was back here, I figured I'd give you guys an update . . .

Just had to run some interference for Meredith. Some dude tried to buy her a drink. She wasn't having it. The last thing she needs is some dude trying to get in her pants. I thought Meredith was going to sock the guy in the jaw . . . Feisty Meredith. I kinda dig it.

Oh, by the way, you'll never guess who did manage to throw a mean punch earlier today. My boy O'Malley. And you'll never guess who he whacked . . . Alex! Man, I wish I could've seen *that*! After acting like a jackass to just about everybody and giving half the hospital the syph, Alex finally got what he deserved! What makes the ending to that story so sweet is that O'Malley was the one who put an end to Alex's reign of terror. Good for George. About time.

Wait until Nurse Debbie hears about this one. I should really instant message her. Wait. I think . . . Why, I think it's the champ himself! O'Malley just walked in with Cristina. Don't worry, I'll be right back!

Back from the Dead

Okay, when I said I'd be right back, I meant later that night . . . *Not* after the brilliant docs up at Seattle Grace found my brain aneurysm, killed me, and then brought me back FROM THE FREAKIN' DEAD. That's right, folks. I am now a testament to the modern miracle of medicine. For 45 minutes, I checked out of this world and was bathed in the luminous rays of bright white shiny light. No fights to break up. No glasses to clean. No drunken bastards to stiff me on tips. It was heaven. Literally.

It's called a standstill operation or something like that. To be honest, that medical mumbo jumbo kinda goes over my head. All I know is that they literally froze my body, drained my blood, stopped my heart, clipped my brain aneurysm, and brought me back to life. And now? I'm as good as new, baby. No more of those killer headaches, either.

There I was, lying on an operating table, looking up at Dr. Shepherd. Thinking to myself—this was the dude who's been lying to Meredith for months. Bastard. You don't just forget you have a *wife*. And this was the jerk about to open up my head and operate on my brain? Seriously? Seriously?? All I could think about was the word "McMarried." I think I even said it as I was counting backwards—"Five, four, McMarried, three, two . . ." and then I was out cold.

You know, if Dr. Married McMoron didn't end up saving my life, well, I guess I would have taken this grudge to my grave. But Dr. Shepherd is part of the reason why I'm able to continue this blog and go on living. The McHero saved my life, so I can't really bad-mouth him anymore. Besides, maybe there's more to the story than I currently know. I'm doubtful, but open to the possibility.

I must admit, part of me is glad I survived the surgery just to see what ends up happening between Meredith and Derek. And, of course, between George and Alex. No, the latter couple isn't an item . . . yet. But if my memory serves me correctly (and don't sue me if I'm wrong because, after all, I just did have BRAIN SURGERY), before I collapsed on the floor of my bar, George had just kicked Alex's ass. I know, it's almost as hard to believe as me surviving this whole standstill thing.

The thought of George and Alex wrestling on the ground like two six-year-olds still cracks me up . . . Hey, it's good to know that my sense of humor is still intact. This just *cannot* be good for Alex's rep. I mean, it's gotta be a major blow to that kid's mojo. As for George, well, I owe my life to him. Without any insurance, I had no idea how to pay for this fancy operation. Somehow, George managed to get a privately funded grant to pay for my surgery. That's why, from now on, George drinks for free down at the bar.

Oh—and if my sweet little kitten of joy, Cristina, thinks that I'm gonna just conveniently forget about her pregnancy, she's got another think coming. Sorry, Cristina. McDreamy is a highly skilled brain surgeon so I still seem to remember *everything*.

I hope one thing's for sure—that Cristina doesn't plan to keep the baby. I mean, the thought of Cristina Yang as a mommy makes me shudder. I wonder if Dr. Burke is ever going to find out . . . Only time will tell. For now, her secret is safe with me. And you. Yes, me and rest of the World Wide Web. Luckily, interns are so busy saving lives that they don't have time to surf the Net.

Pretty soon, it'll be back to working at the bar—livin' the dream and watchin' other people live theirs. Clearly, my date with Walter hasn't happened yet. I hope he doesn't think I'm lying when I tell him I didn't show up because of brain surgery. It does sound a little shady, I admit.

Dude, I wish I could've seen Meredith in the bar tonight, tossing those tequila shots back like water. Okay, I know my recovery's important and all, but I really would've liked to have been there to see Meredith and Cristina *hugging*. That's what I heard they were doing . . .

All right, McDreamy told me to be sure to get some rest, so . . . Good night.

Judy Dolls . . . Seriously!?

Had my first date with Walter the other night. I know, I know, I should be home resting after my recent surgery. But a guy can only sit on his couch and watch reruns for so long. I had to get out of the house and get back to my life.

The moment I saw Walter, I apologized for standing him up a few weeks ago. Can you believe it—he actually believed that lamebrain surgery excuse. What a moron! Just kiddin', Walt.

Anyways, the date went extremely well. Walter seems like a really sweet, genuine, honest guy (and, believe me, there's a shortage of that type here in Seattle). Runs a music store over on Pike Street. I actually like the dude . . . Which, let me tell you, is pretty rare. He picked me up around 8 to take me to dinner. As I climbed into his car (actually, his truck), my wallet fell out of my pocket and underneath his seat. That's when the strangest thing happened. I reached to grab my wallet and felt something really odd under there. It felt like . . . plastic. And hair. And . . . what was this, fabric? It was a freakin' Judy Doll! Right there underneath Walter's passenger seat.

Come on, seriously? He owns a Judy Doll? And I really thought he was gonna be the one. At that point, I should've just told Walter to have a good night and gone back inside my house. Actually, I think I started to . . . Until Walter convinced me that the Judy belonged to his little sister. She was in the car earlier that day. Yeah, right. He expected me to believe *that*? That's almost as bad as using brain surgery as an excuse to get out of a date. I started to think about it and, you know, Walter never struck me as the type of guy who liked to play with dolls. I started laughing. So did Walter, despite his embarrassment.

What's funnier is that there was some dude up at Seattle Grace today who had swallowed *ten* of those bad boys. Yeah, apparently Judies were on this guy's breakfast menu . . . right between Wheaties and pancakes. Okay. Let me tell you something. In all my years of owning the bar across the street from Seattle Grace, I've *never* heard anything as crazy as that! You ever see one of those cute little Judy Dolls? My niece, Samantha, has Chinese New Year Judy and Pretty Pop Princess Judy. Next time I see her playing with them, I'm telling you, it's just not gonna be the same.

Alex came into the bar and told me the whole horrific Judy Doll story. I think he got a kick out of it. Speaking of Alex, something's going on with that kid. I immediately knew something was up the moment I saw Alex reach in his pocket after ordering a beer. He was actually going to pay for his drinks? Okay, this is *Alex* I'm talking about here. You know—Evil Spawn, Rat Boy, Judy Doll–dismembering Alex. He's my boy and everything, but the kid has a running tab at my bar that currently totals $930.67. He *doesn't* pay for his drinks . . . Except when he wants people to smell the smell of open-heart surgery on him or when something big is going on. And I *know* he didn't assist in open-heart surgery today.

Anyway, I'm pretty sure it has something to do with Izzie. Yeah, the same girl featured in the underwear ads that Alex posted up all over the hospital. I hope she didn't forgive him that easily. I mean, I hope she made the kid work for it, just a little bit. Alex mentioned Izzie's name a few times tonight. They worked together on some case involving an abused wife and her son. *Something* is up between those two. I'm sure I'll find out what it is soon enough . . .

So, I think I'm going to hang out with Walter next weekend. Hopefully, he'll leave the Judy Doll at home. Man, I'll never look at those things the same way ever again.

Damn—I've gotta go and order some more tequila. Lately, the interns have been going through that stuff like water.

Instant Message Conversation

JoeKnowsBest—logged on at 6:04 p.m.

JoeKnowsBest:	Okay, I can't take it anymore. Cristina and Burke have been having an affair for a couple weeks and she's pregnant with his baby. There. I said it. OK, bye.
DebbieDoesGossip:	I knew it!
JoeKnowsBest:	Oh please, you had no idea about Burktina.
DebbieDoesGossip:	No, I knew you'd never be able to keep a secret.
JoeKnowsBest:	Well . . . duh.

DebbieDoesGossip:	What is up with this year's group of interns? It's like they all had to take "Screwing Your Boss 101" to graduate med school.
JoeKnowsBest:	There's a new breed of intern at Seattle Grace. They like to get wasted the night before their first shifts. They like to sleep with their bosses.
DebbieDoesGossip:	They like to attach headless Judy Dolls to my stapler.
JoeKnowsBest:	LOL. That's great.
DebbieDoesGossip:	Yeah, if you're two.
JoeKnowsBest:	So, any update on the mistress, the wife, and the attending caught in the middle?
DebbieDoesGossip:	Oh, I forgot to tell you! I overheard Addison talking to some patient of hers the other day. Apparently, *she's* the one who cheated on Derek first.
JoeKnowsBest:	Ah, so *she's* the real McSlut. Derek isn't that big of a jerk after all.
DebbieDoesGossip:	Hello? He could've at least had the decency to tell his girlfriend about his wife at *some* point.
JoeKnowsBest:	Stop yelling at me.
DebbieDoesGossip:	That wasn't me yelling. THIS IS ME YELLING.
JoeKnowsBest:	Seriously. This is how you treat your friends that just went through brain surgery?
DebbieDoesGossip:	You're healed. You went on a date the other night.
JoeKnowsBest:	Jealous much?
DebbieDoesGossip:	How'd it go, btw?

JoeKnowsBest: Excellent.

DebbieDoesGossip: And . . .

JoeKnowsBest: And . . . what?

DebbieDoesGossip: What happened?!

JoeKnowsBest: It's a secret ☺

JoeKnowsBest—logged off at 6:29 p.m.

Mother Knows Best

I see my mom pretty often—she lives right up the street from me. Which probably explains just about all of my issues, but that's not really what I want to get into right now. Look, after listening to other people's problems all night, it's nice to have somebody who will listen to mine. Believe it or not, my mom gives good advice. So it goes without saying that I'm pretty close to her.

Apparently, that's *so* not the case for Cristina Yang and Meredith Grey. Those two do not have the same kind of connection with their mothers that I have with mine. I mean, yeah, I have a love-hate relationship with the woman. It just seems that Cristina and Meredith sorta only have the latter.

But I guess things would be different if I grew up having either one of their mothers—a famous world-class surgeon or a . . . well . . . Cristina's mom is just in a class of her own. I can say this because I saw them both tonight. No, they weren't doing shots of tequila in my bar (hey, that's actually another difference between our mothers). I saw Mrs.—rather, Dr.—Grey and Mrs. Yang—rather, Rubenstein—up at Seattle Grace.

Earlier today, Cristina collapsed in the middle of a surgery. She had a complication with her pregnancy and, sadly, lost the baby. As soon as I heard about it, I rushed up to the hospital to visit my girl. Everybody was there—Meredith, George, Izzie, and

Alex. Everybody except Dr. Burke. I wonder if Cristina ever got around to telling him about the baby? That would suck if Dr. Burke had to find out about the baby like this . . .

Cristina's mom soon arrived after flying up from Los Angeles. Well, Beverly Hills, as she reminds people. Let me tell you, Mrs. Rubenstein is a piece of work. When Cristina wakes up, I'm pretty sure the last person she wants to see is her mother. Cristina's *not* gonna be happy . . .

As I was leaving, I heard some woman screaming her head off about cartoons. George informed me that it was Dr. Ellis Grey. No way, in the hospital?! Yep . . . This whole time, Ellis hasn't been traveling, like Meredith said. Instead, she's been suffering from early onset Alzheimer's . . .

Poor, poor Meredith. I told her that the bar is still open . . . She was thankful.

As a matter of fact, I figured that everybody could use a drink. So, we all headed down to my bar. Even Dr. Bailey came along. And guess who else showed up? McDreamy. He didn't talk to Meredith, though . . . They just kept stealing glances at each other. Yes, still very much in love. Which is kinda bad—I mean, Derek's wife is just a quarter of a mile away. Maybe I should get my mom to come over and talk some sense into Meredith . . . I'm sure she'd have plenty of advice. But then again, Meredith doesn't seem to do very well with mothers.

All That Glitters Ain't Gold

Wow. You should've seen Izzie Stevens tonight. She came into the bar dressed like I've never seen her before. All pretty and . . . glittery. Three guys tried to hit on her, but of course, big brother Joe came in with the save.

Now, I know Izzie used to be a model, but . . . just . . . wow. Apparently, those 48-hour shifts that she's been putting into Seattle Grace haven't affected her modeling figure one bit. She looked pretty hot, even I can admit it. I was about to ask who the lucky guy was, but then Alex came in and, well, I immediately knew. You should've seen Izzie's face light up. Then, surprisingly, that's when things got really strange. It was almost as if Alex froze up when he saw how great Izzie looked. He didn't have his game face on, I can tell you that. You know what else? He didn't even hold the door open for Izzie when they left. Once a jackass, always a jackass. What more is there to say?

Just about the same time, there was another storm brewing on the other side of the bar . . . the Derek and Meredith saga appears to continue. They had been arguing for a little while before Meredith stormed out. And Derek left right behind her. Now, Nurse Debbie mentioned something about divorce papers. I bet that's what all the fuss was about—Derek didn't sign them. Idiot!

Man, if I were Derek, I would've signed those papers as soon as Addison handed them over. I'm not sure I care for Addison too much. For one thing, she hasn't even stepped foot in my bar before. That tells me something. Tell me, who works at Seattle Grace without coming to the Emerald City Bar? Addison, that's who. And that's why I don't like her. Maybe she'll prove me wrong one day, but I'd rather she just got her ass back to New York and left my girl Meredith alone.

Yes, McDreamy has quite a decision on his hands. Meredith or Addison? Two beautiful women. One sad, confused guy. Dude. I can't wait to see how this one pans out.

I'm going to visit Cristina again in the morning. Somebody's got to keep her sane while her mother's in town . . .

Instant Message Conversation

JoeKnowsBest—logged on at 9:25 p.m.

| JoeKnowsBest: | Guess who's here. |
| DebbieDoesGossip: | I know it's not McDreamy—he's sitting in the lobby right now. |

JoeKnowsBest:	What?! What's he doing?
DebbieDoesGossip:	It looks like he's . . . thinking? Why? Why do you care?
JoeKnowsBest:	Meredith is making him choose. Either Addison or her. If he comes to the bar, then he's picked Meredith. If he doesn't show up, then . . .
DebbieDoesGossip:	Well, it looks like he's not showing up.
DebbieDoesGossip:	Did you know Addison wears salmon-colored scrubs? Who in their right mind would pick her?
DebbieDoesGossip:	Joe?
DebbieDoesGossip:	U there? Where'd u go?
JoeKnowsBest:	Sorry . . . Had to pour Meredith another shot of tequila. George, Izzie, and your girl Cristina just came in.
JoeKnowsBest:	Salmon-colored scrubs, eh?
DebbieDoesGossip:	Shhh. Addison just walked up to McDreamy.
JoeKnowsBest:	What are they doing?
DebbieDoesGossip:	Talking.
JoeKnowsBest:	What are they talking about?
DebbieDoesGossip:	I don't read lips, Joe.
JoeKnowsBest:	Well, do they look happy? Angry? Sad? Does it look like Addison is about to yank off one of her heels and stab McDreamy in the eye? Dude, this can't be good.

JoeKnowsBest—logged off at 9:43 p.m.

Instant Message Conversation

JoeKnowsBest—logged on at 10:45 p.m.

JoeKnowsBest: OK. It's been over an hour. Is McDreamy still talking to Satan's whore?

DebbieDoesGossip: No, I think they're done talking. Not sure where they went.

JoeKnowsBest: But . . . they went somewhere? Together?

DebbieDoesGossip: Again, not sure.

JoeKnowsBest: Meredith is still demanding shots of tequila.

DebbieDoesGossip: That's kind of pathetic.

JoeKnowsBest: Hey, leave my girl alone.

DebbieDoesGossip: I'm just—Whoa!

JoeKnowsBest: Whoa! What the—Are you watching the news?

DebbieDoesGossip: Everyone's pager is going off. Jesus—a guy with no leg just came into the ER. And . . . here comes his leg.

JoeKnowsBest: Train wreck. Jesus.

JoeKnowsBest—logged off at 10:55 p.m.

Train Wreck

McSteamy finally made his choice. What the hell was he thinking?! The dude picked Addison? The salmon-colored-scrub-wearing surgeon who moonlights as Satan's whore gets the boy? Seriously?!

All right, I just had to get that out. I feel horrible for Meredith. She's got to be heartbroken. You should have seen her in the bar a couple hours ago. She was pretty drunk (tequila, of course). What's worse is that she was called back to the hospital to deal with that disastrous train wreck. Hey, the smell of charred flesh will probably sober her up pretty fast.

McDreamy did manage to show up . . . Only one problem: He was late. Meredith and company had already left. I just assume that, since he was late, he had bad news for my girl. Poor Meredith. This is going to get the whole hospital talking, I'm sure. I'm a little wary about serving McDreamy here in the bar anymore. He's got some explaining to do first . . .

All in all, tonight actually turned out to be a slow night in the bar. All because some redneck tried to outrun a train. He did a pretty good job of clearing the bar out. Man, time just seemed to stand still. I told you, I hate nights like this. They're worse than the nights when my bar is filled with drunken frat boys from U-Dub who shake their ice at me or shatter their shot glasses after ordering Jäger bomb after Jäger bomb and then proceed to fight over games of pool and darts. But I digress . . .

Poor, poor Meredith. Tonight, she's got to be a train wreck herself.

Walking the Walk

Every night, I see two types of people in the bar: those that are able to throw back the six shots of diesel tequila they order, and those that just talk a big game, eventually chickening out. For you non-barhopping folk, that's the same thing as saying there are those who talk the talk and those who walk the walk. Well, my friends, tonight, Alex was definitely the one who threw his tequila back and walked the walk.

My man came in, turned Izzie around, and gave her a kiss so

hot it made the beer tap dry. He used tongue. And lots of it. I want to know if Alex and Izzie are an official couple now. Somebody fill me in. Is this the next Burktina? Personally, I don't think Alex is ready to settle down just yet. Trust me, some of his old Evil Spawn ways are still hidden underneath his tan, blemish-free skin. But who knows? I could be wrong. I hope I am. Seriously—they make a cute couple. And if anybody could tame Alex, it would be Izzie.

I'm glad everybody was there to witness this monumental event. Even Meredith made it, after her very long, extremely exhausting day. I think she's seen better days. Nurse Debbie told me that everybody was talking about Meredith and the doctors Shepherd today. Meredith supposedly had a bit of a breakdown and yelled at a bunch of people. I would've liked to have seen *that*. If you ask me, Meredith needs to keep her head up. I'll find her someone even more McDreamier than McDreamy himself.

It seems that Derek and Addison are really trying to make their marriage work. Good for them. Derek wouldn't really be the guy that Meredith says he is if he wasn't trying. I mean, they were married for 11 years. They said those vows to each other even before the Emerald City Bar existed. They have to at least attempt to save their marriage, right?

Man, I think I'm a little buzzed right now. Hehe, would you look at that . . . Me. Feeling the effects of alcohol. I'm not drunk, I'm just . . . buzzed. It's all Cristina's fault. Apparently, she ran into some money tonight after selling tickets to her surgery on that terodactyl, I mean tumortoma, no—theateroma . . . Okay, whatever, it's some big tumorlike mass in a person's body. She was buying everybody drinks tonight and she forced me to take a couple shots.

Now, normally, I don't drink on the job. But if you're ever fortunate enough to meet Cristina, then you'll understand exactly why I took those shots. Besides, I've always been the type of guy who not only talks the talk, but walks the walk. I had to oblige.

Congratulations

Damn it! The one night I decide to take off to spend a little time
with Walter, I miss the one person I've been dying to meet—Dr.
Addison Forbes Montgomery Shepherd.

Yeah, she apparently came into the bar tonight with Mc-
Dreamy and two of their friends from New York. Man, I would've
loved to see Addison's expensive-ass heels on the floor of my
bar . . . Right next to all the half-eaten peanut shells my customers seem to leave behind. *That* would've been a classic sight.

I heard one of their friends looked like a poor man's McDreamy.
Supposedly, he got pretty drunk. He started shouting and then proceeded to act like a fool as he stormed out. Congratulations, you're
a jackass! Word on the street is that Addison and Derek were
pretty embarrassed. I wonder what all the fuss was about.

Even though I missed *that* fiasco, Walter and I had front-row
seats for another—Cristina and Dr. Burke's date. Actually, I don't
know if you'd call what we saw a *date*. It looked more like a meeting. Or an interview. I'll just say it looked tense. Very, very
tense . . .

I took Walter to Les Panisse, a hot new restaurant downtown.
As I was chowing down on a really good steak, I looked over and
saw Cristina and Burke sitting just a few tables away. I almost
went over and said hello, but something was weird. They weren't
talking! Just kinda looking around. Really, really uncomfortable.

Don't they have anything to talk about outside the operating
room? Their relationship doesn't exactly scream "healthy" to me.
So, I'm a little worried about those two. It seems like they're really trying to do this whole relationship thing, but neither of them
actually knows what they're doing. It's actually pretty hilarious!

As Walter and I were about to leave, some dude keeled over
in his chair. Seriously. He collapsed. It was a good thing that
Cristina and Burke were nearby. They rushed over to Fainting
Dude and started checking his vitals. It was actually pretty sweet,
the way they were working together. Suddenly their "meeting"

was over and their "date" had begun. Congratulations, you guys act like a real couple now!

Oh—I almost forgot . . . Looks like Dr. Nazi is about to be Dr. Mommy. Dr. Bailey is pregnant! In addition to Derek and Addison, Mini-Nazi was apparently the talk of the Emerald City tonight. I'm so happy for Dr. Bailey. Does this mean she's going to be slicing people open with a baby strapped to her chest in the very near future? One can only hope . . . I've got to go order her some flowers. A congratulations is in order.

Iron Chef Wannabe

Allow me to share a little secret fantasy (as well as a recurring dream) of mine. It's pretty simple and straightforward:

I'm in my house and I seem to be playing host at a lavish dinner party. I see all of my closest friends patiently sitting around an elaborately set table. They're eagerly awaiting the seven-course, gourmet meal that I've spent days preparing. Okay, cut to the staff of waiters I've personally hired as they BURST out of my kitchen, holding plates upon plates of food. My guests are elated! Their eyes go wide. Their mouths drop to the floor. A little bit of drool even escapes my friend Tony's mouth. They begin to eat and delight in every last bite. As for me, well, I can do nothing except smile. Having gone all Iron Chef on their asses, I'm extraordinarily proud of my cooking talent and accomplishment.

All right, so this may come as a bit of a surprise to you, but, all my life, I've really just wanted to be able to do one thing: cook. My customers frequently refer to me as a genius when it comes to mixing alcoholic drinks. However, when it comes to preparing food— well, I'm a complete moron. If I knew my way around a kitchen as well as I knew my way around a bar, I feel like all my problems would be solved. I'd be living in a shiny little happy place. It sounds silly, I know, but jeez, electric whisks are just so sexy!

Anyways. I've got a Thanksgiving dinner party at Meredith's coming up and I've decided to bring a pumpkin pie. Oh, and Walter, too. Yes, we've been going out for a couple months now. You know, I *still* tease him about that Judy Doll. Meredith's dinner party is going to be the first time he hangs out with my friends from the hospital. So I'm kinda nervous. Hopefully, he'll get along with everybody.

Man, I've got butterflies in my stomach just thinking about this pumpkin pie. But I've convinced myself that I'm going to do it! I am going to keep on keep keepin' on and make the best freakin' pumpkin pie in the history of all pies that are pumpkin.

Hey, does anybody out there have any good, old-fashioned, drool-inducing recipes for me? Maybe a pumpkin pie your grandmother used to make? I'm talking something really, really tasty and delicious. Let me know . . .

Instant Message Conversation

JoeKnowsBest—logged on at 6:03 p.m.

JoeKnowsBest:	So glad ur back. I missed you, Deb.
DebbieDoesGossip:	Missed you, too, Joe. My poor Uncle Pete. But I think he had a good run. How was the dinner party?
JoeKnowsBest:	Let me just say—Preston is my new hero.
DebbieDoesGossip:	Preston?
JoeKnowsBest:	Oh, you'd know him as Dr. Burke.
DebbieDoesGossip:	Ur on a first-name basis with Dr. Burke?
JoeKnowsBest:	Yeah. We're buds now.
DebbieDoesGossip:	I guess he pretended to like your pumpkin pie or something . . .
JoeKnowsBest:	Hey my pumpkin pie was amazing FYI.

DebbieDoesGossip:	Nice try. I called your house and talked to Walter. I could hear you freaking out in the background. How burnt was it?
JoeKnowsBest:	That was *you* on the phone? Fine. I stopped by the bakery on the way to Meredith's . . .
DebbieDoesGossip:	So what's the deal with "Preston"?
JoeKnowsBest:	He operated . . . on a turkey.
DebbieDoesGossip:	Of course he did. He's Dr. Burke. That's what Dr. Burke does.
JoeKnowsBest:	He turned cooking into a fine art form.
DebbieDoesGossip:	It was that good?
JoeKnowsBest:	I'm sure. I wish I could've stayed to taste it. Had to get down to the bar. Thanksgiving is—
DebbieDoesGossip:	One of your busiest times of the year. I know, Joe.

JoeKnowsBest—logged off at 6:45 p.m.

Sixth Sense

One of my favorite things about being a bartender is the opportunity to meet and greet people from all walks of life. You know, just about every facet of human existence is alive and well inside the confines of a bar. So it should come as no surprise, then, that I possess a finely honed sixth sense about people. I'm pretty much able to know what someone's all about within the first two minutes of meeting him or her. Personally, I think my razor-sharp people instinct is a gift. It's part of the reason why people seem to like me so much.

Okay, so my point is (and I do have a point), Meredith put this sixth sense of mine to work last night at the bar. Some dude rolled up to her and ended up buying her a drink. I lay low for a little while, casually pretending not to listen to their conversation. (Note: I always do this, not because I'm nosy, but because it's my duty to protect my female customers from the countless number of evil, drunk bastards who come into Emerald City looking to take advantage of sweet, innocent girls.)

Well, I witness a few minutes of heavy flirting along with a bunch of Meredith's cute little giggles thrown in for good measure. Soon after, the guy politely excuses himself to the bathroom. That's when Meredith asked what I thought. We deliberated. And, my sixth sense delivered. I didn't see any fancy flowers. I didn't hear any wedding bells. I didn't feel any long-term-relationship kind of vibe. Yes, this guy was all about the one-night stand. And it turned out that Meredith was fine with that! Right now, all she's up for is a little fun. Why not? The poor girl deserves to have a little bit of that, don't you think? I mean, it's not like she's hurting anyone . . .

Anyways, when the guy got back to his seat, Meredith stood up and took his hand. Then they bolted. It was great! I say, good for Meredith. I'm sure I'll hear all about it tomorrow night, when Meredith's back in the bar. Come to think of it, she's been coming in here a lot lately . . .

Gametime

I hear there's a lady up at Seattle Grace that's about to deliver quints. Quints?! That's FIVE babies in one woman! Now, that's just crazy talk. The media has been covering the story nonstop. I guess it's not every day that a woman delivers FIVE babies. Who woulda thought.

All night, journalists and reporters were coming through the bar. Man, they were ordering shot after shot, beer after beer, Jäger bomb after Jäger bomb. And I thought hospital interns could drink. Anyways . . . Because it was so busy, I almost had to postpone my monthly darts tournament. Almost . . .

But not quite. Yes, every month, I host a friendly little game of darts. And, every month, that friendly little game quickly turns into an all-out war among my customers. There's name-calling, trash-talking, and just a general look-at-me-like-that-again-and-I'll-shove-this-dart-in-your-eye kind of intensity. It's pretty great.

Walter got off work early tonight just so he could make the competition. It eventually came down to me and Walter vs. George and Nurse Debbie. Now, Nurse Debbie, of course, is known for throwing bull's-eye after bull's-eye. Surprisingly, George is also pretty good, but tonight, he just wasn't in the zone. He was off his game. Needless to say, George choked and my team was able to bring home the gold.

I talked to George afterwards (who, I might add, has always been a great sport), and I found out that *something* is on that boy's mind. Or, rather, *someone*. "Who! Who?" I demanded that he tell me the name of the girl who basically just caused him to lose the tournament. But good ole George wasn't talking . . . Okay, so it took a few more shots, but he eventually caved . . .

"Meredith!" he said.

Yikes. Bad idea, I told him. These two do not belong together! They're at completely different places in their lives. Not to mention . . . They're roommates!

George said he plans on asking Meredith out on a date. I begged him, please, whatever he does, please do not call it a "date." If anything, it should be casual, right? He said he's sick of playing games and ready to just bite the bullet. Oh boy. This one should be interesting. Clearly, the upside to being a bartender is that everybody tells you everything. But . . . it's also the downside.

Hot Rum and Cold Feet

I don't have much time to post right now because my fingers are literally drenched in melted butter and brown sugar. Yeah. I decided to (attempt) to make hot buttered rum for the holidays this year. So far so good. But I needed a break so I decided to come on here and post a little something about . . . George.

All right, apparently George chickened out on the whole I'm-going-to-ask-Meredith-out-and-nobody-can-tell-me-otherwise thing. Yeah, my man got a severe case of cold feet and didn't end up going through with it. I saw George earlier and he said he couldn't do it because of some major interference by McSteamy (who, by the way, still calls just to check in after my brain surgery so, yes, I will continue to serve him his usual double scotch, single malt).

I don't know what it is, but something tells me this isn't the last I'm going to hear about George's deep-rooted love for Meredith. Who knows, I could be wrong (but I'm usually right about stuff like this).

In case anybody's interested, here's my father's recipe for hot buttered rum (let me know how it turns out for ya):

Combine all of the following ingredients and then add 2 quarts of boiling water:

> *2 cups firmly packed brown sugar*
> *3/4 cup butter*
> *3 sticks cinnamon*
> *6 whole cloves*
> *1/2 teaspoon ground nutmeg*
> *1 pinch salt*

Cook all of that on low for six hours. Next, add 2 cups of rum. Then, serve this bad boy in a warm mug, but only after you top it off with some whipped cream!

The Doctors Shepherd

So there I was, at work . . . standing where I always stand . . . topping off a pitcher of beer for my buddy Jim . . . thinking about which special drink I should make for the New Year . . . just minding my own business, really . . . When I hear a female voice ask for some of my hot buttered rum. I look up, and there, right in front of me, is a woman who I had never seen inside the Emerald City Bar . . . Addison Shepherd. Finally!

Now, at that exact moment, I wasn't absolutely sure that this was THE Addison Shepherd. Heck, appearance-wise, the only thing I knew about Addison was that she had red hair, wore salmon-colored scrubs, and liked to deliver babies in really, really high heels. I had never seen Addison for myself, so when I served her the drink, I didn't know I was serving the human form of pure satanic evil.

All right, maybe I'm being a little hard on the woman, but I can't help it. My loyalty still lies with Meredith at this point. Maybe that will change, or maybe I'll just ship Addison back to Manhattan in one of the old, cardboard beer cases that currently clutter my storage closet. Who knows?

Anyways. A few minutes later, McSteamy waltzes in and my suspicions are confirmed. Yes, that red-haired patron drinking just a few feet away from me was, in fact, Dr. Addison Forbes Montgomery Shepherd. Talk about a mouthful. What woman needs that many letters in her name? I mean, seriously.

Derek took a seat next to Addison and the two started to talk . . . and talk . . . and talk. I tried to listen to what they were saying, but I couldn't hear much. I did, however, catch the name "Meredith" quite a few times. It looked like Addison was getting pretty upset—and Derek did order a few more double scotch, single malts—so I assume their conversation got pretty intense. Thirty minutes passed and Addison finally got up and left. No "Bye." No "Good night." No "Thanks, Joe, your hot buttered rum was great." Nothing! She left without muttering a single word. After sitting alone for a couple minutes, Derek dropped a wad of cash on the table and took off. He looked pretty contemplative.

I wonder how the Dr. Shepherds will be in the morning. After all, the New Year is approaching and it's all about new beginnings and new possibilities. Only time will tell!

Same Drama, Different Year

Okay, here's a question: If, after having brain surgery a few months ago, you suddenly take a tumble down a black-diamond ski slope and end up diving face-first into a snowbank where you hit the head McSteamy operated on in said brain surgery, would you be worried? Thought so. Well, when this little scenario happened to ME (go figure), I was pretty damn worried, too.

Yes, last weekend, Walter and I decided to take a holiday ski trip up to Whistler. I was skiing down this one slope that I've had some experience with when, all of a sudden, my skis crossed each other. Next thing I knew, I was facedown in a snowbank, having a nice, cold meal of . . . well, snow.

But don't worry! I'm fine! Promise. I even went in to see the main man himself, Dr. Shepherd, yesterday. He took a look and said everything was normal. That was a relief. I wouldn't want to go through a second standstill operation. Something tells me two times *might* be pushing my luck.

During my examination, McSteamy and I somehow got into talking about women. It's funny that people always seem to see me as Joe the Bartender, even when I'm outside of the bar, not bartending. Anyway, I managed to ask how Addison was doing— you know, in the kind of casual, nonthreatening way that I ask such questions. McSteamy sorta paused, stared at me, smiled, and was about to answer . . . when Nurse Debbie walked in! She started rambling about some patient in 4312 that needed something I'm unable to pronounce, let alone spell. So, Mc-Dreamy shook my hand and left to spread even more of his McDreaminess.

So now I'm back in the bar, doing what I do best (and still loving every minute of it). I haven't seen Meredith in a while, so I haven't had a chance to catch up with her. I did see George a little bit earlier. He seemed . . . troubled. I passed him a drink and asked what was wrong. But instead of answering, George stood up and propped his leg up on the bar. Utterly confused, I took his drink away from him. That's when George pointed to the bottom of his jeans . . . torn to shreds. He took off his shoe and pointed to his sock . . . holes everywhere. Apparently, Meredith's dog likes to use George's clothes as chew toys. Poor George. But I couldn't (and still can't) stop laughing!

Well, it's about closing time here. Happy New Year!

Two Can Play That Game: Nurse Debbie Stories

It seems that my pal Nurse Debbie has decided to collect some stories about me. Yeah, she's going around asking everybody up at Seattle Grace for a "Joe Story." Like she's trying to write some unauthorized tell-all book about me and my bar . . . What gives, Deb?

Surely things aren't that slow up at Seattle Grace these days. Right? I mean, doesn't Deb have a debridement or abscess to tend to? I wonder what the Chief is gonna say when he finds out Deb is playing investigative reporter instead of, oh, I don't know, saving lives??

Well, anyway, I guess I'll play along and give Deb a taste of her own medicine. If she wants to collect a couple of tidbits about me, then my new mission is to gather a few interesting tales about everybody's favorite nurse.

And here they are . . . Reprinted from the chicken scratch that a few of my best customers left on their cocktail napkins. Ah, Nurse Debbie stories—you know everybody has at least one . . .

MY DEBBIE STORY: BY ALEX KAREV

Wait a minute, you want me to write down a story about . . . who? Dude. You know I can't remember any of the nurses' names. I couldn't even tell you which one changed the bedpan in Colon Dude's room just a few hours ago. What? Why are you looking at me like that? Dude. Nurses? They're all one and the same to me.

(Ed. note: OK, this is me, Joe, here. At this point, I show Alex a picture of Nurse Debbie on my camera phone. And . . . back to scene . . .)

Oh yeah, OK . . . Nurse Debbie. The nurse that drives crack whore Cristina crazy. Yeah, I like Nurse Debbie. She's actually one of the good ones. I think we both have the same sick, twisted sense of humor.

I remember, one time, when Judy Doll–Eating Dude was in the hospital, I was in the on-call room. I had just bought a bunch of Judy Dolls myself. What? It was for a joke, dude, I told you, stop looking at me like that. Anyway, I was trying to twist off one of the dolls' heads when Nurse Debbie opened the door, looking for somebody. She took one look at all the Judy Dolls and started cracking up. I told her to get out. She kept laughing. I think she was laughing at the fact that I was struggling with trying to get that damn head off of that damn doll. Whatever. Those dolls are pretty well made. Debbie left. Still laughing. Screw her.

A couple minutes later, Debbie was back. I was still struggling with that freakin' Judy Doll head. Debbie sat down next to me and grabbed a doll. She held on to Judy's legs and told me to pull off her head. And, well, we started beheading my dolls! She would hold on to the legs and I would yank the heads right off. Simple. Dude. I was impressed. This chick was all right. Hey, if she wore a little makeup and did something with her hair, I'd even . . . well . . . never mind. Look, Joe, is this enough of a Debbie story for you? Now, pour me another drink.

MY DEBBIE STORY: BY MIRANDA BAILEY

Believe it or not, Nurse Debbie was one of the first people I met up at the hospital. Back before I came to be known as "The Nazi." Back before I was even Bailey. I was just an intern. A clueless, struggling intern. I didn't talk to anybody. Didn't smile at anybody. Didn't make friends with anybody. No, it was me against everybody else. And it was Nurse Debbie who changed that attitude of mine . . . Real quick.

She taught me about manners. And respect. Not just for my patients, but for my fellow interns and superiors. Ah yeah, one of the biggest lessons I learned from Nurse Debbie is this: Don't piss off the nurses. Because if you do, they'll have you jumping through, over, and around so many hoops that you'll be crying yourself to sleep and beggin' for your mama. And if you think I'm joking or exaggerating, clearly you've never seen the wrath of a scorned nurse.

It was towards the beginning of my internship when I made the mistake of pissing off Nurse Debbie. All day, we had been working together on a patient about to undergo open-heart surgery. I don't know whether it was a lack of caffeine in my system or what, but I became increasingly cranky. And I remember ordering Nurse Debbie to go and get me some coffee. Yeah. Thought I was a hotshot surgeon. Stupid and ignorant as little Bailey was. I didn't know my role yet. I told her, "Go and get it done."

Well, she got it done, all right. She got me my coffee. And I enjoyed my coffee. Up in the gallery. Watching Nurse Debbie and a bunch of other fools perform open-heart surgery on my patient. But . . . I got my coffee. And Nurse Debbie got her revenge. You know, I didn't see the inside of an OR for a whole month.

Yeah. Had me runnin' around doing scut for weeks. I deserved it, though. So believe me when I tell you this. You'd rather have me slap you upside your head (and I mean three, four times) than make the fatal error of pissing off a nurse.

MY DEBBIE STORY: BY RICHARD WEBBER

Now, the only reason I'm here in your bar right now is because my wife is standing next to me, physically making me write these words across this cocktail napkin. When Adele heard that you were collecting Nurse Debbie stories, she ordered me to get down here and share my thoughts. I'm a damn fool for being here.

I make it a point to stay clear of bars. But Nurse Debbie is one of the most dependable, trustworthy nurses at Seattle Grace. I'm honored to share a story about her. Even if I am sitting in a bar.

You see, Nurse Debbie is like family. While Adele keeps me in check at home, it's Debbie who keeps me in line at work. As a matter of fact, it's Debbie who keeps my wife informed about exactly what I'm doing up here at the hospital. She's the one who calls Adele when I'm stuck in surgery and won't be able to make it home for dinner. She's the one who reminds me about birthdays, holidays . . . wedding anniversaries. OK, Adele wants me to erase that last part but this is all part of my Nurse Debbie story. No. I'm not erasing it, Adele.

I recall the time Nurse Debbie threw me a huge 50th surprise birthday party down in the hospital cafeteria. I think she got the entire hospital to show up. Pulled out all the stops. A great big chocolate cake. Presents. Streamers. Booked a DJ. And, of course, the party hats. You know, those silly little party hats you wore in elementary school? Yes, sir, Debbie even got Dr. Burke to wear one. I've got the pictures. Somewhere. Ah good, Adele says she'll find the pictures and bring them into the bar sometime.

Those were some good times. I'll never forget how surprised I was when I walked into that cafeteria. Yes, Nurse Debbie is certainly one of a kind. I have the utmost respect for her, as well as for the rest of the nurses I interact with every day.

MY DEBBIE STORY: BY ADDISON SHEPHERD

Of course I have a fantastic Nurse Debbie story. It was Nurse Debbie who introduced me to the world of online shopping. It's true. Look, I'm a world-renowned neonatal surgeon. I work all day, every day. And when I'm not working, I'm thinking about working. So I have very little time to do the one thing that makes every woman truly happy. That is, to go shopping.

Back in New York, it was simple. I had no trouble getting to

Bloomingdale's and Saks. Yes! Even during my shift! I'd either walk or catch the subway. Here in Seattle? Entirely. Different. Story. I haven't had time to find any cute little boutiques or even large, designer department stores for that matter. No. I work my shift, then trek through seemingly endless, rough terrain (that's clearly not made for heels, mind you), and finally get to the trailer that my husband insists—*insists*— we make our happy home in. OK, I'm digressing.

Where was I? Nurse Debbie. Right. So, one morning, not too long ago, I was enjoying my morning latte when I saw Nurse Debbie looking at one of the most beautiful pairs of shoes I had ever laid eyes on . . . On her computer! I hurried over to Deb's screen and asked who made them. Well, to make a long story short, Nurse Debbie and I spent a good hour looking at that particular website. $1,600 later, I had two brand-new pairs of exquisitely crafted shoes on their way to me, via the World Wide Web and priority, overnight shipping. How cool was that?

Since then, I've been obsessed with this world of online shopping. It's like one site leads to another great site which leads to an even better site. Technology is an amazing thing. And you know, I wouldn't have even thought to stop and think about using the Internet to shop if it hadn't been for Nurse Debbie. It's really helped me out so much. It lifts my mood. Strengthens my spirit. But most importantly, online shopping allows me to relax. My husband isn't so happy about this newly formed habit of mine, but go figure. I just blame it on Nurse Debbie. Love her!

MY DEBBIE STORY: BY MEREDITH GREY

Joe. I came here to talk and all you want is a story about Nurse Debbie? Seriously? Seriously! Okay, wow, you're serious. You and Nurse Debbie are actually collecting stories about each other.

I can't stop smiling. What's funny is that everything always seems to come full circle for me. Isn't that weird? Even this, right here—you asking me for a Nurse Debbie memory—I'm telling you, full circle. You see, it was Nurse Debbie who actually told me that your bar existed in the first place. And, it was here in your bar where I met Derek. Now I'm here in your bar attempting to forget about my problems (that have to do with Derek) and . . . writing a story about Nurse Debbie. See, what'd I tell you? Full circle.

Yes, I met Debbie even before I officially started the program. I had just finished filling out a bunch of paperwork up at the hospital. I wanted to get an idea of what my life was really about to become, where I was basically going to be living for the next couple of years, so . . . I gave myself a little tour. Pretty soon, I found myself staring at a group of interns eating together in the cafeteria. They were all laughing, talking about patients—looking like they were actually having fun. Well, they looked exhausted, but still, I could tell that they were enjoying one another's company.

Anyway, I just stared and stared and stared. That was gonna be me in a few days, I thought. It was all starting to sink in, really. Then, in the middle of it all, I heard a woman's voice say to me, "And you'll even drink at the bar across the street with them every night, too." I looked up and it was Nurse Debbie. I smiled at her. She then continued to tell me a few funny intern stories as well as everything there is to know about the Emerald City Bar. She told me not to worry about all of the stress that was about to invade every facet of my existence . . . "You'll always have the Emerald City Bar," she said.

So, Nurse Debbie was kind of my official welcome to Seattle Grace, and, well, to Joe's bar. I wonder if she remembers this story. I've got to ask her. Okay, Joe, so in the spirit of everything coming full circle for me . . . Could you pour me another shot of tequila??

MY DEBBIE STORY: BY DEREK SHEPHERD

It seems like Nurse Debbie and I have been working side by side ever since I moved to Seattle. We've performed numerous operations with each other. Even shared a few laughs. Not too many people know this (and I'm sure many would beg to differ), but

Nurse Debbie really has a great sense of humor. That is, if you find sarcasm funny. And I do. I mean it—I find sarcasm hilarious.

Anyway, one of the most vivid memories I have of Nurse Debbie occurred just a few weeks after I moved here. I was reading a Seattle magazine, trying to figure out what I was going to do the following day that I had off. I still didn't know my way around the city very well. And I still hadn't seen any of the places or famous landmarks that are found in Seattle. It was Nurse Debbie who, while flipping through a stack of patient charts, casually mentioned the ferryboats (you know, in the kind of way that Nurse Debbie casually mentions everything).

Ah, yes, the ferryboats. I had lived in Seattle for six weeks, and still I had no idea that I had a fleet of ferryboats at my disposal. Nurse Debbie told me all about them. I was immediately intrigued and fascinated by these so-called ferryboats. Later on that day, she handed me a piece of paper. It was a full day-trip itinerary. And it was fantastic. It included just about all of the Seattle sights as well as, well, of course, a few rides on the ferryboats.

Since then, I've found that taking a ferryboat across to, say, Bainbridge, keeps me sane. I'm serious. I would start out every single day with a ride on a ferryboat if I could. They're relaxing. Calming. Just me, a cup of coffee, the wind, the water, and . . . the ferryboat. Ah, Nurse Debbie, I thank you. My life in Seattle definitely wouldn't be complete without the ferryboats.

MY DEBBIE STORY: BY CRISTINA YANG

This is stupid. This is a waste of time. I'm pretending to write down a story about that mean old witch of a nurse, Nurse Debbie or whoever . . . Joe isn't looking right now so I'm just writing and writing in order for it to look like I'm actually coming up with a Nurse Debbie story when, really, I'm just trying to fill space with an incoherent train of thought so I can be done with this immature little "game" of theirs and order a drink. I mean, come on, this is a bar—

Okay, I was caught. Izzie, of course, saw what I was writing and told Joe on me. Tattletale. What are we, in the third grade? So I lied. Big deal. Liar, liar, pants on fire and all that crap.

All right, so I guess I really have to write down a Nurse Debbie story because Joe is refusing to serve me until I do.

So. Here goes. Okay. Nurse Debbie. Um.

Okay, you know what? This just isn't something Cristina does. I don't do hugs. I don't do sweet little gestures of gratitude. I don't admit when I'm wrong. And I certainly don't do Nurse Debbie stories.

Maybe I should tell you about the time Nurse Debbie assigned me an afternoon that was chock full of rectals? Or, oh, dude, this is a good one—the time she made me clean up vomit that was left by some patient's brother (yeah, the brother—not even the actual patient) who ran around uncontrollably . . . throwing up. Yeah, those are some good Nurse Debbie stories.

But bad Cristina memories. Thank you, Joe, for making me relive all that. Are you satisfied? I'm done. You know what? Don't even serve me a drink. I was just leaving.

MY DEBBIE STORY: BY PRESTON BURKE

Joe, I've got a great story about Nurse Debbie to share with you on this fine, fine evening. I can sum it up in one simple word: paella. Now, if you don't know, paella is an exquisite rice dish that I particularly like to make on Sunday nights. Especially during the summer. Joe, I'm telling you, there's nothing like it.

So, not too long ago, I was studying the board when I smelled something that I'm not used to smelling in the hallways of Seattle Grace. It was a complex, toasty, almost spicy smell . . . It was paella.

I turned around to follow that smell. I saw Nurse Debbie standing over the nurse's station eating out of a plastic container. When I approached her, she immediately told me that she doesn't share food. I don't, either. I asked her what she was eating, and, well, yes—it was paella.

Apparently, Nurse Debbie had made paella the night before. Those were her leftovers. We talked for a good 15 minutes about paella and the particular recipe she used. It was a bit different than mine. She actually threw a bit of cinnamon into the mix. Cinnamon? Seriously? I told her that she really shouldn't use too many additional spices because it's important not to overpower the taste of the rice and saffron already found in the paella.

At that point, Nurse Debbie challenged me to a paella-making contest. At first, I was a bit hesitant. I didn't have anything to prove. Everyone that tasted my paella fell in love with my paella. But Nurse Debbie persisted. She challenged me flat out, in my OR. In front of interns, other nurses—yes, in front of the entire staff. I had to accept Nurse Debbie's challenge.

We each brought our paella dishes into the hospital the next day. We set up a blind taste test with five subjects: Dr. Bailey, Nurse Boki, Izzie Stevens, Chief Webber, and George O'Malley. The five of them were told to try each dish and decide which one was better . . .

Dr. Bailey chose mine. Dr. Bailey, of course, is my girl. Nurse Boki chose Debbie's. Of course she did. Next, Izzie Stevens picked Debbie's dish as well. I didn't sweat it. Chief Webber, a man of finer taste, enjoyed my paella the best. Finally, it was down to O'Malley. O'Malley. The one I honored by choosing to scrub in with me during his very first shift. I thought he was my guy. Well, I was wrong about him then, and, as it turned out, I was *still* wrong about him. O'Malley picked Nurse Debbie's paella!

I can admit it. I lost. I lost the paella competition. Let me tell you this, though. Since then, I haven't changed my paella recipe one bit. I mean, who puts cinnamon in paella? Nurse Debbie does, I suppose. But I'm not bitter. I love my paella. Cristina loves my paella. And nobody else needs to love my paella.

MY DEBBIE STORY: BY GEORGE O'MALLEY

Okay, so I know that a lot of people around here have mixed feelings about Nurse Debbie. I mean, there are those that really enjoy working with her and scrubbing in on surgeries with her . . . And then there are those that don't think she's very nice. Personally, I think Nurse Debbie is one of the sweetest, most genuine, down-to-earth people I've ever met.

So, yeah, she gets a little cranky. But so does everybody else. And yes, Nurse Debbie has been known to assign lots and lots of scut work to interns she doesn't particularly like. Like Cristina. Oh man, she hates Cristina. With a passion . . .

Like, for example, if Cristina had taken a nasty tumble down three, or even four or five, flights of stairs and there was nobody else around to help her stand up or check her injuries except for Nurse Debbie—well, you know, I don't think Nurse Debbie would even extend a finger to help Cristina get up. No, well, okay, I don't actually know that because Cristina has never taken a nasty tumble down three or four (or even, you know, five) flights of stairs, but if that were to really happen, then I could see Nurse Debbie just passing Cristina by on her way to deliver labs down on the second floor.

But back to what I was saying. About Nurse Debbie actually being a really nice person. Did you know that every year around Christmas she organizes a group of kids from her nephew's high school to come to the hospital and sing carols to patients? Yeah. She'd probably be furious at me for telling you that, because she doesn't really want anybody to know that she's the one who actually organizes the whole thing, because she doesn't really want people to think she's soft, because she's really a lot like Dr. Bailey in that respect, but . . .

Well, I never would've known that Nurse Debbie coordinates all of that every year if her nephew didn't tell me. Yeah, I was talking with Sam—that's her nephew—when his high school group was here this past year and he's the one who told me his Aunt Debbie has been the organizer for the past four years.

See? Nurse Debbie is a really sweet woman. And caring. Oh, and coordinated. Very coordinated, as a matter of fact. I know this because she's a kick-ass darts player. So there you go, Joe. That's my Nurse Debbie story.

MY DEBBIE STORY: BY IZZIE STEVENS

I'm sitting here, writing this down across a dirty cocktail napkin that George just spilt his beer on—seriously, George, learn some freakin' coordination—and I seriously can't think of a single Nurse Debbie story. I mean, I know who she is. She's . . . Nurse Debbie. But I honestly don't think we've ever really talked to each other. Is that weird? It's kinda weird.

I mean, yeah, we've met before. Sorta. Well, it was more like I said, "Hi, I'm Izzie Stevens," and then Nurse Debbie just kinda grinned and handed over a bunch of patient charts. So I guess that counts as an introduction, or actually more like a meeting, not really a conversation, but—fine, it's whatever you want to call it. Nurse Debbie, yes, I know her.

Okay, don't think I'm a bad person or anything just because I don't really have a Nurse Debbie story. I'm really not a bad person. And I do—I honestly, sincerely do—know all of the nurses' names. I do! Hey, I brought in homemade cupcakes at Christmas and every last one of those nurses enjoyed them.

Anyway, it's not like Alex had some great Nurse Debbie memory. Or Cristina, for that matter. Seriously, what could Cristina possibly say about Nurse Debbie? Everyone knows they don't really get along. Not that I'm comparing myself to Alex or Cristina because we are really, really different. I'm actually nice and cordial.

I guess now isn't exactly the best time for me to think of a story about Nurse Debbie. My mind is cluttered with all sorts of stuff. So I can't think of one Nurse Debbie story! What's the big deal? Oh, now I sound like Alex and Cristina. Okay, I feel bad about this. Really, really bad. I feel the kind of bad that you get when you feel it deep, deep in your stomach and your knees go kinda weak.

Nurse Debbie, I'm sorry. I'm truly sorry. I am going to figure out a way to make this up to you. Man, I suck.

You Are What You Eat

Okay, I've witnessed *a lot* of people do *a lot* of crazy things in my bar. I'm talking *strange* things. Foolish, idiotic things. Things I can't repeat right now (hey, my mom reads this blog). I've noticed that these kinds of senseless events are usually the result of either a) one too many shots of Jäger; b) someone crying out for a little attention; or c) some poor sap losing a bet.

However, nothing I've seen in my bar quite compares to the story I just heard from Alex. My man was just in here, telling me about some dude up at Seattle Grace who ate an *entire* novel. All right, setting your friend's hair ablaze after attempting a vodka-induced breath of fire is ONE thing. But eating a novel? Your *own* novel? That, you know, you actually wrote? Well, that's an entirely different, much crazier story. Right?

Let's just say Alex needed several stiff drinks tonight after dealing with Book-Eating Guy. Now, I would've charged Alex (thereby adding to a tab that now stands at $1,072.36), but I sorta felt bad for him. He couldn't stop rambling on and on about his medical boards. I had no idea he had to retake them. He should find out the results any day now, so naturally, the kid is pretty nervous. Wow—I can't imagine life around here without Alex. I know he can be a total jackass, but I've got mad love for the guy.

Alex also gave me quite an earful about some patient named Denny Duquette. Apparently, this guy Denny made quite a connection with Izzie. Isn't Izzie *always* getting attached to her patients? Anyhow, Alex thinks Denny is a pretty good guy—which surprised me . . . in a good way. Normally, if some dude was flirting with Izzie, then Alex and I would be brainstorming a bunch of clever, insulting nicknames. But this time, Alex seemed to like the guy . . . Which makes me think that, in his heart, Alex really wants what's best for Izzie . . . Which makes me want Alex and Izzie to end up together even more.

Oh—I just remembered that I've still got to clean up the mess that Meredith's dog made in my bar tonight. Yeah, that's right.

The dog was actually in my bar. He's cute, in a terrifying, I'll-obliterate-anything-in-sight kind of way. It's true! That little devil-dog destroyed one of my barstools! Took the whole leg off. Really. Freakin'. Annoying.

Initially, I wasn't going to let the little guy into the bar, but Meredith pleaded—she needed a drink and she couldn't leave Doc at home with George and Izzie. I guess the dog doesn't really get along very well with the roommates. At that point, I should've known not to let him anywhere near me. But I did. Who knew he was going to eat a barstool for dinner?

Anyways—Meredith seemed to be in good spirits. We talked for a little bit. I told her I saw Addison and Derek together in the bar before the New Year, but she seemed to be unfazed. I wish I had heard what Derek told Addison that night, but I didn't—they were across the bar, and you *know* how noisy my bar can get. Meredith didn't seem to really react to any mention of Mc-Steamy, so I backed off. It only makes me wonder . . . Is Meredith finally over Derek?

I wish I had more time to ponder that question, but online shopping awaits. Who knew there were so many different types of barstools—aluminum, wooden, swivel, stationary . . .

Super Brawl 2006

Sometimes, it's drunk frat boy #1 vs. drunk frat boy #2 jumping across the pool table. Other times, it's girlfriend vs. slutty mistress wrestling in the parking lot. And still, there are times when it's bar regular vs. out-of-towner duking it out at my monthly darts tournament. Well, folks, tonight it was intern vs. nurse . . .

Yes, Cristina, Meredith, and Alex just went head-to-head with a whole lotta angry nurses. Apparently, the nurses are facing a bunch of short-staffing problems up at Seattle Grace. At least, that's what Nurse Debbie tells me. So they're striking. And they're striking *hard*. Seriously. I'm talking a homemade-sign-raising, war-cry-yelling, projectile-throwing, don't-cross-the-picket-line-unless-you-want-to-lose-an-eye *strike*. Man, those nurses do not mess around.

Tonight, it all started when this one nurse "accidentally" spilled her drink all over Cristina. Okay. Let me fill you in on a little something: You *don't* want to "accidentally" spill a drink all over Cristina. Because if you do (and just . . . *don't*), Cristina will have you eating the same glass that held the drink that is now spilt all over Cristina. Get the point?

Cristina was ready to throw down. You should've seen the death rays that shot out of her eyes. Classic! Alex and Meredith quickly stood up behind their girl, although they were clearly outnumbered. Even so, I firmly believe that the Cristina-Alex-Meredith combo could have kicked some serious nurse ass. Okay, I admit, part of me wanted to see it happen. But my better half told me that a bar brawl just wasn't what the Emerald City Bar needed tonight.

Anyway. On to more important things—WE'RE GOING TO THE SUPER BOWL! Can you believe it? Finally, my team gets a little recognition. And, in honor of this monumental occasion, I'm hosting a huge Super Bowl party down at the bar. If you're in town, feel free to stop by. I'm going all out for this one—food and drink specials the whole night.

Hopefully, all of my favorite interns will be able to stop by the party. That is, if they're not in the middle of some bar brawl or moping around, talking about how much they miss Bailey—who should be due pretty soon, right? I, for one, cannot wait to see a little Bailey running around here. Well, not *here* as in my bar, but *here* as in Seattle Grace. How cute would that be?

At least I know Alex will show up. My man just passed his boards, so he's in pretty high spirits. Earlier tonight, he was talking about Izzie and how he royally messed up *that* whole situation. I think he should do something nice for the girl. And contrary to popular belief, I do believe Alex is, in fact, capable of doing something nice.

Hawks all the way!

@#)$($#*#!!!!

Sorry it's taken me a few days to post. I've just been a little down— you know, with the Hawks losing and all. I hate to lose. Losing sucks. Losing is for the weak. And that's what I am right now. A loser.

Maybe I'm being a little too hard on myself, but I was really pulling for the Hawks to win. I mean, I actually got down on my knees and prayed for that Lombardi Trophy. It's all just so very disappointing. Does anybody else feel my pain? Man, the last time I felt this miserable was when my liquor license expired and I had to shut down the bar for a month. Now, those were some rough times.

Look, the Hawks were robbed. And I'm pissed. And depressed. But, I suppose things could be worse. I mean, I could be trapped in a hospital operating room with my hand touching live, unexploded ammunition that's lodged in some random dude's body. Yeah, that actually makes my little rant about the Super Bowl seem a little petty.

I've been watching the news reports all day and I've never seen anything like this. I'm worried. It's pandemonium! The bomb squad is up at the hospital right now. Yes, the bomb squad. Right across the street. Okay, now I'm officially freaked out.

Hmmm, you know, maybe I should shut down the bar . . . Nah, I've always been an optimistic person. Everything's going to be just fine, right? That bomb isn't going to go off, right? Meredith still has to get back with McDreamy. Addison still has to move back to New York. Cristina and Dr. Burke still have to work out their relationship issues. George still has to meet the right girl.

Alex and Izzie still have to declare their love for each other. And
Dr. Bailey still has to have her baby . . . Right? Right! Right?!?!
Why aren't any of them answering their cell phones?

Half-Day

After careful consideration, I decided to close down the bar early
tonight and give myself a little half-day. I did this for two reasons.
One, somebody told me Dr. Bailey had her baby. Needless to say,
I was itching to get up there and visit her at the hospital. As it
turned out . . . it's a boy!

Let me tell you, he's a real cutie. At least *I* think so. Cristina
disagrees. Yeah, leave it to Yang to say it's a fact that all babies are
ugly until they're three months old. That's what she told me when
I ran into her outside of Dr. Bailey's room. I just laughed. Dude.
You gotta just laugh at Cristina sometimes.

William George Bailey Jones. You know, he kinda makes me
want to have one of my very own. I haven't quite figured out exactly how to make that happen just yet, but . . . I'm working on it.
It's so sweet that Dr. Bailey named her son after O'Malley. Apparently, it would have been even more difficult for Bailey to
have her baby if George wasn't around to act as coach. I always
knew it. O'Malley's a champ.

So, I wonder if the little guy is gonna have any of the attitude
that's passed down from one generation to the next in the Bailey
clan. Nah, I bet he's gonna be sweet, just like his dad, Tucker.
Now, talk about a nice guy. Tucker always makes it a point to talk
to me and find out how I'm doing. Good people, I'll tell ya that.

But back to what I was saying—the second reason that convinced me to close down early tonight was because A BOMB
WENT OFF AT SEATTLE GRACE. Um, yeah, I took that as a
surefire sign to definitely close early. Can you really blame me?

I noticed it was getting quieter and quieter as the night

progressed and the reality of a Code Black actually began to set in. It just wasn't a fun atmosphere. I mean, it's kind of hard to laugh and joke when a bunch of friends are in grave danger of losing their lives just across the street. Fewer and fewer people wanted to drink away their problems. Trust me, that's a first around here.

I actually heard the bomb go off. I swear it shook the walls of the bar. It was terrifying, because you knew—you just *knew*— that somebody was going to be hurt. Or, even worse, dead. Come on, those are my people up there. Friends that I'd do anything for. And to think of a bomb exploding around them? Well, really scary stuff, folks.

I kicked the last few customers out and rushed over to the hospital. The place was a madhouse. Part of the hospital was blocked off—the bomb destroyed an entire operating floor. I soon found out that it was the guy from the bomb squad who lost his life. Dylan. Everybody else was apparently fine. Chief Webber told me Meredith was a little banged up, but not seriously injured.

Overall, it was a pretty intense night. As I was leaving, Alex tracked me down and asked if the bar was open. Said he was in desperate need of a drink. He didn't have any cash, but if I could spot him, then he'd be eternally grateful. Okay, dude, seriously? I just shook my head. Ass. Some things will never change.

Rewind

I think it's safe to say that sometimes we all do things that we know we shouldn't be doing. Whatever the reason—whether it's because we're selfish or because it's the result of one too many shots of tequila—we all make horrible, painful, embarrassing, wish-my-life-came-with-a-Tivo-so-I-can-press-rewind mistakes.

Just last week, for example, I kept pouring drink after drink for an already very drunk Alex. I shouldn't have served him that seventh beer, but I did anyway. Reason? I'm selfish. Hey, at least

I can admit it. Besides, I wanted him to keep talking about Izzie Stevens. Seriously—it's like the dude is in love with her. OK, so that may come as a surprise to many of you, but my boy Alex was talking like he worships the ground that Dr. Bethany Whisper herself walks on. Finally. I think they're gonna make a great couple.

Take Meredith as another example. Now, this is a girl that's definitely made her fair share of mistakes. Mistakes she can't take back. Can't rewind. Can't do anything about now . . .

Just last night, Meredith was in the bar, talking about how she just saw her father for the first time in 20 years. Apparently, she had just come back from his house. Poor Meredith—she was just so sad and looked really, really down. She told me the whole thing was a mistake—she never should've gone to her dad's house in the first place (of course, she told me this after a couple more drinks).

Soon, some dude rolled into the bar and ordered a double scotch, single malt. Sounds familiar, right? That's the same drink that McDreamy orders. Only this time, the dude ordering it definitely wasn't McDreamy.

Come to find out, this dude was Mark. As in Derek's former best friend. As in the guy who Addison slept with back in New York. As in the guy that came to Seattle Grace to bring Addison home!

Yeah. He sat down right next to Meredith. Just the two of them. The dirty mistresses. A scotch in front of him, an empty vodka tonic (about to be a shot of tequila) in front of her. I'm telling you, what a pair.

Mark had told Addison to meet him in the bar after work—which, I knew, was not going to happen. I mean, come on. What woman in her right mind would choose a cocky, arrogant plastic surgeon with facial hair that's just a little bit too manicured over McDreamy? Yes, Addison had made some mistakes in the past, but I've always been a glass-half-full kinda guy, so I'd like to believe that Addison has actually learned from those blunders . . .

But, regardless, Mark kept waiting. After about an hour, he seemed a little pissed that Addison hadn't yet walked through that door. Then he slammed his glass down on my bar (dude, don't ever slam your glass down on my bar), mumbled something about wishing he never even came to Seattle Grace (called it a serious lapse in judgment), and made his exit. Pissy Mark. Let me tell you, for a famous plastic surgeon, Mark is a weak tipper. Hope I never see his chiseled mug in my bar again. And, judging from the way Mark left, I don't think I ever will.

Anyways, Meredith stuck around a little longer to sober up a bit. Said she wished she never made that switch from vodka to tequila. Since George wasn't around (you know, good ole George is usually the sober one who drives Meredith home after these kinds of nights), I called her a cab. I hope Meredith got a good night's rest . . . It looked like she definitely needed it.

Instant Message Conversation

JoeKnowsBest—logged on at 8:12 a.m.

DebbieDoesGossip:	OK. Something really, really strange is going on up here.
JoeKnowsBest:	Let me guess. Some dude is pregnant.
DebbieDoesGossip:	No.
JoeKnowsBest:	Bomb in a body cavity?
DebbieDoesGossip:	Not funny.
JoeKnowsBest:	Hmmm. Train wreck. 2 people. 1 pole.
DebbieDoesGossip:	That's just mean.
JoeKnowsBest:	I give up. Tell me.
DebbieDoesGossip:	Well, the she-Shepherd keeps walking around in an extremely weird manner.
JoeKnowsBest:	What do u mean?
DebbieDoesGossip:	I mean she's kinda doing some odd little leg dance every time I see her. Like, a shimmy. And a shake.

JoesKnowsBest: So Addison Shepherd is not only a world-renowned neonatal surgeon, but she's also a championship ballroom dancer?

DebbieDoesGossip: It's not really a dance. It's like she's . . . itching. In a very, very bad place. And she's trying to relieve the irritation.

JoeKnowsBest: Do u mind? I haven't even eaten breakfast yet.

DebbieDoesGossip: Sorry.

JoeKnowsBest: Well let's stop the presses everybody. Addison Shepherd has an itch!

DebbieDoesGossip: That's not the only thing going on up here today. Something happened between Meredith and George. Something big.

JoeKnowsBest: I just saw Mer last night. She was at the bar.

DebbieDoesGossip: With who?

JoeKnowsBest: By herself. Then that cocky bastard of a plastic surgeon, Mark "I don't even care what his last name is" showed up.

DebbieDoesGossip: YES! I knew it! I am always right. Meredith slept with Mark last night. And George is the only one that knows. That's why, right now, things are really, really weird between them.

JoeKnowsBest: Whoa, whoa, whoa. Slow down, Deb. Mer did not sleep with Mark. I can guarantee it. Mark left the bar early because he was pissed Addison never showed up. Mer went home alone *much* later.

DebbieDoesGossip: Damn u and ur facts.

JoeKnowsBest: Got any other great theories to share, Deb?

DebbieDoesGossip: I'll get back to u.

JoeKnowsBest: K, I gotta go. I feel all . . . itchy. Great. Thanks, Deb.

JoeKnowsBest—Logged off at 8:39 a.m.

Apologies

I know, I know, it's been way too long since my last post. I apologize. Really, I'm sorry. And I'm not going to make any excuses . . . Except for the fact that I've basically been catatonic ever since I found out that MEREDITH SLEPT WITH GEORGE.

OK, yeah, when I put Meredith in that cab a few nights ago, I figured she was going to go home and get a good night's rest the moment her pretty little head hit her pillow. I had no idea she was going to rip George's beating heart out of his chest, throw it into a blender, and grind it up into itty, bitty, tiny pieces by HAVING SEX WITH HIM.

Deep breaths, Joe, deep breaths.

George has stopped by the bar a few times since that ill-fated evening. And I've definitely gotten the impression that he doesn't want to talk about anything having to do with that night. Or Meredith Grey for that matter. I mean, the dude has stopped talking to Mer altogether and started bunking with Cristina and Burke. I'm sure Cristina is thrilled about that!

Personally, I don't think things will ever be the same between Meredith and George. I'm telling you—Right now, things are *bad* between those two.

Just last night, George was here, talking to me about some hot ortho doc he met up at the hospital. Said her name was Dr. Torres . . .

Callie? I know Callie. Dude, she's awesome. Between you and me, Callie can drink like a champ. I, for one, would love to see

O'Malley and Callie together. They'd actually make a great couple. Now, all my man George has to do is actually call her. Yeah, Callie has already handed her digits over. Told you she was awesome.

That's exactly the kind of girl George needs in his life right now . . . A girl that knows what she wants and goes after it. I mean, not too many girls have the balls to be the first one to write down their numbers. Man, George better not sleep on this one. He better call. He has to call. He *needs* to call. I warned him that Callie was the type who expects a guy to call. If he doesn't pick up the phone, a simple "I'm sorry" isn't going to cut it. Nope. He will have lost his chance with her forever . . . So, George. Dude. *Call*.

Anyway, the moment Meredith stepped foot inside the bar, George immediately stopped talking about Callie. He threw down some cash and left. Seriously. Bad sex can really ruin a great friendship. Who would've ever guessed? I was ready to call Meredith out, but she shut me up as soon as I opened my mouth. I guess it's still too soon to tease her about the whole incident.

So, it turns out that Mer has apologized and apologized, but it's no use. George refuses to listen. It's sad, really. Meredith and George made really great friends. I at least want to see them back on speaking terms. Things just aren't the same.

Friends and Lovers

It's been said that best friends often make the best lovers. OK, seriously? This saying couldn't be further from the truth. Well, at least in my experience. Oh, I've tried dating my friends. Really, I have. And the only thing I seemed to have ever ended up with was, well, one less friend. For me, friends and dating just don't mix. I was never able to make it work . . .

I vividly remember when my relationship with my good friend Max turned into something much different than I had ever imagined. Yeah, we went from playing with video games every weekend to playing with a few other things I can't really mention right now.

We dated for about four weeks. Pretty soon, I started to realize something. There are just some things you can tell your best friend that you absolutely cannot tell the person you're sleeping with. Such as . . . who else you want to sleep with.

What?! Don't judge me! I see you sitting there with that look on your face. Judge McJudgster. Let me explain.

Max and I were at the beach and I started talking about some lifeguard and he started to get upset and wah wah wah. The point is, in that one moment, I forgot Max was my lover instead of my friend. Clearly, as I was going on and on about this hot lifeguard who seriously made my heart skip a beat, I was in best friend mode! *Not* lover mode. See? I just can't mix friends with lovers. The whole thing confuses me.

Oh—Don't worry, Walter knows all about Max. And the lifeguard. It was a long, long time ago.

Anyway, maybe I need to tell all of this to Meredith. You know, my little theory about how friends should not date. Because that's exactly what Meredith is doing right now. She's dating her friend, Dr. Derek Shepherd.

Oh, you didn't know? Yes, Meredith and Derek are now friends. Or, should I say . . . "friends." Hey, I wouldn't be Joe the Bartender if I wasn't just a little bit skeptical about this whole "friend" thing. Anyway, these two "friends" have been doing a very interesting kind of dating: dog-dating.

Just last night, Mer was in here telling me all about her so-called newfound friendship with McDreamy. Oh, by the way, she refuses to call him McDreamy anymore. From now on, he's just her good friend Derek. I mean, her good "friend" Derek.

Apparently, Meredith and Derek have been going on hikes with Doc. You remember Doc, right? That evil hell-dog that chewed up my barstool. Yeah, the two "friends" have been touring just about all of Seattle's dog parks together.

Oh man, Meredith is really trying. So far, she tells me, the whole "friend" thing seems to be working. Only, they're *so* not friends. They're dating! Through the devil dog! *So* dating. *So* more than friends. *So* the reason why friends cannot be lovers. And, *so* the reason why lovers cannot be friends!

I think Meredith needs to come to her senses and realize exactly what she's doing by dog-dating her "friend" Derek. I guess she will, eventually. I just hope it's sooner rather than later . . .

Supercuts

Remember when I checked into Seattle Grace after collapsing in my bar a few months ago? Yeah, that whole brain surgery standstill operation thingie. Well, believe it or not, back then, my biggest fear wasn't dying. Nope. As a matter of fact, death was the furthest thing from my mind.

To be honest, the thing I was most worried about was what my hair was going to look like post-surgery.

Seriously—They shave just about your entire head before they can operate on your brain! Now, let me tell you, shaving a gay man's head (when he possesses a full head of beautiful, shiny hair, mind you) can lead to a serious bout of severe depression. Dude, it's one of the ten gay commandments: Thou shall not venture out in public with a bad haircut. It took me some time to get over it, but, in the end, I chose to live instead of being a good, law-abiding gay.

Fortunately, I look good in hats. In particular, this one camouflage baseball cap fit my head extremely well. But, when that hat was off, I was miserable. In the comfort of my own home, with all of the window blinds securely closed, when I looked at my own head of stringy, half-cut hair, I was mortified.

Dude. Bad haircuts suck. And, after my surgery, I had a *bad* haircut. A really, really, bad haircut. I was the embarrassed owner of the worst haircut known to man. Well, I *used* to be. Now, George O'Malley has taken the title. Let me tell you, I'm more than happy to pass the torch. He walked in here tonight with a brand spankin' new 'do. I can only say: Poor George.

The whole sleeping with Meredith while she bawls like a baby thing must've really done a number on George. Maybe it woke him up. It's definitely changed him, I can tell you that. Whatever George has decided to do with his hair is tangible proof that he's a new man. I think it's great. No, not the hair. But, the fact that George is trying something new.

Okay, seriously, maybe he should've just bought some new jeans. A new T-shirt? New shoes always help me when I'm down and out. Yeah, George should've just left the hair alone!

Maybe George's new best friend, Dr. Burke, will say something. I hear that ever since he's started living with Burktina, George and Dr. Burke have become really close. Which, of course, drives Cristina crazy. HAHA. How cute. George is the better girlfriend! At least Cristina has the better hair.

Alex thinks George looks like a hobbit. As much as I hate to agree with Alex right now, I definitely see the whole resemblance to Frodo.

Lately, Alex has really been saying the worst things about people. He's been in here every night, breaking the bar rules by leaving crappy tips, shouting at other customers, and just generally doing all of the evil spawn things that evil spawns do. What is his deal?

Maybe it has to do with Izzie falling in love with a patient. That's right, folks. Nurse Debbie has confirmed it. Izzie is head over heels in love with that dude Denny. Aw, seems like Alex is a little jealous. Something tells me that Alex's ego was just a tad bit bruised when Izzie chose Denny over him. Serves the little ratboy bastard right. Tough love, folks. Until next time . . .

Instant Message Conversation

JoeKnowsBest—logged on at 1:39 a.m.

| JoeKnowsBest: | What have u done with Izzie Stevens? She hasn't been down to see me in forever. |

DebbieDoesGossip:	Don't get me started on Izzie Stevens. She's been busy, Joe . . . Busy falling in love with patients.
JoeKnowsBest:	Wow, so she's really in love with Denny.
DebbieDoesGossip:	She crossed the line.
JoeKnowsBest:	Well, she's human. That line between doctors and patients can get a little fuzzy, I guess.
DebbieDoesGossip:	That's not the line I was referring to . . .
JoeKnowsBest:	Uh, OK . . .
DebbieDoesGossip:	Dr. Model stole my Scrabble board. You don't steal Nurse Debbie's Scrabble board. There's a line. A line that separates nurses from interns, Joe. We're not friends. We're not meant to be friends. There's a line! A line you just don't cross.
JoeKnowsBest:	Dude. It's always about you, isn't it Deb?
DebbieDoesGossip:	That Scrabble board was my baby.
JoeKnowsBest:	Well, steal it back.
DebbieDoesGossip:	No, I can't . . . I thought about it. But, my baby's tainted with Izzie Stevens now. Ick.
JoeKnowsBest:	OK. U've got issues.
DebbieDoesGossip:	Who doesn't?
JoeKnowsBest:	U think of a Scrabble board as your baby. A baby? Do u even hear yourself?? Hello!
DebbieDoesGossip:	Well, not a "baby" baby. But, yeah, a baby.
JoeKnowsBest:	A baby like Dr. Bailey's baby?
DebbieDoesGossip:	Oooohhhh, Joe!! I totally forgot to tell you!
JoeKnowsBest:	What!? What!?

DebbieDoesGossip:	Dr. Bailey took her baby to work today. And, she had Cristina Yang babysit!
JoeKnowsBest:	LOL. OK, now that's funny.
DebbieDoesGossip:	Cristina Yang. Covered in baby. Joe, it was classic!
JoeKnowsBest:	I wish I could've seen that. Next time something like that happens, please take your camera phone out and snap one for me. Please?!
DebbieDoesGossip:	All right. Stevens just passed me. I've got to go.
JoeKnowsBest:	Where?
DebbieDoesGossip:	To make sure my baby is OK.
JoeKnowsBest:	Ur obsessed with a Scrabble board.
DebbieDoesGossip:	More than u know.
JoeKnowsBest:	Dude. Seriously? I at least hope it's the Deluxe Limited Edition.

JoeKnowsBest—logged off at 2:01 a.m.

Rules

Here in the Emerald City Bar, people toss back shots of tequila every single night. They order rounds of Jäger bombs. They throw darts. Play pool. Yell at the television. Talk about their problems. They certainly do not knit. In a bar. With yarn and needles. Someone please tell me why Meredith Grey was in here the other night . . . knitting?!

I mean, seriously—knitting? Meredith is my girl and all, but she was totally freaking the other customers out with the whole knitting thing. Man, I'm telling you, people just aren't used to seeing something like that in a bar. Fights, drunken sorority girls from U-Dub, and some old man in a corner about to keel over while clutching his Jim Beam—YES—those are the things you find in Emerald City. But, knitting? No way. Not here. I'm making that a new rule.

Even Derek and Addison were confused. Now that they're all happily-married-couple, they came in together, grabbed a table together, sat and watched Meredith play with her yarn . . . together. Lately, I hear Derek and Addison have been doing a lot of stuff . . . together, as a matter of fact. The other night, they actually looked happy. It was cute. But there was one thing that struck me as just a little bit strange . . .

When Addison went to the bathroom, Derek walked over to Meredith to make sure everything was OK (I think he was just trying to figure out what, in fact, Mer was trying to knit together—it wasn't looking so good). I swear, people, in that moment, I saw a glimmer in McDreamy's eye . . . It was a glimmer marked by just a touch of chemistry and yearning . . . One that made me feel like, yep, hope is still alive for Mer and Der. Then Addison returned and the glimmer disappeared.

Anyways, Derek and Addison soon left, leaving Mer alone . . . with her knitting. She told me she was making a sweater. Didn't look like a sweater. I'm curious to see how this project of hers turns out.

I still haven't seen Izzie around the bar. It's been a really, really long time. All because of her patient, Denny. Ever since that dude checked back into the hospital, Izzie's been all M.I.A. She's spending every second of her time up there. I'm telling you, she's really made a solid connection with this guy. Hey, don't doctors need to adhere to some unspoken rule about not getting too attached to their patients? If they don't, they probably should, right?

You know, I'd really like to meet this Denny character, but something tells me that's not gonna happen anytime soon. Alex keeps telling me that's *never* gonna happen, because, as he says, the dude is a total goner. I hope he's wrong.

Well, folks, I've got to get to work on a revised Emerald City Bar rules sign. Like I said, at the top of the list: No knitting. I can't take another night of perplexed faces and annoyed customers. Just not good for business!

Regulations

I wasn't kidding when I said I was going to make a new Emerald City Bar rules-and-regulations sign. And, I certainly wasn't kidding about the first rule simply stating: No Knitting.

Meredith came in tonight, again. And, she brought her knitting . . . again. And, I witnessed a sea of perplexed, confused faces . . . yet again.

OK, I'm not trying to hate, but Meredith's "sweater" is still not a sweater. It just looks like a messy clump of yarn to me. The sad part is, Mer has supposedly been working on this thing all day. Izzie has been trying to help, but she obviously hasn't helped enough.

Anyway, Mer took a seat at the bar and continued to furiously concentrate on her knitting. I asked her what she wanted to drink, but she was in some sort of zone. A "Do not disturb me unless you want this knitting needle in your eye" zone.

After a good ten minutes, I had no choice.

I slowly reached out and took hold of Meredith's rapidly moving hands. In a very, very calm voice, I soothingly stated, "Mer? I'm going to take the sweater now."

She put up a pretty good fight, but I eventually managed to get that damn yarn and needle.

I poured Meredith a drink and told her to wipe that sad look off of her face. Even though Mer looks pretty damn cute when she pouts, I didn't want to see it tonight. She asked me for her sweater back. I told her I couldn't give it to her. At least, not in the bar.

I started feeling a little guilty when Mer told me that Doc is sick. Yeah, she had just come from a veterinary clinic with the little guy. Poor Doc. I almost want to take back every bad thing I've ever said about Satan's pet. *Almost.*

Anyway, Meredith's pouting continued. She *needed* that sweater back. Fine. I handed the sweater over. I mean, her dog is sick. I'm no Evil Spawn, people.

We talked for a little while longer and I soon started to realize that Mer wasn't just knitting to take her mind off of her sick dog. Nope. She was knitting—crazily knitting—to take her mind off of her sick dog's veterinarian. It seems that, tonight, Meredith met McVet.

But, Meredith assures me that she's sworn off men. Said she's seriously serious about this whole celibacy thing. It's true. Celibacy, Mer states, is a very important item on her newly revised list of rules and regulations. Yeah. Let's see how long that's going to last. Maybe she should ask her friends Derek and Addison what to do about McVet. Ha! The thought of that made Mer knit a little faster.

The number of customers who couldn't help but chuckle and stare at a frantically knitting Meredith continued to increase by the minute. But I chose to stand by my girl and let her do her thing. Especially when Meredith confessed to me that she saw her dad up at the hospital today. Okay, we all know what happened the last time Meredith saw her dad. Even worse, Meredith apparently met a sister she never knew she had today, as well.

Dude. I had to let her knit. Screw my bar's new regulations. Meredith had some pretty serious stuff to deal with. And if Meredith needed to knit, then Meredith was going to knit. She ended up staying until closing time. Just Mer and Mer's knitting. I gave her a ride home. No questions asked.

O'Malley Reborn

The other night, when Meredith was in here knitting up a storm, I was dying to know if George ever ended up calling Callie.

I couldn't ask Meredith because George still wasn't speaking to her. Well, tonight, folks, the new and improved, so fresh and so clean George O'Malley walked into the bar with none other than Dr. Calliope Torres.

Yes, my boy had a hot ortho surgeon on his arm and a brand spankin' new 'do on his head. Let me tell you, it was really a sight to behold.

And to think I was worried that George wasn't going to follow through. I think I actually believed George would never recover from the whole sleeping with Meredith thing. Well, fortunately, I was wrong. It looks like broken George is well on his way toward a speedy recovery.

Let me just say this: George is totally Callie's McDreamy! You should've seen them in the bar tonight. Flirting by the pool table. Laughing in front of the dartboard. Tossing back shots of tequila. It was great to see George having a little bit of fun . . . About time, right?

Oh, and George's hair! Yeah, OK, it looks a little bit like how a third-grader wears his hair, but, still . . . It's definitely an improvement. Seriously. Anything is better than hobbit-hair.

I didn't know that Cristina finally managed to get George out of Burke's apartment. I knew she was trying, desperately, to live George-free, but I didn't know she actually succeeded. And all she had to do was walk around the place naked one night. Yeah— George seeing Cristina's good girl was enough for Burke to toss him out into the street.

Or, rather, into Callie's place.

As a matter of fact, George stayed with Callie last night. And, get this, she lives in the artificial limb room of the hospital! Dude. Nurse Debbie is going to freak out when she hears this one . . .

Callie lives in the catacombs of Seattle Grace. Has a whole setup that nobody knows about. And, she plays video games down there. How hot is that? Like I said, this is *exactly* the kind of girl George needs in his life. *Especially* after Operation Meredith Grey.

The couple was going to stay at George's old place (Meredith's house) tonight. Hey, he still pays rent there so he can do whatever he wants, right? George was a little bit nervous because, apparently, Meredith and Izzie don't really care for Callie. OK, yeah, maybe she's a little abrasive, but get over it, ladies. This is a good thing for George. Show some respect. Man, I can't wait to hear what happens next with these two. George and Callie, my new favorite Seattle Grace couple.

Instant Message Conversation

JoeKnowsBest—logged on at 12:47 p.m.

JoesKnowsBest:	I'm calling it right now. Satan's Whore does Evil Spawn.
DebbieDoesGossip:	Joe, out of all the sick, twisted things that have come out of your mouth, THAT has got to be the worst one.
JoeKnowsBest:	Hey, I just call it like I see it. I'm telling you. Addison Shepherd and Alex Karev are gonna hook up.
DebbieDoesGossip:	It's not even 1 p.m. yet. Shouldn't u still be sleeping?
JoeKnowsBest:	Is that all u think I do? Sleep, wake up, eat, drink, serve drinks—
DebbieDoesGossip:	And make up crappy stories. Is there something I'm missing?
JoeKnowsBest:	U don't know me at all. That really hurts, Deb.
DebbieDoesGossip:	U come at me with some prediction about the She-Shepherd and Evil Spawn that has absolutely no basis. You give gossip a bad name.
JoeKnowsBest:	Ouch.

DebbieDoesGossip:	I'm cranky. I'm sorry. Fine. Seriously. Why do u think what you think about Addison and Alex, Joe?
JoeKnowsBest:	Well . . . Since u asked . . . Alex was in here last night complaining about Addison. Apparently, she told him that she "owned him."
DebbieDoesGossip:	"Owned him"?
JoeKnowsBest:	That's what I said. Owned him.
DebbieDoesGossip:	Well, she has been assigning him to all of her gynie cases.
JoeKnowsBest:	Dude. Evil Spawn is part of the vagina squad! LOL.
DebbieDoesGossip:	And u think there's some kind of sexual tension between those two?
JoeKnowsBest:	As a matter of fact, I do. Just the way Alex was talking about her. He hates her. *Hates* her. And we all know when an 8-year-old says he hates a girl, he usually pulls her hair when he's secretly fantasizing about her.
DebbieDoesGossip:	True. Well, you've been wrong before.
JoeKnowsBest:	Yes, but, I've also been right . . .

JoeKnowsBest—logged off at 1:01 p.m.

Bull's-eye

Yours truly had the pleasure of seeing McDreamy a few hours ago. He came into the bar, all by himself, took a seat, and ordered his double scotch, single malt. Just like he always does. The only thing, McDreamy didn't look so dreamy tonight. He looked tired.

Exhausted, really. Like he was carrying the weight of the world on his shoulders.

Dr. Shepherd raised his glass to me and let out one big, minty-fresh breath of McDreamified air. I'm telling you, it looked like he was just letting it all out in that one single sigh. His problems, fears, and worries—they were all let loose.

I asked him if everything was OK. He shrugged. I could tell he didn't want to do much talking, so I didn't bother to try. Pretty soon, Derek got up and walked over to the dartboard.

Dude, let me tell you, McDreamy's got an arm. And quite an aim.

With fire in his eyes, McDreamy threw those babies like missiles. Seriously. Missiles that left McDreamy's hand, flew through my bar, and landed in the center of the dartboard. Bull's-eye after bull's-eye. I wonder what was fueling his rage. I can only wonder . . .

Anyway, it must've been a rough day up at Seattle Grace because not too many other people came into the bar tonight. Truth be told, I miss my regulars. Well, Alex soon graced me with his presence, but Alex doesn't really count as one of the regulars I actually miss. Seriously, he's in here just about every night! They've got to be absent for at least 24 hours before you start to miss somebody, right?

I asked Evil Spawn where everybody else was. He said he didn't know for sure, but he could make a few guesses . . .

Let's see, the walking vagina (that would be George) was probably doodling in the hospital dungeons with Hot Ortho Chick (Callie). Miss Bethany Whisper (Izzie) was probably putting down a triple word score with Dying Heart Guy (read: Denny). Oh—the crackwhore (Cristina) was probably attempting to take on a human form at home with Dr. Burke. And, of course, the chick who gets drunk and sleeps with inappropriate men (better known as Meredith Grey) was probably off doing the vet.

Bull's-eye!

So *that's* what had McDreamy's panties in a jumble. He must've found out about Meredith and McVet!

Although, now that I think about it, why would Derek care? I mean, Derek and Meredith are friends, right? The kind of friends that talk to each other about their problems. That go to bars together after work. That go on hikes together with the dog they share. Because . . . you know . . . they're "friends." Right? Riiiiiight. Like *that* was going to last.

Well, I guess McDreamy's arm soon got tired of launching dart missiles because he soon decided to take off.

Meanwhile, Alex continued to enjoy himself sitting at the bar, alone. Just him and his beer. Then he got a little annoyed when I called him a gynecologist. Ha! Well, it's kinda true . . .

Nurse Debbie tells me that Addison is *still* making Alex jump through the gynie hoops up there. Rat-Boy, though, is being a good sport about the whole thing and is trying his hardest to take it all in stride. He told me he could handle anything Satan's Whore throws his way. We'll see about that . . .

Instant Message Conversation

JoeKnowsBest—logged on at 11:07 a.m.

JoesKnowsBest:	Hey—How's ur cat Skittles doing?
DebbieDoesGossip:	Oh, you know Skittles, he's my little survivor. Just a little seizure. He's been through much, much worse.
JoeKnowsBest:	Seriously? Skittles the Seizing Stray. Nice.
DebbieDoesGossip:	Leave Skittles alone. Anyway, have I got a scoop for you!
JoeKnowsBest:	Oh, yeah?
DebbieDoesGossip:	Ohhhhh, yeah. So, I talked to McVet for a pretty long time when I was there with Skittles the other day.

JoeKnowsBest:	And I'm sure you couldn't help but dig for some shiny little gossip gems about Meredith, right?
DebbieDoesGossip:	Well, hello, it was just so easy.
JoeKnowsBest:	OK, what'd u find out?
DebbieDoesGossip:	Well, for starters, they birthed a horse on their first date.
JoeKnowsBest:	Sounds messy. Who wants to end up covered in pony at the end of the night?
DebbieDoesGossip:	I thought it was kind of romantic.
JoeKnowsBest:	Right. What else did u find out?
DebbieDoesGossip:	McVet wants to tell Meredith about his wife.
JoeKnowsBest:	His wife?! Not again . . .
DebbieDoesGossip:	Calm down. This time it's not what you think. His wife died in a car accident years ago.
JoeKnowsBest:	Jeez.
DebbieDoesGossip:	I think this is the start of a wonderful relationship between those two. I mean, clearly McVet feels comfortable enough with Grey to tell her about his dead wife.
JoeKnowsBest:	Dude, McDreamy is and always will be Meredith's soul mate. This McVet guy sounds nice in a Mr. Rogers kinda way, but, come on . . . He doesn't compare to Dr. Shepherd.
DebbieDoesGossip:	Well at least McVet doesn't walk around calling Meredith a whore.
JoeKnowsBest:	You really want to get into this? You'd really choose McVet over McDreamy for Meredith?

DebbieDoesGossip: I really would.

JoeKnowsBest: I guess we're just gonna have to agree to
                        disagree on this one.

DebbieDoesGossip: FINE.

JoeKnowsBest: FINE.

JoeKnowsBest—logged off at 11:31 a.m.

McDreamy vs. McVet

So, Nurse Debbie and I have agreed to disagree about who
makes the better suitor for Meredith Grey. My vote is for
Dr. Derek Shepherd, a.k.a McDreamy. Deb, however, is partial
to Finn Dandridge, a.k.a. McVet. One is a world-renowned neurosurgeon who just happened to save my life several months ago.
The other is a veterinarian.

For me, it's all very simple. Allow me to break it down for you.
Here's a little top 10 list for you to ponder:

#10
McDreamy: Saved my life.
McVet: Haven't even met the dude.

#9
McDreamy: Saves other people's lives. *Human* lives.
McVet: Puts helpless little doggies to sleep.

#8
McDreamy: He's a *real* doctor. He could save Meredith
                        if, God forbid, a life-threatening illness
                        were to strike her.
McVet: He's a veterinarian. Have you *seen* the

tools in a vet's bag? Not gonna save
Meredith . . .

#7

McDreamy: Makes lots of money.

McVet: Again. He's a vet. Don't you get it?

#6

McDreamy: Sometimes smells like freshly chopped
               wood.

McVet: Almost always emits a musty odor usually
               linked to mangy pets.

#5

McDreamy: The best hair this side of the Atlantic.

McVet: Has a head full of pony birth residue.
               Gross.

#4

McDreamy: Wears sexy, form-fitting blue scrubs that
               complement his eyes.

McVet: Puke-green coveralls are so last fall.

#3

McDreamy: All it took was a couple shots of tequila
               to get Meredith into bed.

McVet: A pony birth, a nice guy attitude, a
               shower, a change of clothes and STILL . . .
               no dice.

#2

McDreamy: No baggage. Except the whole wife
               thing. OK, let's just not talk about the
               wife.

McVet: A deceased mom, deceased wife, and an
               alcoholic father? McDamaged much?

#1

| McDreamy: | People! He's Meredith's soul mate. |
| McVet: | Seriously? He's only Meredith's *temporary* McDreamy replacement. |

Evil Misery—Part One

I love it when the gang's all here.

Let me rephrase that.

I love it when the gang's all here and they're happy. When they just throw their heads back and laugh. When they playfully rib each other about who's sleeping with who and who's about to get kicked out of the program for doing so. Oh, the teasing. The mocking. The togetherness of it all . . .

It just reminds me of the reason why I decided to open up the Emerald City Bar in the first place. I wanted to create a safe haven for people to relax and unwind after long, stressful days. The Emerald City Bar is a happy place. And it's my customers who keep it that way—but only when they're actually happy.

Last night, they weren't. Yes, they were all here . . .

Dr. Burke and McDreamy—they stayed in the corner playing darts together the entire time. All angry and aggressive. Derek furious about the vet. Burke irate because of Cristina. Misery all around. By the way, don't they compete with each other at work every day? Why darts? Dudes. Relax.

Meredith, Cristina, and Izzie—these girls couldn't stop staring at the hostile dart game happening across the bar. Meredith was mad because McDreamy called her a whore. Oh, and her dog is still sick and seems to be getting worse. Fine. She has a reason to be cranky. I will let her be miserable.

Cristina was upset because Burke didn't seem to be over the fact that she fell asleep during sex. Seriously? She can't be angry at him for being mad at her because of something that so clearly deserves somebody getting mad at the other person. Or something. Whatever. Burktina has some issues to iron out. What else is new?

Izzie, as well, jumped on the anguished bandwagon and got mad as soon as Alex walked into the bar. Okay, Evil Spawn was within a three-mile radius so, yeah, *somebody* had to get pissed.

And, of course, Alex was incensed when Izzie called him a gynecologist. HAHA. Sorry, makes me laugh every time.

A few seconds later, George and Callie took their seats at the bar. I thought to myself, "OK, finally, some people who aren't miserable." Those two are getting serious and I'm so happy for George. I hope their relationship survives Seattle Grace, because, I'm telling you, that hospital seems to have a habit of obliterating the whole girlfriend-boyfriend thing.

Anyway, George and Callie's cheer soon faded. Probably because they didn't exactly receive a warm welcome when they came in. Dude. Meredith, Cristina, and Izzie can be *bitches*. Don't get me wrong—I love them all to death, but, seriously . . . Callie deserves a chance, doesn't she? I mean, George seems to really dig her.

Yeah, last night, the gang was all here . . . In all their evil, miserable glory. As entertaining as it was, it's much better when everybody's happy.

Evil Misery—Part Two

So, I just had to write a continuation of my last blog. Up until five minutes ago, it was a really slow night for me. Thankfully, I have some time to write . . .

What's funny is that just this morning, I blogged about evil misery. Well, folks, the most miserable evil bastard just left my bar. Let's call him Crazy Psycho Dude.

Crazy Psycho Dude stormed into the bar as I was cleaning off one of the booths. I had been feeling so alone because *nobody* came into the bar tonight. Seriously. The place was empty. The jukebox wasn't even playing music. Yep, it was just me and the bar. I figured something big was going on up at Seattle Grace. What else was new?

Anyway, I had never seen Crazy Psycho Dude before. He looked like he had just been hit by a train. Literally. He was trembling. Sweating, even. His clothes were dirty. He already reeked of alcohol. This dude was a mess. Seriously.

The dude walked right up to me and demanded a vodka, straight up. I lied and told him we were about to close. He asked me for the drink one more time. Actually, he screamed for his drink at the top of his lungs. But I held my ground. In my mind, there was no way in hell that I was going to put a drink in front of this dude's ugly mug.

I was about to call for backup when, very calmly, Crazy Psycho Dude took a seat at the bar. In a really low, almost haunting voice, he said, "Sir. I'd really, really like my drink." He said it simply. Like it was a fact.

Something in the dude's tone made me a little bit uneasy. And what does Joe do when he's uncomfortable? He talks. Oh, man, does he talk. So, I did just that. I talked to Crazy Psycho Dude. I had to find out this guy's deal. Or, at the very least, calm his crazy psycho ass down before he left.

It turned out that he worked at a restaurant not too far from the bar. Well, he used to work there. Until today. Yeah, the dude got fired. The manager kicked Crazy Psycho Dude's ass out onto the street.

I started to feel sorry for the guy. He kept telling me about his family. How he wasn't a good husband. Or a good father. And, now that he'd lost his job, he had no way to provide for them. Man, this guy was miserable.

At that point, he asked for his drink again. Still, I wasn't going to serve him. I offered to call a cab, but he refused. Then, he stared at me straight in the eye and asked, "You ever shoot anybody?"

OK, this guy was evil, too.

It was then when I let my imagination run wild. I'm telling you, all I could think about was the idea that this guy could very well be the kind of guy who keeps women in a man-made well in his basement and says things like, "It rubs the lotion on its skin before it gets the hose again." Seriously? Seriously.

The possibility that Psycho Crazy Dude could actually be psycho and crazy began to dawn on me. Now, I knew I had been lucky enough to survive a standstill operation. But what if I didn't have any luck left? What if *I* ended up in the well? What if *I* ended up having to rub lotion on my skin? What if it was *me*, Joe the Bartender, about to get the hose again?

I asked him to leave.

He asked me, "Why?"

I swallowed. Hard. Like the kind of swallow you hear across a really quiet room.

Then, Crazy Psycho Dude explained, "Seattle Grace is right across the street."

"Um, yeah?"

Crazy Psycho Dude wanted to know if I had heard about the shootings.

"Shootings?"

Crazy Psycho Dude wanted to know if I knew Brad.

"Brad? Dude, what are you talking about?"

Crazy Psycho Dude didn't like being called "dude."

"My name is Petey," he said. Then he jumped up from his seat and ran out of my bar.

Yes. Crazy Psycho Dude was really crazy and psycho. Who the hell was that guy? Petey who? You know what? I don't even wanna know . . . OK, yes I do . . .

Instant Message Conversation

JoeKnowsBest—logged on at 10:38 p.m.

JoesKnowsBest: OK. Tell me what's keeping all of my favorite interns away from the bar tonight. Nobody's here. I haven't even had the pleasure of seeing the wrath of Evil Spawn.

JoeKnowsBest:	I feel so alone.
JoeKnowsBest:	Deb?
JoeKnowsBest:	U there?
DebbieDoesGossip:	Dr. Burke's been shot.
JoeKnowsBest:	WHAT?!
DebbieDoesGossip:	Some crazy guy shot up a restaurant and then just came to the hospital to shoot more people.
JoeKnowsBest:	Wait. Did the guy work at the restaurant?
DebbieDoesGossip:	Yeah. Got canned today. He came here looking for the manager that fired him. He's freakin' crazy.
JoeKnowsBest:	Petey.
DebbieDoesGossip:	Petey.
JoeKnowsBest:	That evil, miserable, crazy psycho dude shot Dr. Burke?!
DebbieDoesGossip:	And a whole bunch of other people. Then shot himself.
JoeKnowsBest:	Well, is Burke OK?
DebbieDoesGossip:	Don't know yet. Joe, there's just so much going on up here. I gotta go.
JoeKnowsBest:	Right. Of course. Call me the second you have a chance.

JoeKnowsBest—logged off at 10:44 p.m.

With the Adults Away, the Kids Will Play

OK, I can spot a fake I.D. from a mile away. So, if you're under
the age of 21, don't mess with me. Seriously. Occasionally, some

random kids will come in here with their random fake I.D.'s and, every single time, I have to embarrass their random, scrawny asses by kicking them outta my bar. Dudes. I've been in the business since your mothers gave birth to you. I know what a real driver's license looks like.

Well, tonight, my patience was pushed to the limit. First I had to deal with Crazy Psycho Dude in my bar. Then I had to deal with the fact that I apparently let Crazy Psycho Dude loose into the night so that he could go shoot up the hospital . . . INCLUDING DR. BURKE. And, just an hour ago, I had to deal with a whole bunch of underaged kids trying to steal beer and tequila.

I thought this was going to be a slow night. A quiet night. Man, was I wrong. I'm glad that the bar is now closed and I'm finally home.

So, not too long after I let a killer run free, these two pimply-faced, high school brats came into my bar and took a seat. I smirked and decided to run with it for a minute. Besides, I needed a good laugh. You know, after that run-in with Crazy Psycho Dude. Who knew he had a gun and was on his way to Seattle Grace?

Anyways, I asked the two in front of me, "What are you boys drinking?"

They looked at each other and chuckled. "Two beers."

I asked to see some I.D. They handed over two of the worst fake I.D.'s I had ever laid eyes on. Seriously. The two boys in front of me were suburban white kids. But, according to their I.D.'s, their names were Kumar Daftuar and Amish Katari. I threw the cards back. Told them to get outta my bar.

Then, four more snot-nosed, underaged kids walked in. Followed by six more. And then two other stragglers. What the hell was going on? I'm a bartender. Not a babysitter.

Apparently, these kids had just come from the same place all of my other customers come from: Seattle Grace. They were friends of Camille Travis—the Chief's niece.

Camille was admitted to the hospital tonight because she lost consciousness while cashing in her v-card at her prom. Poor girl. I can only imagine the look on the Chief's face when he found out why his niece was in the hospital. I hope Camille's boyfriend got away unharmed.

One of the kids told me that Camille's ovarian cancer is back. That's why they all tried to visit Camille at Seattle Grace, but the Chief kicked them all out. Dude. Seriously? The poor—and I'm guessing highly embarrassed—girl missed her prom, has cancer, and you made all of her friends go home? Not cool, Uncle Richard.

I felt bad for the kids, so I told them they could stay. They didn't want to go back to their prom. They had nowhere to go. Plus, I was kinda sick of being alone in the bar all night. Hey, at least hanging out with the high-schoolers would be better than Crazy Psycho Dude.

I warned them, NO ALCOHOL WILL BE SERVED. Surely they remembered prohibition and the whole temperance movement from history class, right? Well, a few of the wise-asses did.

I couldn't help but ask the kids if they had run into anybody named Meredith, Izzie, George, Alex, or Cristina back at the hospital. Unfortunately, none of them did. Which, of course, tells me that those five are *definitely* up to something. Something big . . .

Prom Night

Tonight, at Seattle Grace Hospital, there's going to be a prom. Yes, that's what I said. You read correctly: a prom. An actual high-school prom, complete with cheesy theme and helium-filled balloons. Apparently, there will be many, many balloons.

I knew something crazy was up when I saw Alex walk through my door earlier this afternoon. He raced in, pleading for a drink. Begging me for a beer. One simple little beer to make the lambs stop screaming. Dude, I think he was losing it.

He had just run over from the hospital, on his way to pick up balloons for the prom. I guess Uncle Richard felt guilty about sending his niece's friends away last night and called all of them back for the prom of the century.

Anyway, Alex needed a drink before he could do any more thinking about balloons. Silver, white, and black balloons. But only the shiny black, not the matte. And a helium tank. Alex couldn't forget the helium tank. Oh, and paper, paint, glue, tape, and glitter. Seriously? I handed Alex a beer. It was on me.

Supposedly, Bailey is running this thing. Of course she is. I needed answers. Alex was about to buy 600 balloons. For a prom. At the hospital. Why was Bailey forcing him to buy prom supplies?? Whatever happened had to have been pretty bad . . .

I asked Alex what he did.

Alex told me that *he* didn't do anything. *Somebody* cut Denny Duquette's LVAD wire. *Somebody* wanted to make Denny's heart worse in order to get him at the top of the transplant list, and, as a result, get him a heart. *Somebody?* Somebody.

Now, the only person that would do such a thing would be Izzie Stevens. Right? Come on, everybody knows Izzie is in love with Denny. Alex was about to answer, but instead, he changed his mind and shrugged. Which was fine, because I didn't really need him to answer. I understood. It was fight club. The group was sticking together. Nobody was going tell on anybody.

The good thing is, Denny got the heart. And . . . Denny lives. Could you imagine if, after all that, he didn't? I don't think Izzie would be able to handle it. That's a scary thought . . .

So, Meredith, Cristina, Izzie, George, and Alex are all in this together. Bailey must be livid. The Chief must be furious. Oh, man, not a good day up at Seattle Grace.

I asked Alex how Dr. Burke was doing. He told me Dr. Shepherd operated on him a few hours ago. It sounded like a pretty tough surgery. He could end up having permanent nerve damage. And, guess what—Cristina hasn't even checked on him yet! How messed up is that? You know, Yang talks a big game, but when it comes to dealing with serious issues, she's got to learn not to just run away. I mean, that's her boyfriend. Show some support. Show some love. Be a little human.

Alex finished his beer and took a deep breath. It was time to get those balloons. He needed to pick up his suit, as well. Wait a second, he had to actually go to the prom, too? Apparently, everybody goes to the prom. *Everybody.* Chief's orders. And now is definitely not the time to piss off the Chief.

Seriously? Dude, prom night sucks.

Words

Proms are so overrated. Seriously. Prom should be a dirty, dirty word.

You spend weeks—months—getting ready for the big night. It's supposed to be the time of your life. Friends, laughter, music, and dancing. Such are the things prom memories are made of . . . Right?

Well, then the night's over and all you've got to show for it is a nasty hangover because it was your first time ever tasting liquor when your buddy Chris forced you to try nine different brands of vodka as part of a silly taste-test that you knew—you just *knew*—you shouldn't be a part of in the first place, and the whole thing was going to ruin vodka for you forever. Then you puke all over your date's dress that her mother spent years—not weeks, not months, but, *years*—sewing together.

Right. Such are the things Joe the Bartender's prom memories are made of. Now I actually cringe every time I hear the words "vodka tonic."

Needless to say, I didn't exactly have a great time at my prom. Since my date was my best friend, she eventually forgave me. Her mother never did.

I just told my pitiful prom story to Dr. Callie Torres. I was hoping it'd cheer her up. Because, let me tell you, the girl needed some cheer.

Callie ordered three shots of tequila as soon as she sat down at the bar. I lined them up in front of her. Then she ordered two more: One for her, one for me. Dude. I love this chick.

She looked hot. Wore a tight-fitting black dress and high heels. *So* not like the Callie I knew at all. Then she said she shaved her legs, too. OK, what the hell was going on? Was prom night really that bad?

Apparently, for her, it was . . .

I started to see a little bit of Callie's softer side. A side I'm pretty unfamiliar with. She told me she was humiliated tonight. She had told somebody that she loved him, and George—I mean, that somebody—didn't say it back. The funny thing is, the fact that he didn't say those three little words back made Callie so much more into George—I mean, that somebody.

Saying "I love you" too early isn't fun for anybody. Especially for the person who pulled the trigger and *actually* said it too early. I told her that she's just gonna have to ride this one out. And that she shouldn't be embarrassed by her feelings. That's what makes her Callie. That's what makes her human. Apparently, staying human is a bit of a struggle for the folks at Seattle Grace.

After Callie downed a whisky sour, it all just started pouring out . . .

Denny Duquette is dead.

Wait. What?

Denny Duquette is dead.

When I heard those four words, my stomach dipped. I had never even met the dude. But, still, I felt like I knew him.

I knew that Denny was a good guy who made everybody smile up at the hospital. Cristina told me, even though she despised Denny for making people smile. I also knew that Denny Duquette talked with a little bit of a drawl. Alex told me that one. And I knew that he liked horses, too. Izzie told me so. Oh, man, Izzie.

Callie said it wasn't a pretty sight. She refused to leave Denny's side. I can't imagine seeing something like that—Izzie bawling in her prom dress, clutching what was left of Denny Duquette. Alex supposedly scooped Iz up in his arms and consoled her. Which is kinda ironic, don't you think? Evil Spawn comes in with the save.

Now that she was clearly falling into sad, teary-eyed mode, Callie started to gather her things. I admit, for the first time in a really, really long time, I was speechless. What a night. For everybody.

"Yeah. And I didn't even get to the part about finding two people having sex in an exam room," Callie said, under her breath.

Whoa, whoa, whoa . . . Back up a little bit, Dr. Torres.

Two people? Having sex? In an exam room? Seriously?

Something about the tone in Callie's voice and the look on her face led me to believe that the two people she caught having sex . . . were two people that shouldn't have been having sex. And not because the sex took place in a hospital exam room, but because one of those people was married and the other was dating a vet.

That's right, I'd bet the whole Emerald City Bar that Meredith and Derek finally took the plunge and did the nasty tonight. And the only person besides Meredith and Derek that actually knows? Well, she was standing right in front of me, dizzy and drunk as hell.

What does this mean? *What* does this mean? Will Derek leave Addison? Will Meredith tell the vet? Will Derek and Meredith finally get back together? So many questions. Unfortunately, they can't be answered right now because Callie just whispered four words to me: "I need to vomit."

Enough said. Seriously.

Instant Message Conversation

JoeKnowsBest—logged on at 2:17 a.m.

JoesKnowsBest:	Hello? What's the freakin' deal?
DebbieDoesGossip:	Shhh.

JoeKnowsBest:	Deb? We're on our computers. We're not really talking. You can't really hear me. Shhh yourself.
DebbieDoesGossip:	Remember that train wreck a few months ago? And that man and woman came in together . . . impaled on a pole?
JoeKnowsBest:	Sad. Yeah, I remember. What's that got to do with anything?
DebbieDoesGossip:	Well, we had to choose which one would live. The man or the woman. We had to make that decision. I thought that was the toughest decision anybody around here would ever make . . .
JoeKnowsBest:	I'm with ya . . .
DebbieDoesGossip:	I was wrong.
JoeKnowsBest:	Deb, what could be tougher than *that*?
DebbieDoesGossip:	Choosing between McDreamy and McVet.
JoeKnowsBest:	Oh, I get it. Meredith is standing between them right now, huh?
DebbieDoesGossip:	Literally. In the lobby. They're both calling her name.
JoeKnowsBest:	Well . . . Is she inching towards either one?
DebbieDoesGossip:	Not yet.
JoeKnowsBest:	Who's she making eye contact with?
DebbieDoesGossip:	Can't see that far.
JoeKnowsBest:	What good are you, then?
DebbieDoesGossip:	Wait, I see movement.
JoeKnowsBest:	Who? Who!

DebbieDoesGossip: AGH! My pager. Gotta go, brb.

JoeKnowsBest: Seriously, you can't leave right now.

JoeKnowsBest: Deb?

JoeKnowsBest: Hello?

JoeKnowsBest: Anybody?

JoeKnowsBest: DAMN IT!

JoeKnowsBest—logged off at 2:24 a.m.

Last Call

So far, it's been quite a year here at the Emerald City Bar. I've made some new friends. Said good-bye to old ones. I've heard some crazy stories. Been a part of those crazy stories . . . Contributed to those crazy stories . . . Was the reason for those crazy stories—Okay, I'll just stop right there. The funny thing is, the year isn't even over yet. As a matter of fact, I'd say it's just getting started . . .

I've been going over and over the past six months in my head. Who would've ever thought I'd be sitting here right now with my stomach in knots thinking about Izzie Stevens quitting the program. That's right—Nurse Debbie told me she just quit. Izzie thought she was a surgeon, but now she thinks she was wrong.

Only six months ago, Izzie was an eager little ex-model about to kick some serious surgical ass. Six months ago, she never struck me as a quitter. But, then again, six months ago, she didn't strike me as a chick that would fall for a dying heart patient, sacrifice her medical career, and watch the love of her life die. So sad. So very, very sad.

But I haven't lost faith in Izzie. She's a fighter. She's a survivor. She's a resilient human being. She's Izzie Stevens. She can't go all psycho crazy on me now. Let the psycho crazy people take care of that. Please?

Then there's the whole Mer-Der-Addison-McVet of it all.

If Meredith and Derek really were the two that had sex in an exam room tonight (and I don't know for sure just yet), then they *both* have a lot of explaining to do. Starting with each other.

I guess the sex was bound to happen, sooner or later. It just sucks that McDreamy was still McMarried when it did. He can't keep this from Addison. And Meredith can't keep this from Finn. Dude. I know her dog just died and all, but, come on . . . Sex with McDreamy in an exam room? Meredith should've just kept knitting.

Well, at least it's good to hear that Mer and George are back on speaking terms. I heard they can actually sit at the same table in the cafeteria these days. Which is great, I think. For *both* Meredith and George.

Ah, poor George. My man has had quite a couple of months. And that's a severe understatement. Bad surgeries, bad sex, bad hair . . . Dude. It's been a *bad* six months for my guy O'Malley. I hope Callie continues to change George for the better. Hey, she already fixed his hair. And I hope George's friends finally accept Callie and give the girl a chance. The woman kinda rocks.

Let's not forget about Cristina and Dr. Burke. Or, rather, Preston, my hero. Dude. He operated on a turkey. I saw the whole thing! He helped save my life. The man is a living surgical legend. Some measly little gunshot wound isn't gonna ruin his career. Right? Right. He'll recover just fine. Now, he may dump Cristina's cold ass out onto the street, but that's a different issue.

Man, I hear it took Cristina *forever* to go visit her boyfriend in recovery. George even went to check in on Dr. Burke before Cristina did. So, all her fears about George making a better girl-friend? Well, I hate to say this, but . . . they were true. She needs to get it together. Seriously. The cold, bitter thing only works for so long—It doesn't stay cute forever.

I wonder what Dr. Bailey and the Chief are thinking now that they know for sure who cut Denny's LVAD wire. If these past six months are any indication of what the next six months are going to be like, I'm not sure if I can handle it. What's going to freakin' happen next??

Something tells me that the rest of the year is going to be a crazy, crazy time at the Emerald City Bar. Yeah, there are definitely a few problems that people are gonna want to drown in tequila. Pitchers of tequila. Very, very large vats of tequila. Dude. I must admit, I'm gonna love every second of it.

Emerald City Bar Specialty Drinks

Here are some of my favorite specialty drinks . . . Appropriately named after some of my favorite people from Seattle Grace. If you're over 21, happy trails!

Meredith's One-Night Stand

Both Meredith and tequila are fiery spirits. Both have been sinful and both have been good. But let's face it, the following drink is just sinfully good:

> 1 3/4 ounces of tequila
> 1/4 ounce of triple sec
> juice of 1/2 lime
> 1 teaspoon of sugar
> 1 scoop of crushed ice
> 1 ring of pineapple

Mix all of the ingredients in a shaker. Save the pineapple ring for a little garnish. Pour the mix into a highball glass. Now enjoy. It tastes extra good when you drink this baby in a crowded bar that's filled with hot neurosurgeons. Feelin' a little frisky, aren't you?

Bloodhound Yang

Vodka is one of the most direct and aggressive liquors out there. Drink enough of that stuff and you'll know exactly what I'm talking about in the morning. This next drink is just a tad bitter, too. No wonder I named it after the love of my life, Cristina Yang.

1 1/4 ounces of vodka
1/2 ounce of dry sherry
4 ounces of tomato juice
2 dashes of lemon juice
pinch of salt and white pepper
slice of lime

Combine all of the ingredients in a Collins glass filled with ice. Mix well and throw that lime slice on top. Now plug your nose and take a swig. See? This one has absolutely no qualms about drawing a little blood from her competition.

Izzie Stevens aka Peach Daiquiri

I know what you're thinking: Daiquiris are for the weak. But you really shouldn't underestimate the power of this little drink. Yeah, so it's pretty and it's fruity—who cares?! It may be really nice to look at, but damn it—she deserves to be in this internship program! Um—I mean this drink deserves to be on this menu!

2 ounces of light rum
1/2 ripe, peeled peach
juice of 1/4 lime
1 teaspoon of sugar
1 scoop of crushed ice
1 of those cute little drink umbrellas

Mix all of these ingredients (except the umbrella) in a blender. Pour the mixture into a large cocktail glass. Stick the umbrella on top. Just look at that pretty little glass. Now drink. Told you not to underestimate this one.

The O'Malley

Gin was once known as "the spirit of the masses." The rich and the poor, the young and the old—gin was their best friend. Kinda like sweet ole George O'Malley. He's everybody's buddy. We all need friends like gin and George in our lives.

> 1 1/2 ounces of gin
> 1 teaspoon of honey
> 1 scoop of crushed ice
> lemon juice

Mix the first three ingredients in a blender. Strain the mixture into a chilled cocktail glass. Add as much lemon juice as your heart desires. Now give your best friend a big, silly hug.

Evil Spawn

Alex Karev talks a big game, but I'd like to see him drink more than a couple of these bad boys.

> 1 ounce of 151 proof rum (I told you—evil)
> 1/4 ounce of lemon juice
> Juice of 1/2 lime
> Dash of grenadine
> Dash of sugar
> 1 scoop of crushed ice
> Club soda

Mix all of the ingredients, except the soda, in a shaker. Pour all of that into a large pilsner glass and then add the club soda. It's very possible that, come tomorrow morning,

I'm the one you're calling Evil Spawn. I wish Alex came with a warning like that.

McScotch

Scotch is a man's drink. Sorry ladies. But it's true. Scotch drinkers are fly fishermen. They're wood choppers. They're guys that wear flannel and live in trailers while pondering the complex feelings of the beautiful women that surround them. You know, like McDreamy. They're also the kind of men who drink this:

3 ounces of scotch
1/2 ounce of sweet vermouth
1/2 ounce of dry vermouth
1 scoop of crushed ice
1 lemon, peeled and spiraled in the most masculine way
possible

Pour the scotch and vermouth into a chilled Collins glass. Add the crushed ice and stir. Drape that masculine lemon peel over the side of the glass. Now sip (slowly). What's that? You say you feel like hiking out to the river and catching a nice big trout for your lady friend? Mission accomplished.

Burktini

Simple, smooth, elegant, and sophisticated, my man Dr. Burke makes for a damn good martini. Plus, the martini glass is as iconic as Burke's trademark surgical cap.

2 1/2 ounces of the best gin you can afford
splash of vermouth
2 skewered, jumbo olives

Fill a mixing glass with exactly four cubes of ice. Pour the vermouth over the ice and stir exactly three times. Strain the vermouth. Add the gin to the ice and stir exactly 30 times. Strain into a 3-ounce martini glass—exactly, over the olives. To make a proper Burktini, you have to follow this recipe *exactly* as it's written. Hey, the Burktini is akin to the way Burke operates—an exact science.

Bailey's Bourbon Sour

She's distinct. She's powerful. Seriously, don't piss her off. If you don't watch what you're doing, Dr. Bailey can and will kick your ass, much like the following drink:

> *2 ounces of bourbon*
> *juice of 1/2 lemon*
> *1/2 teaspoon of sugar*
> *1 scoop of crushed ice*
> *orange slice*

Mix all of these ingredients in a shaker. Except the orange slice, of course. Strain the mixture into a chilled glass and garnish with that slice of orange. Don't worry, you'll eventually start to enjoy the sourness—well, Bailey's interns do.

Addison's Julep

Don't you just love it when, out of the blue, something (or someone) comes along and really stirs things up? You know, when something (or, again, someone) comes along just to keep life minty fresh?

> *6 mint leaves*
> *1 teaspoon of sugar syrup*
> *3 ounces of bourbon*
> *1 scoop of crushed ice*
> *brut champagne*
> *mint sprig*

Combine the syrup, mint leaves, and ice in a tall, salmon-colored glass. Pour in the bourbon and stir briskly. Stir it up just a little bit more. Very good. Next, top the mix off with the cold brut champagne. Stir (but this time gently) and then use the mint sprig for garnish. Now toast to your marriage!

Chief's Cape Cod

Here's one that's been around for a long, long time:

> 3 ounces of cranberry juice
> 3 ounces of white grape juice

Pour the ingredients into a chilled glass (over ice). That's it. Simple and straightforward. If you notice, this drink doesn't feature any alcohol. Because the last thing the chief of surgery at Seattle Grace needs is a hangover. Plus, there's that little rumor about Chief Webber once having a pretty stormy relationship with the sauce—hey, you read my blog, right?

GREY'S ANATOMY

Notes from the Nurses' Station

HYPERION

NEW YORK

Library of Congress Cataloging-in-Publication Data

ISBN: 1-4013-0882-1

Hyperion books are available for special promotions and premiums. For details contact Michael Rentas, Assistant Director, Inventory Operations, Hyperion, 77 West 66th Street, 12th floor, New York, New York 10023, or call 212-456-0133.

FIRST EDITION

10 9 8 7 6 5 4 3 2 1

GREY'S ANATOMY

Notes from the Nurses' Station

Welcome to "The Nurses' Station"!

Your Unofficial Source for Seattle Grace Gossip

Most people are fairly familiar with Seattle Grace Hospital. It is, after all, one of the most prestigious hospitals in the United States—patients travel from all over the world to be treated here . . . Physicians from all over the world clamor to work here. This hospital is a Big Deal—Capital B. Capital D.

But how boring is that?

Who wants to talk hospital politics when we could be talking about who's having sex in the on-call room??

(smile.) That's where I come in.

Howdy. My name's Debbie. I'm a nurse—have been since . . . well, let's just say a long time. I run the surgical floor of Seattle Grace Hospital—which means I spend most of my time . . . bossing people around.

I LOVE bossing people around. Especially the surgical interns.

That's also why I love this time of year—it's the middle of the summer, and the beginning of this year's surgical internship program. In just a matter of days, our newest batch of interns will arrive—fresh faced, eager, excited . . .

Like lambs to the slaughter. They have no idea what they've gotten themselves into . . .

That's what's so fun! Every year, a new group of interns is thrown together—and every year, they generate more drama than you could possibly imagine.

My friend Joe (he's a bartender at the bar across the street) and I like to keep tabs on the newbies—it's sort of our hobby. Our own personal in-the-flesh soap opera . . .

That's where my blog comes in . . . It's my way of entertaining you with what I do, what I see, what I know . . . and what we all want to gossip about.

I mean, hell—you work hours like these, you have to get your entertainment somewhere, right?

ALL ABOUT DEBBIE

AGE:	Yeah, right. Wouldn't you like to know?
HOBBIES:	Blogging Playing darts Tormenting surgical interns Karaoke

PET PEEVES:	Loud neighbors
	Patients who hoard their medication
	Changing bedpans
	Anesthesiologists (and yet, I keep
	    dating them anyway . . . What's up
	    with that?)

THINGS I LOVE:	My cat (named Skittles) My job Joe's bar Traveling
FAVORITE FOOD:	Chocolate croissants
LEAST FAVORITE FOOD:	Hospital pudding

AWARDS:	Seattle Grace Nurse of the Year
	    (5 years running)
	Holiday Nurses' Skit—Best in Show
	    (twice)
	Reigning Karaoke Champion
	    (Emerald City Bar—Annual Contest)

Emerald City Darts Tournament
(First Place)

Instant Message Conversation

DebbieDoesGossip—logged on at 3:12 p.m.

DebbieDoesGossip:	Hey Joe? You there?
JoeKnowsBest:	Just waiting out the "lull before happy hour . . ." How R things?
DebbieDoesGossip:	U know what tomorrow is, right?
JoeKnowsBest:	Are you kidding? Bought an extra case of tequila just for the occasion . . .
DebbieDoesGossip:	New Intern Arrival Day. Let's hope no one pulls a 007 the first day the way they did last year . . .
JoeKnowsBest:	Or, let's hope they do. That's the kind of thing that drives interns to drink!
DebbieDoesGossip:	You hope a patient almost dies so you can sell more booze?
JoeKnowsBest:	Dude. I'm a bartender. It's what I do.
DebbieDoesGossip:	Heard the Nazi's planning her usual 48-hour-hazing ritual for the group . . .
JoeKnowsBest:	Love her.
DebbieDoesGossip:	Yes. In many ways, Bailey's my hero.
JoeKnowsBest:	As you are mine.
DebbieDoesGossip:	Shut up, Joe.

| JoeKnowsBest: | The way you change those bedpans . . . it's an art. |
| DebbieDoesGossip: | Seriously. Shut up. |

DebbieDoesGossip—logged off at 3:25 p.m.

They're Baaaaack . . .

They say you should avoid getting sick the month the interns arrive at the hospital. If you're not already dying, the interns are so clueless, they'll probably kill you anyway. So, my friends, a word to the wise: Avoid Seattle Grace Hospital this month at all costs!!!

That's right, folks. It's that time of year—when the newest batch of surgical interns arrives at Seattle Grace . . . As I like to call them: The Virgin Surgeons.

The other surgical nurses and I have a bet going as to which intern will be crowned "007"—Licensed to Kill. My money's on the pretty blonde working with Dr. Bailey (aka the Nazi . . .)—rumor has it she used to be a lingerie model. HA!

This year's group seems particularly green . . . no telling what kind of trouble they'll get into . . .

The residents and attendings like to start the interns out with a BANG. Make a big first impression—in other words, scare the crap out of them . . . Everyone has their own methods.

Dr. Bailey—she likes to run the kids till they drop. A full 48 hours of work for their first shift . . . Sure, it seems a little extreme, but—Hey. This is surgery. A specialty full of jocks and bullies. If you can't cut it, then you might as well figure it out now . . .

And Dr. Burke? He's our cardiothoracic superstar—he chooses one intern every year to scrub in on a procedure their very first day. Usually chooses the intern before they've even shown up for work that day . . .

Some years he picks the cockiest, most confident sucker—to knock him or her down a notch. And some years he tries to weed out the weakest link in the group—demonstrate his version of: survival of the fittest.

Wonder who he'll decide to pick on this year . . .

Medical Royalty

So—it gets better. This year, we have "medical royalty" in the mix.

I've been at Seattle Grace a long time, but even someone new to the hospital would know about the infamous Ellis Grey. She's a legend around here—one of the hospital's most famous surgeons.

And (get this) one of our new interns . . . is her daughter. If only Liz (Ellis's old scrub nurse) were still working—she'd get such a kick out of torturing Grey's offspring . . . I'll just have to pick up the slack in her honor! (wink.)

The interns aren't the only ones who are new this year. Turns out the Chief has brought in some hotshot new neurosurgeon— all the way from NYC.

Haven't seen him yet myself, but the floor nurses are describing him as "eye candy in a lab coat." Of course, those baby blue eyes don't mean a thing if he can't slice and dice in the OR . . . But knowing the Chief, that won't be a problem. Chief Webber has an uncanny eye for talent.

Speaking of which—I lost my bet. Turns out this year's resident "007" isn't the model, it's the intern Burke decided to pick on . . . I think his name is O'Malley.

Burke had him scrub in on an appendectomy, and the kid totally choked at the last minute . . . Lost hold of the purse strings— cavity started filling up with all sorts of nasty . . . Really. How do you screw up an appendectomy?

Oh well. Gotta be up for an early shift in the AM, so I'd better post this and sign off . . . More intern tales to come, I am sure.

The Virgin Surgeons: Descriptions and Predictions

Looks like a long year ahead, given the batch of surgical interns we've been dealt . . . Thought you might enjoy a rundown on some of them . . .

Plus, every year, the other nurses and I like to make predictions about the newbies . . . who's going to have a meltdown, who's going to be the first to kill a patient . . . who's most likely to hook up with whom . . .

(You should know—people hook up in this hospital ALL the time. Especially the interns . . . so, it's always fun to try and guess who will try to get into whose scrub pants first!)

Meredith Grey

Spitting image of her mother at that age . . . Seems quiet, but she's one to watch. Has already started showing the other interns up—in front of the Chief, no less.

Seems distracted, though—there's something else going on with her. A secret, maybe? Again—not too different from her mother.

Already seems to have caught the eye of the new Dr. Shepherd . . . He let her scrub in with him, which is huge for a new intern. She must have really impressed him . . .

Yeah. Definitely one to watch.

Predictions: She'll follow in her mother's footsteps—if she can hack it. And I still say—there's more to her than meets the eye. She's hiding something.

Cristina Yang

Can't stand her already. Cocky. Brazen. Too smart for her own good . . . which, of course, means she'll make one hell of a surgeon. It also means she'll be next to impossible to work with . . .

Heard she drives a motorcycle—which says a lot. About her

being fearless, feeling invincible . . . Or, at least, that's what she wants people to think.

Terrible bedside manner—which could one day be her downfall. Around here, you have to have the whole package—the Chief accepts nothing less.

Predictions: She's TOO confident. I think something will happen to shake up her world . . . I also predict she'll be the first of the group to fly solo—to perform a surgery all on her own.

Izzie Stevens

Former lingerie model. Blonde. Beautiful. Seriously? She does NOT belong on a surgical service. If for no other reason than because—Hello! The other interns are going to eat her alive.

She's learning quickly, though. Already stood up to Bailey once, which—trust me—takes some guts.

And she does have an innate ability to connect with her patients. That's the kind of thing that can't be taught—either you have it, or you don't.

Predictions: First glance tells me she's the one who will melt down and drop out, but then again—I think she also has it in her to surprise us all. I get the feeling she thrives on exceeding people's expectations.

George O'Malley

Ah . . . "007." Feel kinda bad for the guy—he seems so completely out of his element. There doesn't seem to be a cutthroat bone in his body. I take it back about Stevens. O'Malley's totally the first to call it quits out of this group.

He's got the desire to be a surgeon, but I wonder if he has the drive . . .

Plus he's obviously got some kind of puppy-dog crush on Grey—it's a little pathetic.

Predictions: O'Malley will suffer in silence—no way he will ever manage hook up with Meredith Grey. And as for his surgical future? I predict there is none. I give him six months, tops, before he quits the program.

Alex Karev

Now, this guy has what it takes to be a surgeon. Rumor is he has his eye on a career in plastics—sounds about right.

That doesn't mean I like the kid—far as I'm concerned, he's the most obnoxious of the group. And you should see the way he's been hitting on—well—pretty much every female on staff. Definite player.

And my co-worker, Nurse Olivia, seems to be eating it up. She's young. I keep trying to warn her that interns like Karev? Not usually such a great catch, but . . .

Sometimes you just have to learn these things for yourself.

Predictions: Karev will be the standout of the group—he'll show everyone up. (While, I'm sure, hooking up with someone new in the on-call room every chance he gets.)

Who's Who at Seattle Grace?

I realized I've been chatting about all of our surgeons as though you already know them . . . So, to keep from confusing anyone, here's the scoop on some of our surgical staff.

And by scoop I mean MY scoop. Let's face it—I know things about most of these people they would never put in their own personal bio!

Chief Richard Webber

Head honcho—Big Kahuna. Married, no kids, good guy . . . Was an intern here with Ellis Grey, back in the day. The tales I've heard from some of Seattle Grace's most seasoned nurses? Richard and Ellis were . . . um . . . very close. I imagine it must be strange for him, suddenly finding himself as Meredith Grey's boss . . .

Dr. Preston Burke

Cardiothoracic surgeon—deals with hearts and lungs. (Plays the trumpet, believe it or not—we keep trying to get him to play a guest spot at our holiday party . . .) Lowest mortality rate in the hospital. The guy is a machine. Right down to his surgical caps— you should see how he behaves when he doesn't get them back from the laundry service in time for surgery!

Dr. Derek Shepherd

The new guy. Big shot back in New York—and rumor has it, he has a history with the Chief. Unclear exactly what that history is . . . Shepherd goes to some trouble not to talk much about his life before Seattle Grace. What I do know is—he's an incredible surgeon. Definitely adds a lot to our neurosurgical wing—not to mention a little friction with Burke. If there's one thing Burke doesn't like, it's to be upstaged . . .

Dr. Miranda Bailey

I know. I shouldn't have favorites . . . but I do. And my favorite— is Dr. Bailey. She's my kind of people—no-nonsense, tells it like it is . . . And, an amazing general surgeon—she's really begun to shine. She's a surgical resident and the person immediately in charge of those ragamuffin interns. And—damn. You should see her husband—that man is a catch!

McDreamy in Our Midst . . .

Wow. Looked after a patient yesterday that really hit home for me . . . Poor girl came in, all battered and bruised from an assault—I've never seen the OR staff rally around a patient like we did yesterday . . .

As much silliness as goes on around here, when something like that comes through the operating room doors, well . . . it shifts your perspective.

And, get this—not only does it look like she is going to make it through all the trauma . . . but she is one AMAZING fighter. We pulled a good chunk of her attacker's penis—Yes! His PENIS—out of her ruptured esophagus!!!

That's right! She actually bit it off!!

Now, it's a rare moment when Dr. Burke is rendered speechless in the operating room, but let me just say for the record: Burke was definitely speechless.

In fact, I sensed Dr. Burke was a little off yesterday, anyway. Something must have been bothering him . . . If you want my opinion? I think our new Dr. Shepherd is going to give him a run for his money when it comes to taking over as Chief. Haven't heard anything official about it, but I'm around these guys all day. I can tell when something is up.

And as for Dr. Shepherd . . . The staff has started calling him "Dr. McDreamy." Some because they are mesmerized by his amazing head of hair . . . others seem to be swooning over his eyes . . . Me? I like it when he leans on things. There's just something very . . . dreamy when he leans.

I could have sworn I caught him making eyes at that Grey intern. Wouldn't that be typical? Beauty and the Brain Surgeon.

Instant Message Conversation

DebbieDoesGossip—logged on at 7:46 a.m.

DebbieDoesGossip:	OK. I've been watching Grey & Shepherd all morning, and . . . I think you're right. There's something going on between those two . . .
JoeKnowsBest:	Told ya. I'm always right about these things.

DebbieDoesGossip:	Um—remember the time you thought I was dating Dr. Bailey?
JoeKnowsBest:	Old news. That was years ago. I barely knew you.
DebbieDoesGossip:	Or the time you SWORE Dr. Burke was into YOU?
JoeKnowsBest:	I'm still not convinced he isn't, btw.
DebbieDoesGossip:	All I'm saying is—you are not always right about these things.
JoeKnowsBest:	But in this case . . . ?
DebbieDoesGossip:	In this case—I think you may be onto something. Ever since our last conversation, I've been watching Shepherd and Grey, and . . . he goes out of his way to talk to her. Even pulled her into the stairwell . . .
JoeKnowsBest:	I knew it!
DebbieDoesGossip:	But we don't exactly have confirmation yet . . . I'll tell you what I CAN confirm, though . . .
JoeKnowsBest:	That you'll be by tonight for the Champions-Only Darts Tournament?
DebbieDoesGossip:	Karev and Nurse Olivia are getting very cozy. Walked in on them totally making out in the supply closet last night.
JoeKnowsBest:	No kidding?
DebbieDoesGossip:	No kidding.
JoeKnowsBest:	Do me a favor . . . next time you catch Alex with his pants down? Check the pockets for cash. He's running up one hell of a bar tab . . .

DebbieDoesGossip—logged off at 8:14 a.m.

Dead Baby Bike Race Day...

I hate Dead Baby Bike Race Day. We all do. These crazy freaky kids ride their crazy freaky bikes all over town causing all sorts of crazy freaky accidents. It's one of our busiest days at the hospital—and something always goes wrong.

Last year, some guy tried to shortcut through someone's yard, and wound up impaling his leg on their picket fence. Year before that, some woman sideswiped a biker with her car door—and the biker lost his handlebars, two fingers, and a surprisingly deeply pierced nipple ring.

No telling what's in store this year. Late for work. This should be fun.

Dead Baby Bike Race Day, Continued...

As predicted—another crazy bike race this year! One guy came in with bicycle spokes slicing through his abdomen . . . But the best part is? I heard Dr. Grey made out with the guy in his exam room! In front of Dr. Shepherd!!

But I spent most of my time today in the OR with an unlucky pedestrian—we had to declare him brain-dead . . . You should have seen the way Yang and Stevens reacted to this guy . . . Yang was frustrated not to be working on something more exciting, while Stevens? She managed to connect with this guy, despite the fact he was—for all practical purposes—a corpse.

She gets dangerously close to her patients. It's the kind of thing that could really come back to haunt her if she isn't careful . . . First rule of surgery: Learn to keep your distance.

Good news is, we wound up being able to harvest his organs,

including a liver for a patient we all know and love. Altogether, not a bad day.

But boy, these interns are gutsy little rascals! Apparently Yang and Grey confronted Dr. Burke in the MEN'S ROOM of all places!! Only to later use O'Malley to go over Burke's head, straight to the Chief!!

If an intern had tried that stuff back when I first started out? They'd have been out on the street and looking for a new job.

My opinion? Interns these days just don't get the right amount of discipline.

Bethany Whisper . . .

OK. I've seen a lot of practical jokes in this hospital, but today's takes the cake!

Karev plastered every available surface on the floor with photos of Izzie Stevens—shots of her from the most recent Bethany Whisper catalogue!

(Speaking of which, I think I may order the lingerie set she was wearing, in purple—or maybe blue. Because, yes—I DO have a sex life. Nurses have just as much sex as anyone else . . . And, NO—I am not planning to share those details with you. I'd much rather gossip about everyone ELSE'S exploits, thank you very much . . .)

So, hats off to Karev. I LOVE a good practical joke . . . Especially when it involves someone who looks THAT damn good in her underwear—I mean, honestly. That's just not fair.

Liz Fallon

Today started off fun, but turned into a very difficult day for me. Which is why I'm up at 4:30 a.m., typing this blog.

One of our former scrub nurses, and a dear friend of mine, Liz Fallon, passed away tonight. In fact, she was Ellis Grey's scrub nurse until Ellis retired . . . Liz has been terminally ill for a while, so it wasn't a surprise. But it doesn't matter how prepared you think you are for something like that—it's never easy.

I was in the room when she passed. It was a strangely serene moment, even for Cristina Yang, who was the intern who had been attending to her.

It's funny because, before now, Cristina has always struck me as the cold, heartless, whatever-it-takes kind of doctor . . . but I saw something else in her tonight. Something unexpected . . . I think we all did.

Liz would have approved.

Get This Party Started . . .

And I thought pulling a penis out of a patient was weird!!

Today we removed a folded surgical towel out from under one of our patients' lungs!?!? And not just any patient . . . I remember this woman very clearly—I was in on her very first surgery, years ago, when the towel must have been left behind. Burke was there, too—just a first- or second-year resident at that time, if I recall . . . I have a feeling this isn't the last we'll hear about the towel. Mistakes like that rarely float by without major repercussions . . .

But I'm not going to worry about that right now because— guess who just got invited to a PARTY??

That's right! I'm hip. I'm cool. And I'm so getting drunk tonight at the Stevens/O'Malley/Grey house party! I hear Stevens is dating a hockey player . . . hope he brings a few of his hockey buddies to the festivities!!!

Joe's been giving me a hard time all day about this stupid

party—trying to make me feel all left out because the interns hadn't invited the nurses yet . . . whatever. He just likes to think he has his pulse on what's happening at Seattle Grace more than I do—as IF!!

I think I'll wear my new jeans. They are rather sassy, if I do say so myself.

McDreamy's Tail Wagon

Just got home from that party—whew! I haven't done that many tequila shots since the last time I was playing darts at Joe's!

But I just had to share—I ran into Dr. Bailey as she was leaving—in a hurry, I might add. She'd just come from a steamy car in the driveway—and the expression on her face was so strange, I had to go check out the car for myself . . .

And you'll NEVER believe what—or, rather, WHO—I saw hurrying to get dressed in the backseat!?!?! That's right. Doctors Grey and Shepherd were VERY much naked in that car together.

I can't wait to tell Joe that our suspicions have been confirmed. Grey is definitely doing McDreamy!! Oh MAN!— I would hate to be Meredith Grey on rounds with Dr. Bailey in the morning!

Instant Message Conversation

DebbieDoesGossip—logged on at 7:56 a.m.

DebbieDoesGossip: This is an emergency. I need your foolproof hangover recipe. STAT.

JoeKnowsBest: Told you to steer clear of the tequila last night.

DebbieDoesGossip:	Where the heck WERE you? I looked all over at the party and never even saw you!!
JoeKnowsBest:	I know—I got there late. Tried to find you . . . Meet any cute hockey players?
DebbieDoesGossip:	Party was disappointingly void of hockey players . . . but . . .
JoeKnowsBest:	Yes . . . ?
DebbieDoesGossip:	I did . . . sort of . . . make out with my Ex for a while in the corner . . .
JoeKnowsBest:	No!!! Don't go back there, Debbie! Back away from Dr. Taylor!!
DebbieDoesGossip:	It didn't mean anything—he was totally drunk.
JoeKnowsBest:	There's a surprise.
DebbieDoesGossip:	Besides—I have news. BIG news.
JoeKnowsBest:	Dish.
DebbieDoesGossip:	Last night—as I was leaving . . . Bailey caught Dr. Grey and Dr. Shepherd in his car. Naked.
JoeKnowsBest:	Seriously?
DebbieDoesGossip:	Seriously.
JoeKnowsBest:	Guess that explains where she disappeared to . . .
DebbieDoesGossip:	Guess it does!
JoeKnowsBest:	Has Grey shown up for rounds yet?
DebbieDoesGossip:	Haven't seen her—but I have seen Dr. Bailey . . .
JoeKnowsBest:	And?

DebbieDoesGossip: And . . . let's just say there's a reason we all call
                      her the Nazi.

DebbieDoesGossip—logged off at 8:35 a.m.

Ewww

All I have to say today is: "Eeeeewwww."

Have you ever watched those medical shows on TV—you know, the ones where they show you these ridiculously large, grotesque tumors that you NEVER expect to actually see in person?

Well, today? I saw one in person. And trust me when I say—they are every bit as disgusting as you might have imagined.

This poor woman came in with a growth that must have weighed 60 lb or more—it was massive. Truly unbelievable . . .

Anyway—she was in surgery for hours . . . I had to leave before it was over—will have to find out tomorrow how everything went . . .

On another note—had quite the scare with one of our post-op patients today . . . And Dr. Stevens? I think I may have underestimated her a bit . . . She managed to single-handedly remove a deadly clot from our post-op guy—bedside. Just reopened his chest, stuck her fingers (gloved, of course) in there, and—scooped out the clot. Like a pro.

Hate to admit that an intern (let alone a model) has skills, but—it was really impressive. I mean, hey. I've seen seasoned doctors buckle under that type of pressure before—one wrong move, and she could have easily killed him.

Meanwhile—there's been quite the ripple effect since Bailey discovered Shepherd and Grey are "an item." They actually don't seem to be making much effort to cover their tracks . . . it's interesting. I wonder how the Chief is going to react when he finds out . . .

Because if one thing's certain? He'll find out—and he won't be happy about it.

Just Ask Debbie

I get a lot of questions about things at Seattle Grace—so every now and then, I like to take a moment to answer a few of them . . .

Debbie—I was recently at Seattle Grace for an appointment— and it seemed like there were a lot of different-colored scrubs . . . What do the different colors mean?

Every hospital does things differently, but at Seattle Grace, different scrub colors designate different departments (and levels of staff . . .). For instance—most surgical attendings wear dark-blue scrubs, while the residents and interns under them wear light-blue. Pediatric interns usually wear lavender, while ER staff are often in light brown . . . Then, there are the nurses. We pretty much wear whatever we want—just the way I like it.

Deb—What exactly does "scrubbing in" mean? You reference it now and again, but I'm not sure I really understand it.

Scrubbing In—it's how you prepare before surgery. If you are go- ing to have any immediate contact with the patient in surgery, you have to be sterile. So there is a detailed, meticulous process used by surgeons to make sure their arms and hands are as clean as possible before being gowned and gloved.

Now, you can be in an OR without being "scrubbed in"—in that case you would just wear a mask and scrubs . . . but it also means you wouldn't be allowed to touch the patient at all—or in any way enter the sterile field.

Hi Debbie—You and Joe (the bartender) seem like good friends. How did you two meet?

To be honest—I don't remember the first time we met. I'm sure it was at the bar, and I'm sure he was pouring me tequila, but . . .

I do remember the first time we knew we'd be friends. It was years ago now . . .

It was late afternoon—Happy Hour time, and my shift had just ended. I wasn't ready to head home quite yet, so I popped into Joe's for a quick drink and a basket of fried food. (Joe's has some killer spicy buffalo wings. Best in Seattle if you ask me . . .)

It was the day of the first annual Emerald City Darts Tournament—my stumbling on it was a happy accident, really, since I hadn't even been to Joe's more than a few times . . .

So it was time to play—and Joe needed a partner. His (now ex) partner had flaked on him, and . . .

I volunteered. I slammed my beer, stepped up to the board—and my bull's-eye throwing skills helped take us all the way to the semifinals.

But that wasn't what told us we'd be such great friends, actually—it was after we'd lost the semifinals round, and were sitting at the bar, watching the remainder of the competition . . .

Joe congratulated me on my darts-playing skills—I congratulated him on taking my mind off of my difficult day at work . . . We sat there, munching on peanuts and enjoying ourselves as we—began to gossip. Not big gossip. Not important gossip—just . . . silly little tidbits about all of the people we knew in common . . .

So many people at the hospital spend so much time across the street at Joe's—it was kind of a revelation—we shared a connection to almost every person we could think of at Seattle Grace. I saw them at work; he saw them after work—it was fun. Like comparing notes . . .

We've been great friends ever since. Joe likes to say we bonded over darts. I say we bonded over a common love for gossip . . .

(He doesn't call it gossip—he calls it "looking after his customers.") Either way—it's nice to have someone like Joe around to help put things in perspective.

Plus, he mixes one hell of a martini.

Debbie—What's the story with Dr. Taylor? You've mentioned him . . . Joe's mentioned him . . . Will you share details?

OK. Yes—a number of you have been curious about my infamous ex—Dr. Taylor. So, in the spirit of sharing so much about so many other people, I'll go ahead and share a bit about myself . . .

Dr. Taylor is an anesthesiologist at Seattle Grace. Has been for years. Older than I am—fairly handsome, certainly charming . . .

I've scrubbed in on a LOT of surgeries with him over the years . . . And one day, he—well—he asked me out. In surgery. With his crossword puzzle.

He likes crossword puzzles. Does them during operations—the thing is, for a long operation, the anesthesiologist doesn't have tons to do . . . they need to be on hand, you know, in case something goes wrong, but . . . while the surgery itself is happening? Dr. Taylor would usually hang out and do his puzzle. Like clockwork.

So—I got in the habit of asking him for the clues—and I'd help him with parts of his puzzles . . . We were a pretty good team.

One day—during a bypass, I think—Dr. Taylor said there was a clue he needed from me: "Four letters, starts with a 'D,' Middle Eastern food often stuffed with fillings such as almonds, candied lemon peel, and marzipan." . . . I thought about it for a moment, then offered—"A date?"

"YES!" he replied, excited, then added—"That would be lovely—how about tomorrow night, say around 7:00?"

Cheesy? Yes. Charming—well, yeah . . . it kinda was. At least, at the time, it struck me as charming in that geeky way that's also so endearing . . . And for a while, Dr. Taylor and I had a lot of fun—a lot of late nights at Joe's, and . . . well. You get the picture.

But things didn't end well. For one thing—It became clear that he wasn't interested in doing ANYTHING that didn't in some way involve alcohol. Don't get me wrong—I enjoy Joe's as much as the next gal, but . . . sometimes, it's fun NOT to drink.

Especially when you work this hard—this many hours. But not for Taylor—he just . . . doesn't cope well without a drink in his hand. Which was a concern for me.

Anyway—that's the short story. Joe was happy when we broke it off. He never did think much of the guy . . .

Competition Is ON

OK, today—I feel like crap.

The flu's going around—half the nursing staff has been out with it this week already—and there's nothing that makes me feel MORE like crap than . . . dealing with these interns. Especially when they start encouraging our patients' idiotic behavior . . .

Take this gunshot-wound patient today . . . He's been in here before. Not the brightest bulb . . . hires his friends to SHOOT him—as in hold out a gun and pull the trigger—the guy gets gunshot wounds for FUN. Likes the way the scars look or some such nonsense . . . Ask me? He's an absolute moron.

So what did Karev—his doctor—do? Not reprimand this guy for his risky behavior, not educate the guy on just how dangerous this is . . . No. They swapped stories about wrestling. WRESTLING. Like Karev had some latent respect for this dude or something. Unreal. Gimme a break.

Meanwhile, Dr. Shepherd performed a successful hemispherectomy today (in other words, he literally removed half of a little girl's brain!)—I mean, wow. Say what you want about his questionable personal life—(an attending dating an intern? Definitely a bad idea . . .)—But you can't deny that Shepherd's amazing at his job . . .

And don't think for a moment that Dr. Burke hasn't noticed. The competitive vibe between those two is ON. I say, it's high time we had another superstar surgeon around here—it certainly makes things interesting . . .

Psychic?!

I know I'm about to sound like a kook—Usually I'm pretty no-nonsense about this sort of thing, but . . .

There's this guy in the hospital today. A guy who—apparently—has psychic seizures. Now, I really am as skeptical as the next gal, but . . . what's the harm in checking him out, right? I mean, what's the worst that could happen?

So, I popped into his room this morning. Completely routine—nothing special, and—before I could even check his IV—his eyes got all distant . . . Eyelids started to flutter . . . and then he began to mumble things . . . things that (I hate to admit it but) may have just made me a believer.

First he told me that I enjoy giving my colleagues a hard time—which is true . . . if you consider the interns my colleagues.

Then he told me that I wouldn't enjoy my chowder for lunch (which didn't impress me at all, as I had packed myself a tuna sandwich. But, as it turns out, I LEFT the sandwich on my kitchen counter this morning and wound up ordering the cafeteria's soup of the day—Broccoli and Cheddar Chowder . . . which, as it turns out, no—I did not particularly enjoy . . .)

And THEN—He told me I'd lose a patient before 11 a.m. today. And sure enough, at 10:45—my patient in 4114 coded.

Now, it is possible that these were all coincidental little predictions—It's not like I'm totally convinced this guy's really truly psychic, but . . .

Then again . . . Hmmm. Maybe I'll pop in one more time before his surgery. Just to ask another question or two . . .

Instant Message Conversation

DebbieDoesGossip—logged on at 4:33 p.m.

DebbieDoesGossip: So. There's a patient here today who claims he's psychic.

JoeKnowsBest: Really psychic, or really THINKS he's psychic?

DebbieDoesGossip: Unclear.

JoeKnowsBest: Hey—remember the time you and I went to that five-dollar psychic down the street from my apartment?

DebbieDoesGossip: Yeah—and you were convinced she'd crossed over—bringing back a message from your dead goldfish.

JoeKnowsBest: Don't mock. I was young and naive.

DebbieDoesGossip: It was last month.

JoeKnowsBest: And I loved that goldfish.

DebbieDoesGossip: Anyway—I think this guy may be legit. He told me some things . . . things he couldn't have known.

JoeKnowsBest: Like what?

DebbieDoesGossip: Said to stay away from anesthesiologists.

JoeKnowsBest: I could have told you that.

DebbieDoesGossip: He also predicted that one of my patients would code—

JoeKnowsBest: Hello. U work at a hospital.

DebbieDoesGossip: And then he said a close friend of mine would meet someone important tonight.

JoeKnowsBest:	That's nice and vague.
DebbieDoesGossip:	Someone with a "W."
JoeKnowsBest:	A "W"?
DebbieDoesGossip:	That's what he said.
JoeKnowsBest:	And U believe him?
DebbieDoesGossip:	Hey. You believed in the goldfish.

DebbieDoesGossip—logged off at 5:01 p.m.

Syphilis and Mrs. McDreamy? Oh My!

Here's what I want to know. How did our surgical floor single-handedly create its own syphilis outbreak? Who are these people having so much sex? And, honestly—why aren't I one of them?

Not that I want the syph, but . . . I sure wouldn't mind the sex part.

The Chief invoked a mandatory sex-education class for the entire staff today . . . That was fun (not). Although, watching Patricia demonstrate proper condom-usage on a banana? Now, that did have its moments . . .

Meanwhile—all hell has been breaking loose today . . .

The dam burst on Olivia's little love-life bubble . . . Turns out she's been dating George O'Malley—That girl gets around—last I had heard, she and Karev had been hooking up . . . But I guess O'Malley didn't know that . . .

Because he punched Karev in the face tonight as soon as he found out . . . Needless to say, Karev's going to have a hell of a black eye in the morning.

But that's not all . . . I was running some paperwork down to accounting this evening, when I saw a light on in the morgue . . .

Now—that's not so unusual, but then I heard voices. Familiar voices. So I snuck up to the door, and peeked inside to discover . . .

Yang and Stevens performing what looked like . . . an autopsy? Now, I'm a stickler for paperwork. All authorizations go through me, and I knew DAMN well I hadn't seen any paperwork about an autopsy on one of my patients, so . . .

Just as I was about to turn around, march upstairs, and find Dr. Bailey—she found me. She'd already figured out what her two troublemaking interns were up to and . . . well . . . I'd be lying if I said I didn't stick around to listen to her yell at them.

Funny thing is—once they made their case, I think she was just as fascinated as they were about what they'd found . . .

Surgeons. Butchers first—everything else second.

Meanwhile—there was something else fishy happening tonight . . . in OR 2. When I did make my way back to the surgical floor, I noticed that OR 2 looked as though it had just been used for a surgery.

I know the room hadn't been booked for anything . . . went back to the board just to double-check and, sure enough—nothing. When clearly SOME kind of surgery had been happening in there. An unscheduled surgery. A secret surgery . . .

What is this hospital coming to??

To top it off—as I was reporting in for the second half of my double shift tonight—you'll never BELIEVE what, or rather, WHO, I saw in the lobby . . .

Looked like Dr. Shepherd and Dr. Grey were about to head out for a dinner date or something when . . .

The most ravishing redhead imaginable (no kidding—it's as though the rain outside hadn't so much as dampened her hair) waltzed into the lobby, made a beeline for McDreamy, and . . .

. . . introduced herself as—HIS WIFE.

His wife, people. McDreamy is McMarried!?!?!

I'm bursting at the seams. I have to talk about this with someone—anyone.

I have to find Joe.

Instant Message Conversation

DebbieDoesGossip—logged on at 8:18 p.m.

DebbieDoesGossip:	Joe? Are you there? You better be there—because I have NEWS you will not believe!!!
JoeKnowsBest:	Me, too.
DebbieDoesGossip:	Mine's better. You first.
JoeKnowsBest:	Derek's married.
DebbieDoesGossip:	Damn it!! How did you know that??? His wife hasn't been here an hour!! How could you already KNOW that??
JoeKnowsBest:	Meredith's here—turns out tequila makes her talkative.
DebbieDoesGossip:	Totally stole my thunder. U suck . . . Busy night?
JoeKnowsBest:	Just took some aspirin. Killer headache.
DebbieDoesGossip:	That bites . . . Wait—Grey's there? At the bar? I thought you said she never comes to the bar . . . ? Well . . . Except for the FIRST time she came to the bar—the night she went home with McDreamy—guess we'll have to call him something else now, like—what? McMarried?
DebbieDoesGossip:	Joe—are you ignoring me or do you have customers there?
DebbieDoesGossip:	Hello? Joe? U There??
DebbieDoesGossip:	. . . Joe?

DebbieDoesGossip—logged off at 8:46 p.m.

Joe

I am beside myself.

My shift ended three hours ago, but I can't bring myself to go home. I'm at a loss. I keep bursting into tears. I . . . don't know what to do.

Last night, Joe was brought in to the hospital . . . My Joe. Bartender Joe. Lovable, invincible, one of my very best friends—JOE.

He has an aneurysm—a really hard-to-reach aneurysm. This is serious. And scary. And—so sudden. They want to operate today.

So . . . aside from watching over Joe like a hawk (and giving him a hard time about scaring me like this . . .), I've done the only other thing I can think of to do . . .

I've ordered him muffins.

It may sound silly, but I happen to know Joe loves muffins. He has an inexplicable love for muffins. So I've started up a collection on the floor to get him the biggest damn basket of muffins I can find . . .

I may not be able to fix him. Or promise him he'll make it through this intact, but . . . I can buy him muffins. That I can do.

I've been going to Joe's bar every Thursday night for years— even before I left County Hospital and got my job here . . . Joe's bar is such an institution around here . . . I can't imagine what things would be like if . . . No. I won't even type it. I'll just look forward to him recuperating, and to my Thursday-night $2 beers and dart tournaments.

Joe will be back at the bar, cheering me and my dart team on in no time. I can feel it.

I just hope the cost for this hospital stay doesn't break him— I know things have been tight lately, partly because he's so good-natured about letting customers not pay their tabs . . . I always pay mine, but . . . Not everyone is quite so conscientious.

Oh! And you know that secret surgery happening last night?
Turns out it was for Chief Webber! McDreamy performed secret
BRAIN SURGERY on the Chief!!

I know I started this blog just to gossip—but there's entirely
too much drama going on right now, even for me . . .

Guess the Chief's OK, though—which is a relief. At least, he
must be OK—I heard he really lit into Shepherd when he found
out he's been dating Dr. Grey . . . Apparently they were kissing or
something when he woke up in recovery . . .

(Between you and me—how dumb is that??)

And now that the Chief is out of commission? Dr. Burke has
been asked to take over as Interim Chief. Yeah—that did NOT
go over so well with Dr. Shepherd, I can tell you that much . . .

I have concerns about Burke as chief, though . . . The man is
an amazing surgeon, but an administrator? I guess we'll find
out . . .

Boy. Can you tell that I'm putting off going home? I just keep
sitting here, typing away, watching Joe out of the corner of my
eye. It's sort of like—as long as I can watch over him, I know he'll
be OK . . .

Is that lame?

Whoa—Yang just walked into Joe's room and vomited into his
toilet. Weird.

A Moment to Honor Joe . . .

I passed a "Get Well" card around the floor and gave it to Joe—
thought you might like to hear some of the messages:

Joe—Your muffins were tasty—wait, I'm talking about your gift bas-
*ket, not, like—in a dirty way. You'll pull through dude—**Alex***

Hi Joe! Oh my gosh—we are totally rooting for you. Can't wait to
see you back at the bar, serving us drinks, watching us go home with

LOSERS . . . *Seriously, though—We love you! xoxo Olivia!!*

*Hey man—Sorry I can't write too much right now—working on something big—as in really BIG because—well, all I'm saying is— I've got your back. Really. So don't sweat it—everything's going to be great—I mean, maybe not for sure great—but hopefully great because, well, at least, that's what I'm hoping. But don't worry about that part. Just . . . hang in there, man. OK. Bye.—**George**. P.S. Thanks for not laughing at me yesterday when I snorted beer up my nose. Really appreciated that.*

*I'm not kidding. You utter one word about what you overheard me and Meredith talking about last night—I'll kill you myself and make it LOOK like an aneurysm.—**Cristina Yang***

*Dear Joe, You're in supergood hands—Dr. Burke is amazing, and so is Dr. Shepherd (at his JOB at least . . .), so don't worry about a thing. I'll be up in the gallery making sure things go smoothly . . . **See you soon, Izzie***

*Joe—never thought I'd perform a standstill—let alone on you. See you on the other side . . . **Dr. Shepherd***

*Dude—Are you kidding me? First time you set foot in this hospital, and you're forcing Burke and Shepherd to perform surgery together??? You always were one to rock the boat, my friend! **Best . . . Nurse Tyler***

*Joe—Please don't die. Otherwise, who's gonna serve me free beers?—**Scooter***

*Hey Joe—So bummed you're in here because that means the dart tournament's cancelled for tonight—OK. I'm also bummed because they are going to kill you then bring you back to life . . . but you have to admit, that's kind of cool . . . Much Luv.—**Nurse Liz***

*Been through a lot together, over the years, haven't we, Joe? Thanks for being my support system when I needed one—now it's my turn to be yours. I'm here if you need me . . . **Bailey***

OK. I hate writing messages on these things, but for you? Anything. Get well soon—I know you'll pull through this surgery like a pro—because if you don't? I'll never forgive you. Love and Hugs and Happy Thoughts. **Yours, Debbie**

Update on Joe

Whew.

You know how sometimes you don't realize how tense you are until . . . you begin to relax? And as soon as you let even the tiniest relaxation in—suddenly every part of your body starts screaming in pain?

Yeah—that's me right now. But I'm so not complaining—because the reason I can relax is—Joe is OK.

His surgery went well, he's already in recovery—awake, alert . . . it's a huge relief.

I haven't even been home yet. Haven't slept. Haven't done anything but gorge myself on Joe's basket of muffins. But it's all worth it because—honestly—I wouldn't have wanted to be anywhere else . . .

Meanwhile—it's been interesting watching how the new Dr. (as in Mrs.) Shepherd has been integrating herself into Seattle Grace . . .

Turns out the Chief asked her to come here for a special fetal case—seems she's some kind of big, important fetal surgeon . . . So she's a visiting surgeon—in for one very high-profile case . . . already getting some attention from the press. I'm not usually one to speculate, but . . .

Knowing the Chief? I bet he wants to offer her a permanent position. He knows what a coup it would be to have a specialist like her at the hospital . . .

Then again—maybe that's my sleep deprivation talking. Could be she's in and out of here by next week. Clearly, from McDreamy's reaction to her, that's what HE wants!

The New Chief

Told you Burke wouldn't know how to handle his stint as Chief—you should see the surgical board today. It's a disaster.

He's bumping surgeries right and left to make room for—what? A guy who swallowed a bunch of Judy Doll heads of all things, and another who—frankly—will be lucky to even make it off of that table . . . ?

This morning, I took the back route to my morning coffee and ran into Burke, in his full-on "Chief" lab coat and button-down shirt . . . checking his reflection out in the window.

Burke's enjoying his new position—but, I'm telling you—he has no idea what he's actually doing. For everyone's sake, I hope the Chief recovers quickly . . .

Because here's the thing—when the board is a mess, and the staff is on edge—it's people like ME who wind up feeling the brunt of it. The nurses. Not the attendings, not the interns—the nurses. There's just no respect.

Speaking of respect—there's something strange going on between Dr. Yang and Dr. Burke—they seemed fine before—perfectly normal, but . . . I've started to notice that the two of them . . . are acting very awkward around each other.

I can't quite place my finger on it—because it's nothing unprofessional or anything, but—there's just something . . . off. Almost—and I don't even know why I'm using this analogy, but—they are acting a little bit like a couple who have broken up—but still have to be around each other every day.

That's nuts, of course—right? I mean, Burke, of all people, would never—could never—especially not with an intern, but . . .

Well. Now that I think about it, I guess . . . it could be possible. I'm going to have to talk to Joe about this one.

I feel sorry for this kid we have in here today . . . car crash victim. His dad's the one on the table—the one in such bad shape . . . I've heard a few rumors about the kid's father—doesn't sound like the nicest guy . . .

And I heard from Dr. Stevens that the kid may be donating part of his liver to his father . . . Can you imagine having to make that kind of decision as a teenager? To decide whether or not to give his own father a chance to live . . .

AAAA! OK, there's a headless Judy Doll tied to my stapler. See what I mean? Absolutely zero respect.

Instant Message Conversation

DebbieDoesGossip—logged on at 5:30 p.m.

DebbieDoesGossip:	Call me crazy—but I think something's going on between Yang and Dr. Burke.
JoeKnowsBest:	What? No welcome back? No glad you're home? No happy you're back after brain surgery?
DebbieDoesGossip:	OK—seriously. The sympathy thing only works for so long. You've been home a week. And I've already come over to check on you twice.
JoeKnowsBest:	Never gets old.
DebbieDoesGossip:	Quit stalling. What's the scoop on Burktina?
JoeKnowsBest:	Who says there's a scoop on Burktina?
DebbieDoesGossip:	Oh, there's a scoop. I can feel it.
JoeKnowsBest:	Did I tell you the dart tournaments are starting back up again? Nurse Liz is WAY psyched.
DebbieDoesGossip:	OMG—you really ARE stalling. What do you know??
JoeKnowsBest:	Nothing . . . ?

DebbieDoesGossip:	You're holding out on me! Unacceptable.
JoeKnowsBest:	Dude. I just had brain surgery. Chill.
DebbieDoesGossip:	U suffering from short term memory loss?
JoeKnowsBest:	No.
DebbieDoesGossip:	Then I will not chill.
JoeKnowsBest:	Cristina swore me to secrecy. On my life. I believe her when she says she can hurt me.
DebbieDoesGossip:	Oh come on. Since when does your loyalty lie with an intern???
JoeKnowsBest:	Swear you won't say a word. Not even on your blog.
DebbieDoesGossip:	That's a tall order.
JoeKnowsBest:	Swear it.
DebbieDoesGossip:	OK.
JoeKnowsBest:	OK?
DebbieDoesGossip:	I said OK!!
JoeKnowsBest:	OK . . . Only . . . Nope. I can't do it. I'm chicken.
DebbieDoesGossip:	You're kidding, right?
JoeKnowsBest:	What can I say? Cristina scares me more than you do.

DebbieDoesGossip—logged off at 6:03 p.m.

Expect the Unexpected

Some days things around here just hit too close to home.

One of our interns collapsed today in the OR . . . Not just any intern—we're talking Cristina Yang. We were in the middle of a tumor resection—Burke was grilling her about the surgery (like I said before—something strange is going on between those two . . .)

And Yang was totally unfocussed. Not answering his questions . . . swaying a little . . . I was just about to say something when—One minute, Burke was cauterizing blood vessels—the next . . . Yang was on the FLOOR.

Now—Burke doesn't usually get flustered, but I'm telling you—this clearly shook him up.

I mean—we've all seen our share of newbies get a little queasy at the sight of blood and ooze and all that—but by now? Shouldn't be an issue—especially not with someone like Cristina Yang . . .

I think there was something much more serious going on with Yang—her face was just . . . ashen. Don't know exactly what was wrong with her, but it can't be good.

And all this after the most unsettling news of all—Ellis Grey was admitted to the hospital today.

That's right—Ellis Grey. Seattle Grace legend. Meredith Grey's mother . . . And you should have seen her.

Kicking and screaming—literally. I couldn't believe my eyes . . . You have to understand, back when Ellis was at Seattle Grace, SHE was the Cristina Yang of her class—aggressive, brilliant, tough . . . To be honest, she scared me a little. But no one could deny her talent—she's still one of the most skilled doctors I've ever worked with . . .

But you should see her now. Heard through the grapevine she's suffering from early onset Alzheimer's . . .

When they wheeled her in, I froze for just a moment—in shock. Then I glanced over from my station, and saw Meredith Grey, peeking at her mother from around the corner.

Until now, I can't say I've been Grey Junior's biggest fan, but . . . I wouldn't wish that kind of situation on anybody. It's enough to just . . . break your heart.

Instant Message Conversation

DebbieDoesGossip—logged on at 7:36 p.m.

DebbieDoesGossip:	OK—I'm so coming by for a drink tonight.
JoeKnowsBest:	Bad day?
DebbieDoesGossip:	Like you wouldn't believe . . . Cristina Yang collapsed during surgery today!!
JoeKnowsBest:	OMG—is she—
DebbieDoesGossip:	Alive. Still in surgery right now.
JoeKnowsBest:	Jeez.
DebbieDoesGossip:	But that's not all . . .
JoeKnowsBest:	There's more?
DebbieDoesGossip:	Ellis Grey came in today—as a patient.
JoeKnowsBest:	What??
DebbieDoesGossip:	She's not well. Alzheimer's. Early onset. U should have seen Meredith. I think all she wanted to do was hide . . .
JoeKnowsBest:	Which means I may be seeing her in here tonight, too . . .
DebbieDoesGossip:	Wouldn't doubt it. It's hard, you know, seeing people you admire—people who are so tough become . . . so vulnerable.
JoeKnowsBest:	Yeah.

DebbieDoesGossip:	Yeah.
JoeKnowsBest:	I have news that might cheer you up . . .
DebbieDoesGossip:	Hit me.
JoeKnowsBest:	Got a new dartboard.
DebbieDoesGossip:	No!! Really?
JoeKnowsBest:	Saving it for you to be the first to try it out. U up for a game tonight?
DebbieDoesGossip:	Get ready to lose.
JoeKnowsBest:	Looking forward to it.
DebbieDoesGossip:	U R the best, Joe.
JoeKnowsBest:	I know.
DebbieDoesGossip:	And so modest.
JoeKnowsBest:	I know.
DebbieDoesGossip:	Thx for cheering me up . . .
JoeKnowsBest:	Anytime, Deb. Anytime.

DebbieDoesGossip—logged off at 8:07 p.m.

Elevator Antics

What's up with all of this pulling the elevator "Stop" button? C'mon, people. It's getting ridiculous.

Today it was Dr. Bailey—Don't these doctors realize that when they pull that button, they inconvenience patients and visitors—who then turn around and start complaining—to ME??? Honestly.

Lunched with Tyler today (another nurse on the floor—tall guy—most everyone has a crush on him) and would you believe he spent the day ushering Dr. Yang BACK to her hospital room?

She was actually rounding with her IV in tow—I'm torn between thinking she's nuts and admiring her determination . . .

I did have a chance to meet Dr. Yang's mother this afternoon— on her way to get a mocha latte or something. Now THAT woman is a handful . . . She spent a good twenty minutes grilling me about Dr. Burke . . . I think she thinks he and her daughter might make a nice couple. Ha! I wonder what she knows that I don't . . . ?

I'll tell you what I do know. Cristina's collapse? Was the result of an extrauterine pregnancy. That's right—Cristina was pregnant. No one is talking about it, really—but everyone knows.

Ooo! Almost forgot the best gossip of the day—the Doctors Shepherd put on quite a show by the elevators this morning . . . Divorce papers were waving, insults were flying—Look. I'm not one to stick my nose in other people's business—(OK. I am.) But . . . with sparks like that between those two? Goodness. I think I'm going to enjoy having Addison Shepherd at the hospital.

Oh jeez. I just saw Ellis Grey hurrying down the hall in scrubs—I should really go—Wait.

Here comes Dr. O'Malley, chasing after her. The Chief has him on babysitting duty at the moment . . . Can't say I'm surprised. Most of these kids don't know their Seattle Grace history the way I do . . . A LOT of things went on around here before the Chief was actually "the Chief."

Chief Webber has a vested interest in looking after Ellis Grey. They go back a long long way. Not that I would want to resurrect any old rumors, or anything. After all, the Chief IS happily married, but . . .

All I'm saying is, it doesn't surprise me in the least that he's keeping such a watchful eye over Ellis Grey.

Stormy Weather

If there's one thing I hate—it's lightning. I've lived in Seattle a long time, and the rain? Not a problem . . . but when it comes to lightning, well . . . I just don't like it. Makes me very uneasy.

Like disaster could strike at any moment . . .

Kind of like this poor kid they wheeled in here this morning— rookie cop. Gunshot wound to the chest . . . I swear, the whole police force is here to check in on him . . . which is sweet and all, but for heaven's sake. They are making me as edgy as the damn lightning, asking me every two minutes how the kid is doing . . .

And these stupid lights keep flickering. I hope it's not danger- ous for me to be on the computer . . . ?

Oh! Apparently there's a guy here watching porn movies in his room—now don't you think that's GOT to be against hospital policy or someth—

Stormy Weather 2

Sorry about that—our power went out.

As in "move all the critical patients, walk around with a flash- light, Holy crap—the elevators are stuck with a critical patient inside!" kind of out.

That's right—the gunshot kid was trapped in the elevator on his way up to the OR. The damn elevator was stuck—the kid, O'Malley, and Karev were inside. And then—the kid started to crash. Burke had to talk them through emergency heart surgery in the elevator!!

But it gets better—Because the real news is—Karev froze. Burke handed him the scalpel . . . and Karev totally choked. Couldn't bring himself to go ahead and open the patient up. He just stood there—until O'Malley stepped in and saved the day.

Which means my prediction was wrong. Karev was NOT the first of the interns to fly solo—it was O'Malley. Once he was "007"—and now he's the "Heart in the Elevator Guy."

No one can stop talking about it—the cops in the waiting area couldn't stop congratulating O'Malley . . . Everyone wanted to know how he managed to pull it off all on his own—

One of our orthopedic residents—Dr. Torres—pulled me aside and grilled me for like twenty minutes about O'Malley and his elevator antics . . . All the while, Karev has just been . . . so quiet. Watching and seething. It's pretty clear he's feeling jealous of O'Malley right now . . .

Just goes to show—anyone can surprise you.

Heard a rumor Karev has other problems, too—apparently he didn't pass one of his board exams. Has to retake it—and pass— or he's out of the program . . .

Never would have pegged that one, either—but like I said— anyone can surprise you.

Is that—? I smell fire.

And I hear chanting—Oh no. When Dr. Shepherd got me to approve that Shaman coming to visit one of his patients, I did NOT approve the use of fire!

That's it. I'm going down there this instant! Taking advantage of my good nature like that—I can't believe I let myself fall for the McDreamy charm! I could kick myself!

Instant Message Conversation

DebbieDoesGossip—logged on at 6:32 p.m.

JoeKnowsBest:	You there? Is your power acting funky over there?
DebbieDoesGossip:	Sure is. We're on backup generators right now. Big drama happening.
JoeKnowsBest:	Bigger than me beating your darts score?
DebbieDoesGossip:	You WHAT?
JoeKnowsBest:	Just kidding.

DebbieDoesGossip:	Not funny.
JoeKnowsBest:	What's happening over there?
DebbieDoesGossip:	Elevator's stuck. O'Malley's performing heart surgery inside.
JoeKnowsBest:	OK—that totally trumps my darts score. Are you serious???
DebbieDoesGossip:	Oh yeah.
JoeKnowsBest:	That's insane.
DebbieDoesGossip:	Tell me about it—Just got an update—he's done. They're about to transport the guy to an OR.
JoeKnowsBest:	Wow.
DebbieDoesGossip:	Wow is right.
JoeKnowsBest:	Never would have pegged it.
DebbieDoesGossip:	I know. 007 just flew solo.

DebbieDoesGossip—logged off at 7:07 p.m.

Train Wreck

Technically, my shift was over hours ago, but . . . I just got home.

I've been at the hospital all night—called back in after that big train wreck yesterday evening. (You probably saw it on the news. Big deal—really gruesome.)

Anyway—I tried to crawl into bed and sleep the moment I got home, but I just haven't been able to stop my mind from buzzing.

Can't stop thinking about it all—the burn victims, the

amputations . . . we even had an impalement. Yes—an impalement. Two poor train travelers skewered by a metal pole . . .

But that's not what's bothering me.

I was in the Pit most of the night—mostly minor injuries. Just a bunch of frightened people. Except for this one woman. She was there with a friend of hers—and she wasn't fazed in the least. Chatting on her phone (which—by the way—had the world's most ANNOYING ring ever)—Busting Dr. Karev's chops (so, immediately—of course—I liked her!) . . .

She was fun. No-nonsense. She and I hit it off—I even managed to hook her and her friend up with some after-hours jello cups, even though the cafeteria was closed.

And then—out of nowhere—she just died. Literally fell out of her chair, onto the floor—dead.

She wasn't even a patient. She was just there, watching after her friend and—I guess she was suffering from some internal bleeding that none of us knew about. One minute, she's on the phone—and the next . . .

Well. It just hit me hard for some reason. Maybe because she seemed so unaffected by the train wreck, by all of it. When actually, she was more damaged than most of the patients around her . . . Tough on the outside. Bleeding on the inside.

Not to get all somber on you, but I guess we all feel like that now and again . . .

Btw—on a gossipy note (because you KNOW I can't blog without at least a little tidbit of gossip), I saw that Meredith Grey walking around all night pulling a banana bag along with her on an IV pole.

Which could only mean one thing—she was called back from Joe's . . . drunk.

What on earth could have compelled her to come to the hospital drunk?? Guess I'll never know . . . Wait, what am I saying? Of course I'll know . . . because Joe's gonna tell me!

In fact, I bet whatever it is—it's all anyone will be talking about by tomorrow.

Instant Message Conversation

DebbieDoesGossip—logged on at 1:35 a.m.

DebbieDoesGossip:	Grey is walking around here like a zombie . . . Was she this bad before the train wreck?
JoeKnowsBest:	Pretty much.
DebbieDoesGossip:	So, are we guessing McDreamy didn't pick her?
JoeKnowsBest:	Don't know for sure—he arrived here so late . . . she was already gone.
DebbieDoesGossip:	Yikes. So you think—?
JoeKnowsBest:	That no, he didn't pick her, didn't choose her, didn't love her . . .
DebbieDoesGossip:	Really? You think he doesn't love her?
JoeKnowsBest:	I think he's not ready to admit it.
DebbieDoesGossip:	Because of his wife.
JoeKnowsBest:	The guy is a mess. A very confused mess . . . With really good hair.
DebbieDoesGossip:	Grey's a mess, too—U should see her right now.
JoeKnowsBest:	All I'm saying is—if he WAS planning on picking her, he wouldn't have been so late—or so guilty-looking.
DebbieDoesGossip:	He looked guilty?
JoeKnowsBest:	Really guilty.
DebbieDoesGossip:	Hell of a night.
JoeKnowsBest:	You can say that again.

DebbieDoesGossip: Hell of a night.

JoeKnowsBest: OK. I was kidding.

DebbieDoesGossip—logged off at 2:12 a.m.

Something to Talk About

What did I tell you? The entire hospital is buzzing today about Meredith Grey and the Doctors Shepherd. I'd feel sorry for her if it weren't so obvious she knew what she was getting into—dating an attending!

Here's the thing. Any idiot can tell it's eating her up inside. The girl looks like a zombie. But that's just life—I say, leave your personal life at home, and when you come to the hospital, act like a doctor. Not some lovesick teenager.

Now—You'll never believe how my morning started . . . With a stolen patient!!

Cristina Yang managed to SWIPE a patient off of the Psych floor, and sneak him onto the surgical service!! Who does she think she is?

There are rules in this hospital for a reason. There is a protocol to follow, something she and her little cohorts (Stevens and Grey, of course) should respect!!

I've had it up to HERE with their shenanigans. So I put my foot down.

I've taken the system into my own hands and have spent the day TRYING to teach Yang a much-needed lesson. You should see the pile of rectal exams and disimpactions I've been saving up for her.

Reminds me of a lesson I had to teach Dr. Bailey once upon a time . . . She was a terror when she first started here, let me tell you! And I'd be lying if I told you she was easy to train . . . But I look at it this way:

If I could break the Nazi? Then I can sure as hell break Cristina Yang.

Not that the case she stole wasn't pretty outstanding—I'll give her that. She's got a good surgical eye, that's for sure. I swear to you, her stolen patient (a man) looks, for all the world, as though he's eight months pregnant. Haven't seen so many people interested in one of our patients like that since . . . well . . . since ever.

Stevens put on quite the display today—yelling at Karev in the hallway—something about him not kissing her goodnight? Now—everyone around here has noticed the on-again, off-again flirtation between those two . . .

But I hadn't realized there was anything else going on . . . Sounds like the elevator isn't the only place where Karev has a problem with his follow-through.

Oh! And did I tell you there was a fire in one of our ORs today? Broke out in the middle of one of Burke's beating-heart surgeries. The patient's heart just burst into flames. Whoosh! Like a wildfire . . . it was nuts!

Glad the patient was OK. Seems weird she could survive it, but . . .

Oooo . . . here comes Yang. I'll just keep typing so it looks like I'm very very busy as . . . Wait. Is she accusing Dr. Bailey of being the one who is torturing her today? Oh, this is good. This is better than I could have ever hoped . . .

I'll tell you what I'm about to tell Miss Yang right now. If she'd shown just a little bit of respect, she could have saved herself a VERY long day.

Kiss to Build a Dream On . . .

Just to follow up—I went to Joe's tonight after work . . . Big darts night with me and the other nurses . . .

And I wish I could describe to you what I saw—I can't possibly do it justice. But it was, perhaps, the most unbelievably sexy, make-your-heart-skip-a-beat, devastatingly melt-in-your-mouth kiss I have ever witnessed . . .

. . . between Alex Karev and Izzie Stevens.

I guess her little fit in the hallway today worked, because . . .

Goodness. I've still got chills thinking about that kiss . . . Joe will back me up on this. Karev definitely followed through on THAT.

Official Seattle Grace Pool

What's Inside the Pregnant Dude's Belly? ($20 buy-in)

Nurse Tyler	a big cyst
Nurse Olivia	some kind of underdeveloped twin?
Alex Karev	an alien, dude.
Dr. Bailey	mesenteric teratoma
Cristina Yang	~~fat fluid fetus~~ a teratoma!!!
Izzie Stevens	Unfair. Cristina's totally cheating.
Nurse Liz	hot air
Janis (lab tech)	really big intestines
Scooter	I think he swallowed a shoe or something
Raj (*from Psych*)	It's nothing. A hysterical pregnancy. That's it.

Alice (lunchroom chick)	Too much of my chili
Dr. Torres	Abnormal bone structure
Patricia	His twin
Nurse Darren	a second stomach
Daisy (in Accounting)	a baby?
Ray (the paramedic)	Dunno. But it's gross, man.
Eric (Radiology)	a time capsule
Courtney (the pharmacy)	swollen tissue from an allergic reaction
Dr. Montgomery-Shepherd	Tell ya one thing—it's sure not a baby

Gotta Have Fate

You know how I love to start my day? OK, with a chocolate croissant and some strong coffee. But do you know how I love to start it even more?

With gossip. Wonderful juicy embarrassing gossip like only Seattle Grace can deliver. Today was no exception.

First, as I was purchasing my coffee and croissant from the coffee cart just outside the hospital, I saw Dr. Shepherd (the Mrs.) pull up right next to Dr. Grey (the mistress) in the parking lot. Nice.

THEN—as Grey was doing something strange to her forehead (still not sure what, although she has been walking around all day with the most ridiculous Band-Aid on her forehead—I mean, what self-respecting surgeon wears Hello Kitty to work?)—Mrs. Shepherd waved to her.

Waved to the woman who USED to bone her husband. Ahhhhhh. Is it wrong that I enjoy other people's misery? Probably.

But then, as if my day were fated to get even better, Dr. Yang cut in front of me in line to get her coffee—AND a coffee for Dr. Burke. Now—I was miffed. And pretty positive she cut in front of me because I made her day hell last week, but . . . then it dawned on me. None of that matters because—HELLO. She was getting a coffee for DR. BURKE.

They were laughing and flirting all the way back into the hospital—So what? Does that mean their romance is back on? Is it out in the open? Do they get a free pass now that the Meredith/McDreamy of it all has come to the surface?

Oh jeez. I have to go. Can't a nurse get so much as a lunch break around here? It's ridiculous. This hospital is so under-staffed with nurses right now we're all having to pick up the slack—and it BITES. Just saying.

And guess who won't even get Thanksgiving off next week? That's right. The rest of my family will be enjoying their tasty turkey, and me? I'll be here. Adjusting to the temp attending who'll be covering that day. I hear it's some doctor from Mercy West. I just hope it's not the freak we got last year. That guy gave me the creeps.

OH! And by the way—I know I have to go, but I simply can't sign off without mentioning the most fantastic piece of gossip of all!

Dr. Bailey . . . she's pregnant!!!

Instant Message Conversation

DebbieDoesGossip—logged on at 3:17 p.m.

JoeKnowsBest:	You didn't tell me!
DebbieDoesGossip:	Tell you what?
JoeKnowsBest:	That the Nazi—is pregnant with a Mini-Nazi!!
DebbieDoesGossip:	I just found out myself.

JoeKnowsBest:	It's all anyone is talking about today!
DebbieDoesGossip:	Really? No one here seems to have noticed . . .
JoeKnowsBest:	Because she's the Nazi! They're all afraid to say anything.
DebbieDoesGossip:	She's not that scary—especially not now . . . I mean, I think she's going soft. I saw her talking to her belly . . .
JoeKnowsBest:	Maybe we should throw her a shower?
DebbieDoesGossip:	Throw the Nazi a baby shower?
JoeKnowsBest:	Why not? Bet she'd love it!
JoeKnowsBest:	. . . Deb—you there? Hello? Debbie?
DebbieDoesGossip:	Sorry—took a minute for me to recover. I fell out of my chair from laughing so hard—you were saying?

DebbieDoesGossip—logged off at 4:30 p.m.

Too Much Turkey, Too Little Time

Happy belated Thanksgiving, fellow Seattle Grace gossipers. Alas, I have some sad news to report. On Thanksgiving Day, my dear old Uncle Pete passed away. Got the call while on duty at the hospital—cut my day a little short, as you might expect.

Didn't even get a chance to swing by Joe's to guzzle down any of his specialty Turkey-Day Tequila Surprises (two-for-one on Thanksgiving. Can't beat a deal like that . . .).

You would have liked Pete. He was a nurse, too—a real pioneer. An activist for Equal Male Nursing Opportunities—a man ahead of his time. You may not know this, but I come from a whole family of nurses: Aunt Lucy, my sister Val, all my cousins,

Pete, and even my Great Grandma Byrd. Guess you could say the urge to nurse is part of our gene pool.

I was, however, privy to ONE spectacular point of interest before I had to leave.

I was manning the nurse's station—so I had a front-row seat to watch McDreamy and Dr. Grey duke it out over some gomer. (As in—a PVS patient. Persistent Vegetative State. Broccoli Head. You get the picture.) . . . She insisted the guy had opened his eyes and LOOKED at her—I swear, sometimes I wonder how she even finished med school . . .

McDreamy (rightfully) put her in her place, turned to leave— but then . . . You could see the transformation on his face. He stopped, turned back around, and flashed her those big blue McDreamy googly eyes that (yes, I'll admit it) even make ME melt.

Between you and me? No way McDreamy is over Dr. Grey. He can parade around, put up a good show about working things out with that wife of his (who—it turns out—goes to the same salon as my friend's daughter's sister-in-law, and—I'll just say it—she spends a small fortune getting her hair that color of red . . .). But the truth is—it's painfully obvious.

If I were a betting woman, I'd bet on him making another play for Grey. Maybe next week, maybe next month—who knows . . . But that relationship isn't over. Or, at least I sure hope it's not. Because it's JUST so much fun to gossip about!

But I missed out on the rest of the drama because—that's when I got the call. About my dear Uncle Pete. Poor guy. Stuffed himself on too much of Aunt Lucy's famous Rice Krispies stuffing. Very sad. But, at least, he died happy.

Seattle Grace Secrets: Best Places to Have Secret Sex in the Hospital

So, the other nurses and I have been collecting a list of everyone's favorite places to have sex in this hospital . . . allegedly.

And boy—you'd be surprised by some of the answers . . . Here are some of my favorites:

ALEX—The Chief's office. But don't tell anyone I said that.

BURKE—I won't answer that.

YANG—Supply closet. Third floor.

GREY—Seriously?

IZZIE—Like I would know? Like I've had sex ANYWHERE in months?!?!?!

O'MALLEY—Not sure. But, like, maybe under the bottom of the stairwell would be cool . . . or maybe the roof might be nice. Only kind of windy. And there'd be bird poop. So . . . never mind. Not the roof. But . . . what about the tunnels?

ADDISON—You get this is grounds for harassment, right?

BAILEY—The on-call room. And the gallery if it's after-hours. And the spare patient room on the fourth floor. Oh—and the library isn't half bad . . .

OLIVIA—A spare bed in the ER, behind the curtain.

DR. CALLIE TORRES—The artificial limb room.

CHIEF WEBBER—My office. But don't tell anyone I said that.

McDREAMY—I'm always partial to cars, myself.

TYLER—Dude. Anywhere's cool with me.

PATRICIA—Conference room. Early in the morning.

DEBBIE—Please. Like I'm giving my spot away for everyone else to use, too??

Dreaming of McDreamy

This just in. I'm supposed to be rounding on the patients in recovery, but I had to pause just for a moment to share some of what I just heard . . .

According to Nurse Inyeshka (who heard from Nurse Bitty after Tyler spoke to Liz who said that SHE was in the ladies' room at the same time as Dr. Grey and Dr. Yang . . .)

Apparently Dr. Grey has been having—how should I put this?—some "racy" dreams . . . starring none other than—Dr. McDreamy.

Ha! Rumor has it the dreams can get pretty darn graphic, and—usually—take place in the shower. They say our dreams can sometimes reveal our deepest thoughts. Wonder what this says about Dr. Grey?

Actually—I don't wonder at all. We ALL can tell she still has the hots for McDreamy . . . All right—I have patients waiting. Better get back to work . . .

Big Things, Little Things

Well! I was certainly greeted with a big welcome back to the hospital after my Thanksgiving absence . . . and I do mean BIG.

In the form of a penis. With a sit-up-and-salute, damn-that's-GOTTA-hurt, neverending erection!

Heck of a lot better than that crazy woman on the new Shepherd's service who just gave birth to quintuplets. But I'll get back to her later . . .

The young man with the erection was surprisingly pleasant. And talkative. Oh yes—he did want to talk. So, who would I be if I didn't listen? It's not like Dr. Grey stuck around to talk to him all that much, although it was clear he would have liked her to do so . . . It's funny how some people just . . . find it easy to confide in strangers.

And yes, my friends, confide he did. Here's the scoop:

Apparently Dr. Grey has been frequenting Joe's almost every night since Thanksgiving—this nice young man had seen her there a few evenings in a row. (I've fact-checked this information with Joe. All true.)

So, Erection-Boy thought Dr. Grey was cute, wanted to ask her out, finally worked up the courage, and . . .

It turns out she had some very specific "eligible bachelor" criteria. She wanted to know if he was married, disease-free, or a doctor. As he was clear on all counts, they hit it off . . . Had a few drinks, shared a few secrets, then went home for (his words) some "unexpectedly mind-blowing" fun. And given what I've . . . um . . . seen of him? I don't doubt it.

Now, about those quints—oh man. Even if I were a "kid-person," I don't think I'd ever be up for five at once. Especially not if all five were being born with major health issues. Starting tomorrow, the surgical floor's going to be inundated with little-baby surgeries. It's just nuts . . .

I stopped by NICU tonight before heading home, just to take a look at the little critters.

There was one—I think her name was Emily—that caught my attention more than the rest. Maybe because she seemed the tiniest. There was just something about her that . . . caught my eye. All the others need these major surgeries, but Emily, well . . . I think I'll probably stop by to check on her in the morning, too. I think Dr. Stevens was the intern assigned to Emily's case . . .

Speaking of Dr. Stevens—she caught my attention as well. She just looked really sad—or distant—or something. Nurse Tyler told me it's probably because of the rumor he had heard about Nurse Olivia and Dr. Karev BONING (again) in the on-call room . . . but I've yet to get official confirmation.

Surely Olivia's smarter than to go back down that road again, right?

Oh—did I tell you what happened to Dr. Karev today? He totally screwed up the orders for one of his patients—readjusted the guy's sodium levels so quickly, the patient probably won't ever recover.

I'm not kidding—I've seen cases like this before. You want my opinion? The guy's a goner. Which would make Karev the first of these interns to make THAT kind of mistake. The kind that can't be repaired.

It's so much worse that being a 007—then, at least, you're just "licensed to kill." This could turn out to be . . . well, I guess we'll find out tomorrow.

As for me—I stopped by Joe's tonight after work to partake in his newly reinstated darts tournament. Wound up with O'Malley on my team. Now, there was a time I would never have let him on my team, but after the elevator incident, I figured—hey. He might be great. He could really come through in a clutch. Plus, I've seen him play darts—he's not half bad . . .

But O'Malley was not so great after all . . . Threw the whole game. I even let him use my hand-crafted designer darts from Scotland, but to no avail. That's the last time I ever team up with O'Malley, I'll tell you that much.

It's one thing to put up with these interns on the surgical floor, but when it comes to my place on Joe's Dart-Tournament-championship plaque, well . . . A gal's got no choice but to defend her title.

Seriously.

Not Easy Being Mean

There's something in the air. Because everyone is MEAN today.

Usually, Seattle Grace is a really pleasant place to work. Lots of friendly faces, witty banter, we even have pretty decent coffee at the cart by the hospital's front entrance . . .

But today? People are grouchy. And snide. And just plain mean . . . even me. I'll admit it.

How am I mean? Well . . . I stuck Olivia with Dr. O'Malley.

I didn't mean to, exactly, but there was this patient today who required treatment in the form of leeches (yes, leeches—those slimy little bloodsuckers), so . . . I assigned Olivia to deal with the leeches.

Which meant she also wound up dealing with O'Malley. The day after she screwed his best friend by screwing Alex. Not the most pleasant scene.

What O'Malley probably doesn't know, though, is that he really hurt Olivia's feelings. I had a long talk with her yesterday at Joe's—she's been really torn up about the George thing . . . I'd had no idea she felt so close to him.

Now—I understand what it's like to want to lash out . . . But that little Olivia. She never MEANT to sleep her way onto O'Malley or Dr. Stevens's bad sides . . . she just DID. And boy, did O'Malley let her know it.

I found her later in the ladies' room, crying in one of the stalls . . .

Another big meanie? Dr. Montgomery-Shepherd.

I heard she decided to "teach" Dr. Stevens a lesson. Now . . . I'm all for toughening these wussy interns up. Always try to do my part along those lines, in fact . . . but what Addison did? Forcing Stevens to spend the night reviving a baby she KNEW had no chance in the first place?

Well . . . that just takes it to a whole new level. I sure hope the lesson was worth it.

I think the only person NOT on edge today was Dr. Bailey— which is almost as startling. I saw her "cooing" to one of the quint babies. The Nazi—making goo-goo noises. It's like—an oxymoron!!

But the thing that gets me at the moment (I'm working the night shift tonight—at the OR nurse's station right now) is what I'm watching, right here, from my seat behind the counter.

You may remember that Dr. Karev made a pretty grave mistake yesterday with one of his patients. Very bad call—and the patient is definitely paying the price. Doubt he'll wake up. Not good. I heard Dr. Shepherd came down on Karev earlier today—really hard.

And now, I'm watching Karev across the way, sitting with his gorked patient. Just sitting at his bedside . . . waiting. For the guy to die . . .

McDreamy came up a bit ago, told Karev to go home, but he wouldn't . . . Karev said he didn't think anyone should die alone.

Now, Karev may not be able to keep his business in his scrub pants, but that boy does have a conscience. He does. Whether he's ready to admit it or not.

Twinkly Lights and Tinsel

Ah . . . the holidays. That chipper time of year when everything around you is covered in twinkly lights and tinsel. I used to be a big fan—decked the halls with glee . . .

But lately? It's all I can do to get my holiday cards out before Valentine's Day.

Not for lack of holiday spirit—don't get me wrong. But with the hours I've been working these days? Forget about it. The Chief REALLY needs to do something about our nursing work-load . . .

This year, that huge monstrosity of a tree the hospital always puts up in the lobby will just have to be enough tree for me (no kidding—the thing's at least two stories high) . . .

OK—that's the second time today I've turned around to dis-cover Addison Shepherd has STOLEN my Elegant Memories catalogue. I GET that she needs to find a gift for her mother-in-law. I even get how stressful that can be (especially the Christ-mas after cheating on your mother-in-law's son) . . .

But—hello? Addison. Get your OWN monogrammed cashmere throw order form. Just saying.

Poor little Justin's back under the knife today. He's a regular in our cardiac Ped's unit—some of us have watched him grow up over the years—I can remember his very first surgery, back when he was teeny tiny . . . The kid's outgrown his heart—three sizes too small, you might say. But Burke's got a transplant match ready for him, so—I just hope the heart takes. That would be such a nice holiday blessing . . .

I have to tell you about the conversation I overheard in the ladies' room this morning—it was Dr. Bailey, talking to her BELLY. That's right—she was informing her unborn baby that she would under no circumstances tolerate it kicking during surgery today.

Only the Nazi could find a way to reason with a fetus. Don't you just KNOW that's going to be one well-behaved kid?

Oh jeez—I'm covering the floor, and there is this one family that, I swear, has single-handedly given me a migraine. Could they be any louder?? Could they page me any more often?? And what's worse—they remind me of MY family. As if I don't get enough chaotic family time of my own this time of year?

Aaah! All right . . . I don't know exactly what just happened, but Cristina Yang literally collided into me—with a Christmas tree under her arm. While yelling something to O'Malley about— her boobs? Yeah—I don't even want to know about that one . . .

One thing I do know, though, is that Karev has to retake the practical for his board exams—tomorrow. Only a few days after KILLING a patient. And only a few weeks after FREEZING in an elevator with a heart surgery.

Any bets on whether or not he'll be able to pull it off? Tyler put $20 on Karev freezing up again . . . Ask me? Could be a pretty safe bet.

Oh, great. Someone just came in with an impacted candy cane . . . I mean, really, folks. What could spread the holiday cheer more than that?

P.S.—The annual Nurses' Holiday Bash is coming up next week . . . We're holding it at Joe's. I'll be sure to fill you in on all the behind-the-scenes action. Hopefully Nurse Ginger will hold her eggnog a little better than last year when she started flashing her Peppermint Patty underpants.

Instant Message Conversation

DebbieDoesGossip—logged on at 8:43 a.m.

DebbieDoesGossip:	So we're all set for the holiday party, right?
JoeKnowsBest:	Deb—I've hosted it how many years in a row? It's under control.
DebbieDoesGossip:	We need eggnog. And the sound system ready to go—and my mix? You've got my holiday medley I burned for you, right?
JoeKnowsBest:	Are you like this with the interns? Because if so—no wonder they drink so much . . .
DebbieDoesGossip:	Ha ha . . .
JoeKnowsBest:	You got your skit ready?
DebbieDoesGossip:	Oh yeah—this year will so top last year's . . .
JoeKnowsBest:	Dunno. Nurse Tyler's impression of the Chief was killer.
DebbieDoesGossip:	It WAS good, wasn't it?
JoeKnowsBest:	And your version of Bailey? Priceless.
DebbieDoesGossip:	I DO do a good Nazi.
JoeKnowsBest:	You can't top it.
DebbieDoesGossip:	Can too.

JoeKnowsBest: Can not.

DebbieDoesGossip: Watch me.

DebbieDoesGossip—logged off at 9:02 a.m.

My Very Own "12 Days of Christmas"

There's something you should know about me. I like to sing.
I don't have a great voice, I don't even have that much rhythm,
but—Oh yes. I enjoy belting out a tune.

Every holiday season, the nurses get together to let loose at a
holiday shindig—we host it at Joe's . . . and it's a blast!

We exchange Secret Santa gifts (thanks for the crocheted
booties and the bottle of gin, Ginger!). We reminisce about our
least favorite patients this past year (mine was the pregnant guy,
Olivia's was the toilet-water drinker) and our favorite patients
(it was unanimous—we all love Joe) . . .

We do impersonations, give out prizes (Nurse Liz was the BIG
winner this year with a killer imitation of Addison Shepherd. Totally rocked those salmon scrubs!) . . .

And we sing songs. This year—mine was quite the hit.

I created my very own version of "The 12 Days of
Christmas"—Nurse Debbie style. So I thought I would share it
with all of you . . . Here it goes:

> *On the twelfth day of Christmas, Chief Webber gave to me:*
> *12 less hours a shift*
> *11 legible orders*
> *10 respectful surgeons*
> *9 free drinks at Joe's*
> *8 of Izzie's cupcakes*
> *7 syph-free nurses*
> *6 weeks of scut for Yang*

5 interns changing bedpans!
4 times more flattering scrubs
3 of Grey's guys
2 dancing Shepherds
. . . and a partridge in McDreamy's hair!

Happy Holidays, everyone!

First to Go?

So, Tyler and I were taking our coffee break this morning, when we created a friendly little "Beginning of the Year" wager . . .

Well, not a wager, exactly. As I've mentioned before, I am NOT a betting woman. But a friendly poll, let's say . . .

And I thought I'd open it up to the rest of you Seattle Grace Gossip Junkies.

Here it is—now, Tyler hasn't been at this quite as long as I have—but I've seen year after year of interns come and go—and when I say go, I MEAN go.

Basically every year, at least one intern will burn out, break down, run away screaming—seems like there's always ONE in the bunch who, well, just can't take the heat.

So that's what Tyler and I were pondering over our gingerbread-flavored holiday lattes—which of this batch of surgical interns is most likely to throw in the towel, give up surgery, and embark on a less bloodsucking career as . . . a dermatologist or something?

Will it be O'Malley—formerly known as 007?

Stevens—recently cut down a notch by that crafty Mrs. Shepherd?

Karev—let's face it, the guy had to retake his medical boards.

Yang—if you push as hard as she does, you're bound to burn out just as quickly . . .

Or Grey? Quite a pedigree to live up to—while surrounded with all sorts of McDreamy distractions . . . ??

Tyler votes for O'Malley. Nurse Liz thinks everyone will stay. Nurse Olivia says Karev (but I think that's just because he's seen her naked) . . . As for me, well . . . I'm not quite sure anymore . . .

But if there's one thing this job has taught me over the years, it's to expect the unexpected . . .

So what about it? Who (if anyone) do YOU think will be the first to burn out of the program?

All You Ever Wanted to Know . . .

OK. So—you know what a hectic schedule I have . . . Particularly since the Chief hasn't approved the new budget to hire more nurses, and we are literally running ourselves RAGGED these days . . . but that's a story for another day . . .

I had a few moments this morning—my first morning off in I don't know HOW long—and realized . . . I haven't had a chance to post comments to any of YOUR comments . . . (Which is a shame, because some of you have some REALLY good ones.) So . . .

I wanted to take a moment now to answer some of your questions. I scanned through the posts, found some of your most commonly asked (and most interestingly stated) questions—and here are my answers (hope they quench your enquiring gossipy minds!):

Do the doctors at Seattle Grace interact on a personal level with the nurses?

Now—are you talking "jumping each other's bones in the on-call room" personal? Seems to me, you probably mean something a little different . . . The fact is—the hospital is a little like high school. People have their cliques. People like their cliques. People stick to their cliques. And most of all, people make fun of all the other cliques.

My clique, for instance, is pretty much me, Tyler, Olivia, and Nurse Liz—Oh, and Joe. But then, he's in everybody's clique, isn't he? And what we love—even more than torturing the interns around us—is laughing at them.

Because, in case you hadn't noticed? They do some really dopey things. Hello? Guy falls off a building, lands on a pigeon, and O'Malley wears the bird beak around his neck all day? You get my point.

What's up with Webber's offer to Dr. Montgomery-Shepherd?

Here's what I know (or have—ahem—happened to see while innocently walking slowly by the fax machine)—Webber made one HELL of an offer to Addison. Now, I don't know exact numbers, but he's practically offered her her own wing—that's way more than he's done for Burke, or than he did to entice McDreamy into coming to Seattle, for that matter.

Some people think Webber has a soft spot for the Shepherds patching up their relationship—but between you and me? The Chief is first and foremost one heck of a businessman. You should SEE the hotsy-totsy (and by that I mean generating Big Bucks) traffic Addison has generated around here. It's crazy. People from all over the country fly here just so she can treat them . . .

All the more reason, in my opinion, the Chief can afford to hire a few extra nurses . . . but like I said—that's another story.

Have you noticed how flirty Dr. Karev is around Dr. Grey?

Are you kidding? Have you noticed how flirty he is around EVERYONE? Hell, he's even hit on me a few times, and—trust me—it was only because he needed something. That kid knows how to work a room, that's for sure.

That said—he and Grey do seem to have a certain . . . rapport. Interesting you should bring that up, actually . . . I'll keep more of an eye out for it from now on . . .

What about Meredith and McDreamy? Are they EVER going to get back together?

Now—I get that a lot of you are all romantic and stuff. I've been known to read a romance novel or two myself, back in the day . . . but—um, have you forgotten? We're talking about an attending— a married attending—and an intern. If there's ANYTHING discouraged around here, it's that . . .

Then again—I have noticed that those two keep "bumping" into each other—in the hall, in the cafeteria . . . in that elevator. Oh MAN do I see them getting off the elevator together a lot— it's weird. They always look a little bit . . . flustered? I don't think anything is actually going on with them, but I do know one thing . . .

Addison sure seems to have started taking the elevator a lot herself. She's watching her husband like a hawk—and who can blame her? Joe told me that she and McDreamy had one HECK of a blustery conversation not long ago at the bar, so . . .

Hmmm . . . time will tell, I guess!

And finally: Debbie, I like your style. Are you single?

Hard as it might be to imagine—I am single. And looking. I'm a Gemini; I like to travel; I don't eat eggs, but I do cook; I enjoy cheesy movies, playing darts, karaoke, and sports. Oh yes—big sports fan. Do not EVEN mess with me on game day.

So, if there are any takers out there, swing on by Joe's and buy me a beer. I'm there all the time . . .

Instant Message Conversation

DebbieDoesGossip—logged on at 4:23 p.m.

DebbieDoesGossip:	Can't believe you went skiing and wiped out so badly. U want MORE brain surgery??
JoeKnowsBest:	Thx for the sympathy. Warms my heart, Deb.
DebbieDoesGossip:	U and Walter have a nice time?
JoeKnowsBest:	Fantastic. Wish vacation had been longer.
DebbieDoesGossip:	Always.
JoeKnowsBest:	U making a New Year's resolution this year?
DebbieDoesGossip:	Gonna try.
JoeKnowsBest:	Right—for like a week. Remember last year's?
DebbieDoesGossip:	No more dating anesthesiologists.
JoeKnowsBest:	Broke that one. And the year before that?
DebbieDoesGossip:	No more tequila on work nights.
JoeKnowsBest:	Totally broke that one. And before that?
DebbieDoesGossip:	No chocolate croissants. No tormenting interns. No laughing at the freaks who work in psych—yeah, yeah. I get your point.
JoeKnowsBest:	So what's the resolution you're planning to break this year?
DebbieDoesGossip:	I don't want to tell you now.
JoeKnowsBest:	Because I'll find out anyway?
DebbieDoesGossip:	Because you're going to mock me.
JoeKnowsBest:	OK. No mocking.
DebbieDoesGossip:	Promise?

JoeKnowsBest: Sure.

DebbieDoesGossip: OK then . . . my resolution is . . . to gossip less.

DebbieDoesGossip: Hello?

DebbieDoesGossip: Joe?

JoeKnowsBest: Um . . . yeah. Good luck with that.

DebbieDoesGossip—logged off at 5:08 p.m.

New Year's Resolutions . . .

Everybody makes them—how about you? Any good New Year's resolutions out there? Mine was going to be: Gossip Less. Only I've already broken that one so, here's my new one: Take No Guff.

Which, at the moment, means figuring out what to do about all these extra shifts my nurses and I suddenly have to cover . . . I mean, honestly—Why should the interns get time to go home and do laundry, but not us? The Chief is on this whole "let's enforce the 80-hour work week" edict that, honestly, may be the death of me.

Because—you know who picks up the slack when the interns are pulled off their shifts? Me and my nursing staff. But does the Chief seem to care if WE are overextended? Does anyone notice when WE have exceeded 80 hours a week?

I've said it before; I'll say it again. Something around here is gonna have to give.

Meanwhile—I have more elevator-related gossip for you. Rumor has it (from a very reliable source—as I'm sure you know, it's hard to do anything around this hospital without somebody noticing) that Dr. Shepherd was making googly eyes at Dr. Grey on the elevator again! Does he have no shame? At least, I assume googly eyes must have been involved . . . it was certainly something big enough for Addison Shepherd to sport her signature evil eye when getting off the elevator . . .

Plus, I heard from Tyler that he overheard the Chief and Mc-Dreamy talking about some fancy Alzheimer's program . . . wonder if that has anything to do with Dr. Grey's mother? Wouldn't that be an interesting tidbit of information for Addison Shepherd?

On other notes—I noticed Dr. Stevens making nice with Dr. Karev (so did Olivia, btw—and she was JUST as surprised as I was). Don't know what that's about, but Stevens is a lot more forgiving than I would be if I were her . . .

Still haven't heard about Karev's boards results . . . although he did bogart my computer today to research what turned out to be a very tricky catch. Diagnosed this crazy guy (in for eating his own novel, of all things) with mercury poisoning. Amazing the things people will do to themselves . . .

O'Malley was on a tear—heard he got himself kicked off of the case he was working on . . . At first I figured Addison was just overreacting, maybe just in a bad mood after the elevator incident this morning, but . . . turns out O'Malley really overstepped his bounds with a patient's family. Yikes. If he's not careful, that's exactly the kind of thing that could get him into trouble around here . . .

Oh! And Denny Duquette was in to get his new heart again . . . he's such a good guy. Been in and out of here for a while—we all love him around here.

Such a bummer that his heart didn't come through . . . I know Dr. Burke will do what he can, but . . . I've seen Denny's charts. He's the epitome of positive thinking—then again . . . I'm telling you. That poor guy doesn't have much more time left.

Are they kidding? The Pit just called—no one to cover because the Chief sent all the interns down there home. Is he kidding? Does he think we can run this place by ourselves???

Joe Stories

I'm not sure why—but it seems like everyone at Seattle Grace has their own "Joe Story." Maybe it's because Joe is a really good listener. Or, maybe it's just because his bar is the only place to find alcohol within walking distance of the hospital . . . Whatever the reason, everybody has:

A Joe Story.

Hell, I have like—fifty.

I've decided to collect a few—give you a little insight into one of my closest friends. I mean—I talk about the guy so much, I might as well tell you a little more about him, right? And, since Joe touches so many people's lives around here, it seems only appropriate to let them talk about Joe . . . in their own words.

MY JOE STORY: BY MEREDITH GREY

Well . . . I guess the thing I remember most about Joe is the night I was at his bar and he collapsed—that was scary. Not just because he crashed to the floor (which, by the way, is really sticky and gross and covered in peanut shells) or because it was seriously raining like CRAZY that night, but because—that was the same night I was supposed to go out for an amazing dinner with my boyfriend at the time, only I found out that he was actually . . . married.

It was a hell of a night.

But that isn't really the story I want to tell about Joe. Because, since then? Joe's become a good friend. He's really been there for me. And I've been there, in his bar, a lot.

So it's been nice on those nights when I don't feel like going home quite yet, to see Joe's familiar face as I walk into his bar. He's always there. With a smile. No judgment. He looks out for me. And I appreciate that.

Actually, Joe and I have developed a bit of a shorthand lately . . . sort of a code for the random guys in the bar that I really don't (or, sometimes really do) want to talk to . . .

Like, for instance: If I'm sitting there, with a perfectly full drink, and some annoying guy a few seats away tells Joe he wants to buy me a drink—Joe's my first line of defense. First, Joe'll ask if the guy is a doctor. If he is? Forget it. I don't want to date any more doctors. I don't want to get drunk with any more doctors. No more doctors, I say. So—Joe will refuse to sell the guy the drink . . .

Now, if the guy isn't a doctor, then Joe will ask the guy if he is, has been, or is currently anywhere remotely close to being married. If the guy hesitates, even an instant (a dead giveaway is if the guy unconsciously touches his wedding-band finger), then the dude's out. No drink. No chance.

But if both of those criteria are met—not a doctor, and not married—well, then . . . Joe will agree to fix the drink. He'll deliver it to me and (with a very subtle nod toward Mr. Potential) ask me: "Ready for a refill?"

If I'm interested in the guy (and sometimes I am), then I'll shrug. Take the drink. But if not—I just refuse the drink.

Works like a charm.

So—I guess that's really my Joe story. That Joe helps me sift through the guys at his bar to see if any of them are worth my time.

Or, at least, worth an extra shot of tequila . . .

MY JOE STORY: BY CRISTINA YANG

Joe story? I don't have any Joe stories. Except that I'm convinced he waters down all my drinks.

Wait—OK. I know my Joe Story.

Joe was my very first (and maybe only) chance at scrubbing in on a standstill surgery—a once-in-a-lifetime opportunity, and I was right there—in the operating room while Burke and Shepherd literally stopped Joe's heart, performed their operation, then brought Joe back to life.

It was incredible.

And—yes. Joe knows things about me—things I don't openly share with other people—but that's because he's an eavesdropper.

And he's nosy. And annoyingly perceptive about things I'd just as soon he stop butting in to . . .

But back to the standstill surgery. Did you know that we had only 45 minutes to complete the entire operation, or else Joe's body—his brain—could have been permanently damaged? Nuts, right? It's an extremely rare operation—only a handful of surgeons in the country are even qualified to attempt it, and . . .

Oh yeah. I was there. In the operating room. Freezing my ASS off.

They have to keep it so cold because they lower the patient's body temperature to slow his blood flow. Sort of like self-induced hypothermia. SO COOL, right?

It was AWESOME.

Oh yeah. I know. You wanna know about the stuff Joe knows about that I don't want other people to know about, right? Forget it—I know you, Debbie. The minute I tell you, you'll tell everyone else in the—

OK. Debbie. Stop calling me chicken. I am SO not chicken. I am the opposite of chicken. I am like the LEAST chicken intern EVER, OK???

Fine. You wanna know about something? Here it goes. When I stole the "pregnant dude" patient, I intentionally stashed him in a room I knew YOU—yes, YOU, Debbie—would stumble upon. Why? Because I wanted to bug you. You and your perfectly filled-out paperwork and your attitude like you know everything and we're just idiot interns. I was TRYING to mess with you. That's right. MESSING with YOU.

So—how's that for chicken? Wanna try to make my life hell, now? Got a few disimpactions piled up to hand off to me? A few cases of explosive diarrhea? No problem.

Bring it on, Debbie. Bring it ON.

MY JOE STORY: BY GEORGE O'MALLEY

Oh man—Joe's a good guy. Like, a really good guy. I don't know how many times he's listened to my stories, given me advice, you know. He really cares. Which is—well—now that I think about it, I guess that's what all bartenders do. Listen to people's problems, but . . .

I'm pretty sure with Joe, it's different. I mean, he's JOE.

This one time, I accidentally locked myself in Joe's bar's bathroom for like—well, a really long time—not on purpose or anything, it's just that I couldn't get the lock to unstick after I was finished, and—the more I tried to unstick it, the more stuck it got, and . . . I guess it didn't help that my arm was in a sling, actually—since I had just dislocated my shoulder the day before and I could only really use one hand . . . I dislocated it from falling down the stairs. At the hospital. But that's a long, uninteresting, totally NOT my Joe story, so . . .

Anyway. Joe? He figured out what must have happened, and he rescued me. Broke the door open, let me out, and—you know what the cool thing was? He didn't even tell anyone. Not one single person. Ever. I was so embarrassed—and Alex Karev? He and Izzie were at the bar that night (I wasn't really hanging out with them—they were more, like, making out in the corner, but . . .). If Joe had wanted to? He totally could have told Alex—who would have mocked me about it forever . . .

As it is, Alex just mocks me about my shoulder, or rather, the thing that resulted in me hurting my shoulder. (OK. I wasn't planning to talk about this, but I kinda slept with this girl I really liked only it didn't go so well and then she told everybody we know—or at least, I thought she told everybody when it turns out she didn't actually tell them only by then I had told everybody which is why I wound up falling down the stairs—and . . .)

Whatever. That's what Alex is making fun of me about these days. So it's just as well he didn't have the bathroom thing to add fuel to the fire, is all I'm saying.

Joe's a good guy. He never told a soul. He just poured me a drink (on the house) and went back to his bartending business.

Of course, then I tried to pick up the drink with my hurt arm and, well, I spilt it down my front and had to go back to the bathroom to clean myself up.

I just didn't lock the door behind me that time.

MY JOE STORY: BY IZZIE STEVENS

OK—Joe is great and all—I mean, he did at least show up on time for Thanksgiving AND he brought pie—big plus. But sometimes, he can really drive me nuts—like really REALLY.

The thing is—he likes to poke fun at me. He says it comes out of love—but OH MY GOD—could he please just STOP kidding me about the steamy kiss Alex planted on me at Joe's bar? C'mon! It's old news already!! Can I help it if I happen to blush (yes, even now, even though it is TOTALLY water WAY under the bridge) every time he mentions it?? I have fair skin, OK? I blush easily. It has nothing to do with how Alex dipped me back off of my bar stool and gave me that hot, hot, hot, unbelievably heart-stopping—never mind.

I don't even care anymore. It's not like I still THINK about that kiss or anything. No way. I'm over it. I'm over him. So totally over Alex and his too-little-too-late attitude it's not even funny.

And NO, Joe. You did NOT overhear me talking to Meredith about how just the thought of that kiss gets me all tingly inside. I was talking about my VIBRATOR, OK?? Got it?? Get it??? Enough already. Stop making fun of me and pick another target.

Or I'll tell Walter that you would have forgotten his birthday if I hadn't reminded you. See how you like THAT, OK???

Love,

Izzie

MY JOE STORY: BY MIRANDA BAILEY

I was the only female intern my year.

I didn't have many friends. I didn't talk all that much—at

least, not when it wasn't about work. We didn't pal around together the way the interns do now . . . at least, I didn't. It was a very tough, very exclusive, very competitive boys' club.

And I had to not only measure up, but outshine every damn one of those testosteroney know-it-alls. So I did. Day after day, shift after shift . . .

You remember, Debbie. Because you gave me as much hell as the boys did, only . . . from you? It was somehow easier to take . . . Anyway . . .

I got in the habit of stopping by Joe's after my shifts at night . . . Too tired to go anywhere else, and too wired to go home right away. Back then, my husband was working almost as much as I was—trying to make a name for himself as the new kid at his firm . . . And let me tell you, there is nothing more lonely than working a 20-hour shift, heading home to see your husband, only—to have him not be there. In fact, it's pretty awful . . .

So I'd stop by Joe's to unwind—alone. All alone in the corner booth with my bourbon and my feet up on the chair in front of me to keep them from throbbing too much. After a few weeks of this, I guess Joe noticed—wanted to make sure I was OK, but he didn't invade my space. Didn't try to pry, or to get me to open up.

He just got into the habit of having my favorite bourbon on the rocks waiting for me when I got off of work. He'd amble over, set it down in front of me, and say: "Good to see you again, Miranda. Let me know if you need anything else, OK?"

It was nice. And it was just what I needed. I didn't even mind him calling me by my first name . . . And it wasn't for a long time—not until the night that I lost my first patient, that—as it turns out—I DID need something else.

That night, I walked in—as usual. Only, I was really upset. Holding it inside, but—I was hurting. I sat down, Joe came over, and this time—he didn't ask me if I needed anything else. He just knew that I did. So . . . He sat down with me. Just sat there. And had a drink with me. In total silence.

After who knows how long, Joe squeezed my hand, stood up, about to head back to the bar . . . Then he looked at his watch, and said: "It's Wednesday. Your husband gets home early on Wednesdays, doesn't he?" I nodded. Still quiet. And Joe just said: "Bet he'd be really happy to see you tonight."

I still smile when I think about that—Joe just knew exactly what it was I needed to hear. I headed right home, found my husband, curled up next to him, and . . . told him all about my day. All about losing my very first patient—it's a terrible thing. It's the kind of thing a surgeon never forgets. I remember the patient's name, his diagnosis, his voice, the color of his eyes . . .

Anyway—What can I say? Joe just knew me. He knows me. For a long time, now, I guess. And the truth is? I'm a better person for it.

MY JOE STORY: BY PRESTON BURKE

For a long time—I didn't have a Joe story. Not because I didn't like the guy—he seemed nice enough, but . . .

I just didn't spend all that much time in his bar. I like to go home at night to my apartment. Maybe practice my trumpet for a little bit. Spend some quality time recharging before my next big day of surgeries. It's how I focus.

But that's begun to change. Because of my girlfriend.

She likes Joe's. She likes to go there with her friends after a long shift. That's where she unwinds. Plays some darts. Drinks a few beers. She lets loose.

And she usually doesn't invite me to come along. It's a part of her life she likes to keep private . . . So I still go home at night. To my apartment. Where I like to recharge, only . . . it feels a little empty now. Because I—I miss her, I guess. And she's not there. She's still at Joe's, without me.

This bothered me for a while. Probably more than I was willing to admit at the time, but . . . then I had a chance to talk to Joe. It was at Thanksgiving, actually—while I was helping Dr.

Stevens baste her turkey, and while my girlfriend was out at the store, looking for wine . . .

Joe was there. As a guest, not a bartender, and . . . I asked him. About his work. About his customers. He mentioned having not seen me in the bar much, that sort of thing. But then—he asked me: "Hey, Dude—how's your trumpet playing going? I hear you're really good."

It threw me. Because I knew—after having Joe as my patient, after all of his follow-up appointments, even after all of that . . . I had never mentioned to Joe that I play the trumpet. Not once.

And there's really no one else who would have known about it—other than . . . my girlfriend.

Turns out, even though she doesn't always want me there with her at Joe's, it isn't that she's shutting me out of her life completely. She still talks about me—brags about me, even. Which means she's thinking about me. And looking forward to seeing me when she gets home.

Just as much as I'm looking forward to seeing her.

So that's my Joe story—Joe helped me see a side of my girlfriend I just . . . wasn't sure I'd ever get to see.

And for that, I am thankful.

MY JOE STORY: BY DEREK SHEPHERD

OK. I'll tell you the same Joe story I told Dr. Burke when he asked me (as I operated on Joe's brain, mind you) about my Joe story. (No names, of course. I'm a gentleman.)

I went to Joe's bar the night before my first day of work at Seattle Grace. It was a . . . difficult time for me. I'd just moved here, I didn't really know my way around, and . . . I had left a lot of unfinished business behind in New York.

I was trying to start a new chapter in my life. And I was—well, I was nervous about it, frankly. Second-guessing myself. All I wanted was—for one night—to forget about my worries and—

for the first time in a long time—allow myself to have a nice evening. Which I did.

I met someone—a woman. A beautiful, disarming, remarkable woman . . . We hit it off. We had a few drinks. We shared a few laughs—God, I loved her laugh . . . and . . .

She took advantage of me. Or maybe I took advantage of her? No—she took advantage—SOMEONE definitely took advantage, and . . . anyway.

I like to think of it as my introduction to Seattle. It was an evening I'll never forget—as long as I live. And it was—as Joe likes to remind me on a regular basis—all thanks to Joe.

MY JOE STORY: BY RICHARD WEBBER

I'll tell you a Joe story. Happened just the other night.

I'd had a really tough day. Old friend of mine—Ollie. She's like a mentor to me. Seen me through some of my hardest times. Nothing romantic, mind you—just a big support to me over the years.

And she walked into my ER—my hospital—about as close to death as you could imagine. So I had to operate on her. And try to save her life. After all the times she had been instrumental in saving mine . . .

I was reminded of so many things . . . SO many things I haven't thought about in such a long time. I needed to take a moment, before going home. Before seeing my wife, and . . .

I walked across the street to Joe's. Sat down on one of the stools. And I . . . ordered a vodka tonic. That had always been Ollie's favorite.

Now—I don't drink. Haven't in a long, long time. It's just that . . . I wanted to order a drink. Just to have it there—on the bar—in front of me. I don't know why. I didn't plan on drinking it—I just wanted it there.

I sat there a while—looking at the drink. Threw some cash on the countertop and gathered my coat. Joe noticed me leaving, noticed I hadn't touched the drink, and—mentioned that I hadn't tasted it . . .

"Yeah, I know," I said. "Turns out I didn't want it after all . . ."

Joe had this funny look on his face—then handed me back the cash. And he said, "Just as well . . . I think I forgot the vodka anyway." He took a sip of the drink. "Yup. Tonic and tonic. Sorry, bro. Want another?"

He played it off like a mistake—but . . . I don't know. Something in his look told me he probably served me straight tonic on purpose . . .

Because that's the kind of guy Joe is—he looks out for people. Quietly—but he does.

MY JOE STORY: BY ADDISON SHEPHERD

I don't really know Joe all that well. I mean, I haven't exactly been in Seattle all that long . . .

I had a "Joe" back in New York. His name was Greg, actually. He bartended the place Derek—that's my husband—and I used to haunt. It was fun—not much like Joe's, really . . . A lot more swanky. Big cushy pillows and funky lights. But it was homey to us. I remember red. Lots and lots of red everywhere . . .

Loved that place. And I loved Greg—always put an extra olive in my martini without me even asking . . .

Anyway—back to Joe. He seems nice. Very polite. Very friendly. Very funny . . . makes a mean hot buttered rum, I'll tell you that much!

It's funny, though. I always get the feeling Joe knows more about me than I know about him . . . It's like—he almost knows what I'm going to say before I say it. Like if I try to tell him some detail about my day—it's as though he's already heard about it—although I don't know how . . .

And when it comes to Derek—I don't know. It's probably all in my head, but . . . I get the feeling Joe hears an awful lot about all of us at Seattle Grace. Like he already knows who we are and what we do before any of us set foot in his bar . . .

That's ridiculous, right? I mean, he's a bartender. Not a psychic. I'm being paranoid. That's all. Paranoid about the things I can't control . . .

Well, and also about the fact that Joe's is like the ONLY place Derek ever wants to go out to . . . there are so many places to get drinks in Seattle, and we always wind up at Joe's. It's like the place is really special to him for some reason—but not special to me, which almost makes him like it more.

I'm being paranoid again. Apparently that's all I do lately. Whatever. I'm late for a consult.

MY JOE STORY: BY ALEX KAREV

Dude. I'm not filling out your stupid survey, Debbie. Joe's a cool dude. He lets me run a tab that I never pay. He was like my first (and only) buddy out here when I first started work in Seattle— pretty much for that reason. He provided booze I didn't have to pay for. Which is cool, since I'm pretty much always broke. So— Whatever. I'm not filling out this survey. Joe almost died, then he saw me hug George O'Malley—a moment I'd just as soon forget, anyway, so . . .

Like I said. Bug off.

You Never Know Your Last . . .

We never know when our "last" time for many things will be . . . Our last cigarette. Our last breath. Our last day of work before barging in on the Chief in his operating room . . .

Let me back up.

I want to start with my drive home from work not so long ago.

It had been a pretty typical day . . . Spent most of my time shuffling one of our perma-res patients around (as in "permanent residents"—the ones who refuse to leave even after they should be discharged).

But I have a soft spot for this particular patient, because once upon a time, she was a high-kicking, sequin-wearing Broadway hoofer—sings the heck out of all the old standards, even now . . .

But back to my story . . .

I was driving home when—out of nowhere—I veered off the road and into a ditch! Thank goodness it was so late there was no one else on the road, but . . . nevertheless, it was really freaky . . .

And that was when I realized—I'd fallen asleep at the wheel. I was THAT tired. Can you imagine?? It was at that moment, as I was waiting for AAA to come tow my car, that I knew—I had no choice but to take a stand.

My nurses and I were overworked—to the point of exhaustion—and it had to stop.

So, the Seattle Grace nursing staff gave the Chief official notice—that unless he hired additional nurses, and reduced our mandatory overtime substantially . . . we were going on strike.

Believe it or not—he called our bluff.

So—5:59 p.m.—the last minute of my last shift pre-strike—was my moment of truth. First, I locked myself in the bathroom stall, allowed myself exactly 60 seconds of hyperventilation, and then . . . I left. Tied on a surgical cap. Marched into OR 2. And interrupted Chief Webber's surgery to give him final notice about the strike.

My heart has never beat so quickly—I mean, it's one thing for me to harass interns. Another for me to raise an eyebrow at the residents here and there, but . . .

Walking in on the Chief (uninvited) in the middle of surgery? That was a first, even for me.

And—let's hope—a last.

Nurses' Strike 2006—Fair Hours! Fair Wages!

Day One

4:30 a.m.
Debbie here. Reporting from the front steps of Seattle Grace Hospital, where Nurses' Strike 2006 is fully under way. We're armed with hot coffee, glazed donuts, and more picket signs than you can possibly imagine.

Spent most of last night making the signs—I'm particularly happy with my "PROUD TO BE A NURSE" signs. Bold. Succinct. I think they make the right statement.

5:20 a.m.
Interns have started arriving. Yang was the first to brave the picket line—managed to make it through with only a few stray bits of donut in her hair.

Oooh! There goes Stevens—hold on. Totally just pelted her with my bagel—Wait!! She just told Olivia to "enjoy her syphilis"! Nice. Very nice.

Now I wish my bagel had been covered in cream cheese.

6:15 a.m.
O'Malley still hasn't made it through the line. Starting to feel bad for the guy. Think I'll send Olivia over to talk to him . . .

7:00 a.m.
I have to admit—I have a newly found respect for Dr. O'Malley. Turns out he's a union guy, and he's decided to join our ranks out here in front of the hospital. Good for him!

10:35 a.m.
Getting worried about some of my patients inside. Just saw Mr. Miller from 3716 wandering around in the lobby with his IV pole

(and his gown wide open) when I KNOW he should already be up in radiology for his CT this morning . . . Hmmm . . .

11:05 a.m.
We've come up with a plan—going to see if O'Malley's on board. Think we may have figured out a way to check in on our patients without crossing the picket line . . . We're sending in George.

12:30 p.m.
OK. Cristina Yang just came out on her lunch break and pelted US with half a dozen tuna sandwiches.
   Oh yeah. It is SO on.

5:45 p.m.
Still going strong—although my feet are killing me, and I'm really regretting that I loaned my mittens to Nurse Tyler. Looking forward to tonight—we're all planning to grab a drink at Joe's when we're done for the day.

Debbie's Phone—Transcript of Text Message Conversation

DebbieDoesGossip:	U there?
JoeKnowsBest:	How's the strike?
DebbieDoesGossip:	Loud. Good. Cold. Caffeinated.
JoeKnowsBest:	People crossing the picket line?
DebbieDoesGossip:	Some are. Some not.
JoeKnowsBest:	I'm watching on the news.
DebbieDoesGossip:	I'm waving my sign at the camera!
JoeKnowsBest:	U R? Wait—there—I see you. Nice sign.
DebbieDoesGossip:	Thx.
JoeKnowsBest:	Is—that O'Malley?
DebbieDoesGossip:	Yup. Union guy.

JoeKnowsBest:	Really?
DebbieDoesGossip:	Proud to be a nurse.
JoeKnowsBest:	I can see that.
DebbieDoesGossip:	U coming over to deliver more coffee soon?
JoeKnowsBest:	U bringing the crew over to buy beers from me later?
DebbieDoesGossip:	U know it . . .
JoeKnowsBest:	Then I'll see you soon!

End of Text Message Transcript

Day Two

1:20 a.m.

Damn! You missed the most fantastic fight at Joe's tonight . . . OK—he may not have found it fantastic, but . . . I know I did!

But before I get to that, I overheard some tasty gossip that I know you would want me to share . . .

First, apparently Dr. Grey intubated a DNR patient yesterday—not good. No telling how she'll handle the stress when she has to undo it. Especially given what she just found out . . . Turns out the Chief has been secretly visiting Ellis Grey in the nursing home—and Grey Junior is NOT happy about it.

I don't blame her—but I do wonder exactly how much of Ellis and Chief Webber's history together Meredith actually knows? Wonder if that would make her less or more upset about Webber's visits?

Rumor also has it that Bailey's new replacement has the interns squirming for the Nazi's return. Especially Yang—she kept muttering things like "Heal with love, my ASS" under her breath when they were at Joe's . . . Karev seemed to be eating it up . . .

But I haven't gotten to the best part—In retaliation for

Cristina's insensitive tuna fight, we (the nurses) decided to strike back . . . by "accidentally" spilling a vodka collins all over her lap.

And—Oh Boy—was Yang ready to duke it out—We're talking full fledged ready-to-throw-the-first-punch kind of angry . . . Man, it was fun to get under her skin like that! Too bad Grey defused the moment by dragging Yang out the door (and O'Malley, too, since—as it turns out—they were his ride). And right when he and I were finally kicking some serious dart-throwing butt, no less . . .

6:00 a.m.
O'Malley is really boosting morale around here—he arrived this morning with warm chocolate croissants. Be still my heart; I could kiss him. They are, after all, my favorite.

1:00 p.m.
Negotiations are under way—Word from Patricia (the Chief's right hand) is that she thinks there's a good opening for some movement . . . Fair hours! Fair wages!

7:45 p.m.
Holy moly. Just took a coffee break with one of the temp nurses—she's an old friend of mine, actually—usually works at a tiny clinic downtown (and, coincidentally, she is also an avid reader of this blog!) . . .

And according to HER—moments ago, McDreamy followed Meredith Grey into a supply closet!! My nursing friend was going to delve deeper—maybe dig up more gossip for me by walking in on them, but . . . when she got to the closet door, she could hear . . . Meredith crying.

So, my friend left them alone. And came out here for coffee with me instead . . . Wonder what Meredith was so worked up about?

8:47 p.m.
Guess what? The Chief has agreed to our terms!!! Can you believe it? Which means I'm back on shift as of tomorrow morning . . .

Reporting from the front steps of Seattle Grace, this is Nurse Debbie . . . Signing off.

Code Black

Two words you NEVER want to hear in a hospital: "Code Black."

Greetings, readers. It's good to be back post–Code Black. Because, let me tell you—it's been quite a ride.

First of all—for those of you who don't know, a Code Black means there's a bomb—or some type of explosive—in the hospital. It's like a "911" page, only—fifty MILLION times more scary . . . because we're healers. We work to save lives. Not worry about whether or not we'll be exploding our patients (or ourselves) into teeny tiny little charbroiled pieces.

So—the short story is: We had a Code Black.

We had a bomb in a body in one OR. And Bailey's husband having brain surgery in the next OR. Bailey was upstairs giving birth. Interns were having sex in supply closets (what's wrong with the on-call room is beyond me . . . ?), and there I was— stuck in the OR next to the bomb. Scrubbed in to Dr. Shepherd's super–brain surgery. Trying to save Tucker Jones despite the fact we all might be blown into smithereens at any moment.

It was . . . pretty intense.

But that's not all. I was there when Dr. Shepherd found out that—the person with her HAND on the bomb? It was Meredith Grey. HIS Meredith Grey. The Meredith Grey he's been so desperately trying to ignore and forget and move past, but . . .

I know what I saw in McDreamy's eyes when Dr. Yang told him the news.

It was panic.

And as he went back to the surgery—to finish up Tucker's operation—he could barely contain himself. The transformation in his posture—his intensity—his breathing . . . Every one of us could tell. Dr. Shepherd was holding it together—but he was also dying a little inside . . .

Finally, as we were just wrapping up, Dr. Shepherd asked me to do him a favor—just to check on the status down the hall. See if the bomb was still there, if it had been removed—if Dr. Grey was all right . . .

So I moved carefully to the OR entrance—we'd been carefully prepped not to move too heavily or quickly—the slightest tremor might set the bomb off . . .

I cracked open the OR door, looked slowly around and—I saw her. Dr. Grey was only a few doors away—basically doing the same thing that I was.

She stepped out of her OR—and into the hallway, I believe to see the bomb squad guy who was leaving. Maybe to call out—to thank him for his help, and then—

That's the last thing I remember.

The bomb exploded. There was a wave of heat. The air seemed to crackle.

The OR door flew back, slammed into my head, and . . . I was out. Woke up a few hours later, as a patient. Had a few stitches from the debris, a big gash on my arm, and a killer headache. Was told I suffered a pretty hefty concussion.

So, I've been trying to recover. They kept me a day or two for observation—I think Dr. Shepherd felt responsible for me getting hurt—wanted to make sure there was nothing else wrong before clearing me to come back to work . . .

Joe's been fantastic. He came by every day—usually with Walter—to wish me well. Brought me all the latest gossip magazines.

Word has it, Grey escaped with just a few cuts. Refused to even stay at the hospital for a checkup.

And I guess that's the latest.

I will say this—if you ever plan to step into the wake of an exploding bomb? Seattle Grace is a pretty nice place to recover.

Especially since you'll get treated by a doctor as hot as McDreamy.

Instant Message Conversation

DebbieDoesGossip—logged on at 10:13 a.m.

JoeKnowsBest:	Debbie! I'm so glad you're back at work! I've missed our midday conversations!
DebbieDoesGossip:	Yeah, yeah. Don't get all mushy.
JoeKnowsBest:	U feeling back to normal?
DebbieDoesGossip:	Pretty much. Thx again for all the flowers, btw. And all the visits. And for sending Walter over to my place to feed my cat while I was cooped up here as a patient.
JoeKnowsBest:	No worries. That's what I'm here for. U coming by tonight?
DebbieDoesGossip:	Might. Trying to take it easy—my stitches come out tomorrow.
JoeKnowsBest:	U gonna have a cool scar?
DebbieDoesGossip:	What is it with guys and scars? Karev asked me the same thing this morning!
JoeKnowsBest:	Dudes like scars. What can I say?
DebbieDoesGossip:	Wow. Speaking of dudes—a very good-looking one just walked up to my station . . .
JoeKnowsBest:	Oh yeah?
DebbieDoesGossip:	Made a beeline for Grey. Why do they always make a beeline for Grey?
JoeKnowsBest:	Dunno. She's not my type.

DebbieDoesGossip:	AAAAAAAAA!!!
JoeKnowsBest:	What?
DebbieDoesGossip:	AAAAAAAAA!!!
JoeKnowsBest:	Deb? What are you AAAAAA-ing about???
DebbieDoesGossip:	You'll never believe this.
JoeKnowsBest:	Believe what?
DebbieDoesGossip:	That hot dude that was just hitting on Grey?
JoeKnowsBest:	What about him?
DebbieDoesGossip:	McDreamy just punched him in the face!!!!

DebbieDoesGossip—logged off at 10:24 a.m.

First Day Back

You know that first day back to work after you've—say—been home with a cold? Or maybe out on vacation? Or sometimes, still recovering from a long weekend?

Yeah—that's nothing compared to my first day back at work after recovering from a BOMB explosion!!

Quick status report—I'm fine. Little dizzy, still—but Dr. Shepherd assures me that's normal. So, I'm taking it slow (half shifts this week—which is possible mostly because of the new nurses the Chief has hired since the strike) and trying not to push myself too hard.

Although, I can't say the same for Dr. Grey.

To catch you up—she was in the hallway when the bomb exploded, too. She and her patient had been moved to another OR—just a little bit down the hall (and apparently NOT directly above the main oxygen lines to the hospital) from where I was assisting Dr. Shepherd with his surgery on Bailey's husband . . .

All of the Seattle Grace ORs are in the same area—I noticed some of you were confused by the geography. All of our surgeries happen on the same floor, in the same wing, in operating rooms that are all within a few feet of one another . . .

Despite Dr. Burke's bomb patient no longer being next door to us, he was still in an OR only a few yards away. Just far enough to avoid a major catastrophe—apparently NOT far enough away to avoid me getting knocked around by the explosion.

And—let me tell you. I have rarely seen Dr. Shepherd as livid as he was when he found out that Dr. Grey's roommates had taken her home rather than keep her at the hospital for tests. Some (like, for instance, his WIFE) might say he was overreacting a little bit . . . (After all—Grey IS a doctor. Her friends are doctors. If they think she's fine, if she thinks she's fine, then—she's probably fine.)

Frankly—I was ready to go home to my own bed as well, but—like I said before, I think McDreamy was trying to be overly cautious.

I heard (today, at the coffee stand) Dr. Stevens talking to O'Malley—saying that McDreamy actually came to their house the night of the explosion to see Meredith!! Guess he isn't above making house calls to be sure she's all right . . .

Meanwhile—I'm back at work. Things are getting back to normal. Everyone is still a little shaken up over having had two men—how should I put this?—Pink-mystified, I guess. It's weird watching the clean-up crew in the OR hallways, repairing the damage, knowing that—only a few days ago—well . . .

Never mind. I don't really want to talk about that anymore.

Other news—Dr. Grey seems to be coping pretty damn well . . . I guess if you look death in the face like that, and survive it—then maybe you become reinvigorated or something?

All I know is—she definitely had her flirt on today, when the dashing Dr. Sloan paid Seattle Grace a surprise visit.

Dr. Mark Sloan, as it turns out. Superfamous plastics guy—in town from New York. And boy—did he make an entrance.

I was on the computer—pretending to work, but actually instant messaging Joe—when this very tall, very chiseled hunk of a man—wearing a VERY well-fitting T-shirt—ambled over and started hitting on Dr. Grey. It was Dr. Sloan—although I don't think she realized that at the time . . .

Still—she most definitely did NOT deter him!

But the best part is—as I sat there watching—out of NOWHERE—Pow! Dr. Shepherd punched the guy—right there in the foyer. It was nuts! And—as it turns out, it was also for good reason . . . I've learned (through—what else?—the hospital grapevine) that Dr. Sloan is ALSO the reason McDreamy left New York.

Ah—I'm so glad to be back!

So—of course, once I found that out, I've been keeping a close eye on Sloan, Shepherd, and Shepherd all day—here's what I've learned:

Mark is here to win Addison back. He still loves her. And he still wants her. And this is confusing for her because—Well, let's face it—it's hard to love someone who doesn't love you back. And it's nice to be wanted by someone who DOES love you, but . . .

Anyway—I saw Addison in the ladies' room—I think she had just come from some sort of conversation with Dr. Sloan, because—she was upset. And she was teary . . . and her mascara was running. So I lent her some tissues and a little powder and . . . I have to say—I feel badly for her—she seems to be trying so hard to make up for her mistakes in her marriage—and yet—they just keep coming back to haunt her.

Of course—it probably doesn't help that her husband seemed more concerned about Meredith Grey's life than his own when they both were in danger . . .

But back to today.

There was another interesting turn of events—In that same coffee-cart conversation . . . Izzie and George kept saying something about "being doers" now—about making a bigger effort to go after what they want.

So—I guess I shouldn't be so surprised to have accidentally walked in on Karev and Stevens (no—they didn't see me—I snuck out quickly and quietly) in the supply closet this evening when I was looking for the extra banana bags. They—well—they definitely sounded like they were enjoying themselves . . .

And—as for O'Malley—I've noticed a change in him today. Like I said—maybe facing such an intense situation (the bomb) has put new life into people's psyches—because George . . . well . . .

He seems to have something big on his mind. Like he's on a mission—and nothing is going to stop him until he does what he's setting out to do—he's being a "doer."

Only—I have a suspicion that his "doing" has something to do with Meredith Grey. When he's not following her around today, or approaching her at all the wrong moments (I saw him try to ask her out on a date this afternoon, and it's as though she didn't even hear him—she was all flipping through a phone book or something . . .), he's talking about her, mostly with Izzie . . .

I've got a soft spot for George since he sided with all of us during the strike. He really showed me what a great guy he really is, and . . . I don't know. It just seems to me like he's on the brink—the brink of doing something drastic.

Oh boy. I just hope it doesn't backfire on him.

The O'Malley Report

I know!! I'm a lame lame busy busy really bad blog updater lately—and I apologize. To all of you. I never realized hiring new nurses around here would actually make my life busier . . . Short-term business, of course—but somebody (apparently ME) has to show the new nurses the ropes around here . . .

Let them know which coffee cart NOT to buy coffee from. Teach them when to make sure they KNOCK before entering certain supply closets (you know as well as I do that if the closet door is closed? There could very well be somebody naked in there!). Show them which on-call rooms have doors that lock (and which don't . . . very important detail if you, say, plan on using the beds for more than sleeping . . .). Help them snag the best lunchroom seating (and by best I mean the seats with prime locations—where you can overhear the most juicy gossip . . .).

You know. All the most important things about working at Seattle Grace.

But in my online absence—Oh MY! So much has been going on, I hardly know where to start . . . So I'm just going to dive right in . . .

First up: Dr. Callie Torres.

Now, this is a woman who knows what she wants, when she wants it, and exactly how to get it. She's one of our most talented orthopedics residents—she specializes in cracking, snapping, popping, and setting all sorts of bone-related injuries. She's a bit of a loner, really keeps to herself.

Heard she spends a lot of time down in the artificial limb room . . . Don't know exactly what that's all about, but I do know that she's smart and she always gets her job done efficiently—no fuss. Which I can respect. I am not fond of fuss.

And the big rumor is . . . she has the hots for none other than—George O'Malley.

Now, honestly, I feel like I should have seen this coming. Not only because—as we all know—opposites often attract . . . But remember earlier in the year—when I told you about O'Malley performing emergency heart surgery—solo—in the malfunctioning elevator?

The thing is—Dr. Torres pulled me aside that day. Actually—she cornered me in the tunnels while I was trying to shortcut to the cafeteria to snag some overcooked mac and cheese, but that's not the point.

The point is, Torres cornered me in the tunnels to grill me about George O'Malley. Kept calling him the "heart-in-the-elevator guy" which—at the time—didn't seem all that strange. I mean, he HAD just performed surgery in an elevator! The whole hospital was talking about it . . .

But now that I think back to it, she was asking me all sorts of questions about him . . . Wanted to know who his friends were, where he lived, whether or not I had worked with him much . . . What was he like with patients? With the other doctors? Did he have pet peeves? Did he have a girlfriend?—Stuff like that.

At the time, it seemed like innocent curiosity—appropriate enough . . .

But now? I think she must have had a crush on him—even way back then . . . And clearly, getting to treat him as a patient recently sparked her to make a move . . . Speaking of Dr. Torres treating O'Malley as a patient—I have to update you on his situation with Meredith Grey.

Let me put it to you like this:

There I was. Minding my own business the way I mind my own business every day. Manning my post at the nurse's station. Updating the chart on this kid who'd come in that day after being smacked in the head with a baseball . . .

(If I'd known then that one of the kid's dads would later vomit into my shoes, I would have probably transferred off of that case . . . But as they say—Hindsight is always 20/20.)

So there I was. Updating my paperwork, when—I overheard voices. Raised, heated, slightly frantic-sounding voices coming from somewhere down the hallway. Nurse Olivia (who was standing right next to me at the time) started listening more closely . . .

"Is that . . . that sounds like . . . George," she said . . .

And sure enough—in that instant—O'Malley burst through the hallway's double doors, and hurried right past us, with Meredith Grey, Izzie Stevens, Cristina Yang, and even Alex Karev in tow.

They were all following after him as he bolted into the stairwell, started trotting down the stairs, and (literally) yelled at the top of his lungs that—He and Meredith Grey had had SEX!!!

I think it was at that moment that Olivia (again, literally) fell out of her chair.

Now, keep in mind, we have those super-rolly chairs and a really slick linoleum floor, so sometimes, if you aren't careful, the chairs do have a tendency to roll right out from underneath you, but . . .

Still. Olivia fell out of her chair. Because, HELLO. George and Meredith had apparently had some sex!!!

But that's not all. Because just after that unexpected outburst, O'Malley fell, himself, headfirst—down the rest of the stairs. Bruised himself all up, banged up his knee, and—yes—dislocated his shoulder.

Which is when Dr. Torres stepped onto the scene. Or, O'Malley stepped into her ER—but you know what I mean.

Torres reset O'Malley's shoulder, and has been paying special attention to him ever since. Picking him for cases, asking him to scrub in on some of her procedures . . . and last night, just as I was starting my evening shift, I saw O'Malley dial her number on his phone (she was standing only a few feet away from both him and me, mind you), and he asked her out on a date.

Now—that takes some balls. Him calling her up—right there, in front of patients and hospital staff and—well—a lot of people—and asking her out? It's a new side to George. A side I've only seen glimpses of before—like when he refused to cross the picket line, and joined us nurses when we were on strike.

I like this new, improved George. He's got some guts. And it appears as though he's finally STOPPED pining for Meredith Grey, so . . . I say, Go, George. Good for him . . . Now, if I could just convince him to do something about his new haircut. It is really really really disastrous.

(Just saying . . .)

So—I'll have more updates for you soon . . . Next up? Meredith Grey and the Dr. Shepherds . . . There's all sorts of strange stuff happening there . . . Like . . . I think maybe THEY think the three of them think . . .

They're all FRIENDS???

Yeah, right.

"Friendly" Neighborhood

OK. You've done it. I've done it. We've all done it. Every single one of us has dated someone, broken up with them, then said—in that masterfully cruel and totally ridiculous way: Let's just be friends.

But we didn't really MEAN it!!!

That's where I'm confused about what's happening right now with Meredith Grey and Dr. Shepherd . . .

They seem to REALLY believe that they are—indeed—genuine friends. I've heard them talking to each other about it. I've heard Meredith talking to the other interns about it. I've heard Shepherd talking to his wife about it—And I have to say—I really do NOT understand it.

Take yesterday, for example. We lost a few patients—back to back to back. Had the whole hospital on edge, frankly, because we all know that a series of deaths like that usually means there are more fatalities to come (at least, if you believe in superstitions . . .)

Anyway—yesterday morning, just after the cluster of fatal surgeries, Addison Shepherd decided to hand out good-luck hot chocolates . . . (Only to the surgeons, mind you. Did she think to give ME a hot chocolate, even though I was scrubbed in on her deadly surgery that morning, too? Of course not. No cocoa for the nurses. But that's a different story altogether . . .)

So Addison gave Meredith a hot chocolate. Then she gave Derek a hot chocolate . . . and the look on his face was pretty much priceless! He commented on the gesture—on Addison including Meredith—and Addison told him, if he's friends with Meredith, then she's friends with Meredith. Simple as that . . .

Only, obviously, it's SO not that simple. It brings me right back to my question:

How on earth can Meredith Grey be genuine friends with McDreamy?

He's her married ex-boyfriend co-dog-owning BOSS. The same married ex-boyfriend co-dog-owning boss who keeps making googly eyes at her in the hallway, and sneaking up behind her in the elevator, and showing her time and time again that he clearly STILL has feelings for her!!!!

I'm sorry. I'm projecting a little bit here. I guess the situation just hits a little close to home for me . . .

The thing is, I dated someone here at the hospital for a while myself. He wasn't my boss, exactly, but he was technically my hierarchical superior . . . (And, no, I won't bore you with the story of our ill-fated romance. No reason to rehash the past, right?)

And even after I broke it off (he was, as it turns out, a little bit wacky), he and I tried to be friends. Or, I tried. And he just tried to find other ways to get back into my pants.

All I'm saying is, in my experience, the friend thing? Never works. Even when you mean for it to work? It never does . . . Especially in this case.

Nurse Liz said she saw Meredith talking to McDreamy in the scrub room. (She's a pro at reading lips, btw—something about a deaf aunt or something.) And she's pretty sure she saw Meredith telling Derek about having had sex with George.

I mean—isn't that taking the whole "friend" thing a little too far?? Maybe not. Maybe I'm projecting again. Maybe they are mature, sensitive adults who know how to handle the intricacies of friendship better than I do . . .

I mean, anything's possible, right?

By the way—as long as we're talking about being friends, not being friends, being more than friends . . .

Izzie Stevens? Totally needs to reexamine her priorities these days . . . I'm not the only one who has noticed JUST how inappropriately close she's been getting to Denny Duquette (one of our in-house heart patients) . . .

The guy's a charmer, I'll give her that (yes, even I get a little weak in the knees when he drawls out his words with that semi-Southern charm . . .), but . . .

More on that later. Looks like I've got a patient in 4213 with an ice chip stuck up his nose. Gotta run!

K-I-S-S-I-N-G

Before I begin—if anyone reading this works at Seattle Grace, and has seen my Scrabble board (you know the one—I keep it in the lounge under the counter with the napkins and the plastic drink stirrers?), let me know. Because it's missing.

I like to play Scrabble on my slow evening shifts. I love my Scrabble. I MISS my Scrabble. Please, RETURN me my Scrabble!!!

But back to the gossip . . .

Izzie Stevens is out of control.

Denny Duquette was rushed back into the hospital recently—and he hasn't been well enough to go back home since . . . His heart is ready to give out completely. He's been in bad shape for a while, but—Wow. He just seems to be getting worse and worse and worse . . . if they don't find a donor heart for him soon, well . . . It's just so sad watching someone die, waiting for a match like that . . .

That said, his spirits seem unusually good, all things considered. I'm sure his rosy outlook is due, in part, to the fact that he's been receiving a lot of extra attention from none other than Little Miss Izzie Stevens.

She's a good doctor—that's not what I'm saying. And she has a wonderful bedside manner—I've witnessed it myself . . . but with Denny? She's crossing a serious patient/doctor line—a line that, frankly, is only going to get her into trouble.

The other night, I saw her bring a bag full of goodies into his room—after hours. She wasn't on duty . . . But she WAS all decked out with her curly hair and curvy jeans . . . We're talking a tablecloth, juice, plastic wine glasses . . .

Yeah—that is NOT how you visit with your patient. Even if you ARE off duty. There's a line. And she's choosing to cross it. When she totally knows better.

But that's not all—because last night? After we had to rush Denny back into surgery (on the night of the fatality clusters—like

I said before, everyone was superstitiously on edge), I saw something SO wrong—

I saw Izzie KISS Denny Duquette. Her patient. On the lips. In his room. After surgery. She kissed him because he didn't die . . . She kissed him because if you ask me? She's clearly falling in love with him.

I mean—Okay. Interns sleeping with their attendings—not a good idea. Pretty much always against the rules, but . . . whatever. It happens. It's fun to gossip about. It's not the end of the world or anything . . .

But falling in love with your patient? Now, that's an intern mistake that's next to impossible to come back from—it's beyond taboo. It clouds your judgment in the most fundamental way—there's a reason surgeons don't operate on their family members. On the people they love—it's because it's so difficult to make the proper decisions.

I'm worried about this. Really really worried. I'd like to talk to Dr. Bailey about it—give her the heads-up, see if there's any way she can intervene, but . . .

It's probably not my place.

And you should see the way Alex Karev has been skulking around the halls these days! He's on a tear—the tiniest thing will set him off. And there's no way it isn't because Izzie suddenly doesn't have time for him . . . Alex is so jealous of Denny, it would be funny if it weren't so darn intense . . .

I have to say—on this, I understand where Karev is coming from.

Earlier, when I was taking a coffee break outside, by one of the benches, Karev came up. Slammed down onto the bench beside me. Looked a little like he was ready to punch somebody.

I told him that if I smoked, I'd offer him a cigarette—but since it's such a nasty habit, and I've seen firsthand just how disgusting those shriveled black smokers' lungs look—all I could offer him was a stick of gum.

He didn't say a word, but he took two pieces. And began to chomp on them—furiously.

I heard later that Izzie had just dumped him a few minutes before . . .

Man, that's gotta sting. Dumped for a dying heart patient. Yikes.

Knitting, Knitting, Everywhere!

OK, first things first—I found my Scrabble board. In Denny Duquette's room. Where he and Izzie Stevens had stashed it!!

So . . . I took it back. And waited for Izzie to hunt me down (which she did) and ask for it back (which she did) just so I could reply, "How much is it worth to you, Dr. Stevens?"

Turns out, it's worth a lot! She started fishing around in her pockets for all sorts of jewelry and cash, when I stopped her. I mean—I do like to taunt people, but I'm not entirely heartless! I settled on a price that isn't monetary—it's more like a skill. Something I've always wanted to do: learn how to knit.

Izzie's been knitting up a storm all over the hospital today, so . . . I bargained three months' worth of knitting lessons out of her. We start tomorrow night—I'm actually really looking forward to it. Already bought myself a set of needles, and some yarn. A lovely shade of butter yellow.

Meanwhile—I think Alex Karev is really letting this whole Izzie/Denny thing get to him. He's just . . . raw lately. Off his game. Emotions too close to the surface.

Like this afternoon—you should have seen Karev blow up— yes, BLOW UP—at Dr. Burke. I guess Burke thought Alex was being too blunt with one of their patients or something . . . but MAN! When Burke pulled him out into the hall to discuss it, Alex went nuts. He was loud, all up in Burke's face—practically snarling. It was intense. And a little creepy. And completely out of line . . . except that . . . Alex did have a point.

He kept talking about how, though he may not be the nicest

guy in the world, at least he's honest with his patients. At least there's that . . .

And I tend to agree with him. I'm not one for sugarcoating things (yeah, yeah—I can hear all of your sarcastic comments about that already) . . . I just don't believe we should sugarcoat things for our patients.

What is it with all of the knitting today?? Just saw Meredith Grey walking around with a strangely shaped piece of knitting herself . . . Glad I picked Izzie to give me lessons, and not Grey. From the looks of her knitting, Grey has no clue what she's doing . . .

Actually—apparently she's been a little out-there all day. Dr. Torres came up to me earlier, looking a little shaken . . . so I asked her if she was all right. Told her she looked a little pale (and if you've met Dr. Torres, you know she is usually ANYTHING but pale!).

She paused, then told me that Meredith Grey had just been smashing a plaster cast with a hammer—like, smashing it to smithereens. And that it worried her when she thought about Meredith as the woman who broke George's heart. That clearly, Meredith had some serious issues—and they were, in Callie's words, "a little bit freaky."

Now—for someone to freak Torres out? That must have been some SERIOUS cast-smashing!

I didn't say this to Callie—but I think I may have an idea as to why Meredith was on such a tear today . . . I'm pretty sure I saw Meredith's father—Thatcher—wandering around the hospital earlier . . .

I can't be sure—it's been so many years, and he looked really different, but—yeah. I do think it was him. In which case—I'm not surprised Meredith was getting a little bit freaky. Last I heard, she hadn't exactly been a big part of her father's life . . .

It's either that—or the fact that Addison is under the same freaky delusion that she and Meredith are all buddy-buddy friends now, just like Meredith and Derek. Addison was all happy and chummy and FRIENDLY with Meredith today . . .

Here's my question—when did this happen? When did they get all "Hey, we've both boned the same dude, but who cares? Let's braid hair!"

Seriously??

I liked it better when they were at each other's throats. So much more fun to gossip about!

My McVet

Not to veer too far off course—I know this is a blog about HOSPITAL gossip—but I just had to share an interesting tidbit with you about my visit this morning . . . to my vet.

You may have heard me mention my darling cat Skittles. I've had him for years—he's a charmer, that cat (well—except when he claws his way up my expensive silk curtains . . .). Anyway—last night he was acting a little strange—bumping into things. Not walking straight . . . So I got worried. And this morning (as I had the late shift at work) I took Skittles in to see Dr. Dandridge. My vet.

Now—Skittles and I are very fond of Dr. Dandridge (he actually insists I call him Finn—but the nurse in me has a hard time not referring to him by his title . . .). He's the best vet around— amazing with the animals. Handles anything from itsy bitsy kittens to horses—he does it all. There's usually a wait list just to get an appointment—that's how popular Dr. Dandridge is . . .

Of course, if you ask me, I don't think it hurts his popularity that he's charming, good-looking, and single—not that Dr. Dandridge has always been single. He was married once . . . sad story. He doesn't talk about it much—And now he lives alone in his rustic apartment right upstairs from his office . . .

But I'm off point. The reason I'm telling you about my McVet is because—as I sat there this morning, waiting for poor Skittles's appointment—Guess who walked in to pick up his dog?

McDreamy. I share my McVet with McDreamy.

I tell ya—having both of those deliciously handsome men standing together right there in front of me? Not a bad way to start my morning. Not a bad way AT ALL!

Instant Message Conversation—

DebbieDoesGossip—logged on at 8:08 p.m.

DebbieDoesGossip:	Guess who I saw at the vet's office?
JoeKnowsBest:	Vet's office? Is Skittles sick?
DebbieDoesGossip:	I saw McDreamy. I share my McVet with McDreamy.
JoeKnowsBest:	Which means you also share your vet with McMeredith Grey.
DebbieDoesGossip:	Huh?
JoeKnowsBest:	She and McDreamy have joint custody of their dog. So his vet is her vet.
DebbieDoesGossip:	Seriously?
JoeKnowsBest:	C'mon. I told you that.
DebbieDoesGossip:	No you didn't.
JoeKnowsBest:	AND—McVet asked her out. On a date. I KNOW I told you that.
DebbieDoesGossip:	NO. You DIDN'T.
JoeKnowsBest:	Yes I did! She was in here, all knitting, and swearing off men—

DebbieDoesGossip:	I remember the knitting.
JoeKnowsBest:	Next thing I know, she's heading out to date the vet!
DebbieDoesGossip:	Dude. I'd remember you telling me something like that.
JoeKnowsBest:	Well, then. I MEANT to tell you.
DebbieDoesGossip:	You're letting me down here, Joe. You're my most reliable non-hospital source of gossip. You dish, I dish, remember? It's what we do.
JoeKnowsBest:	I dish. I totally dish. Don't diss my dishing.
DebbieDoesGossip:	If I'd known Grey was dating my vet, I could have pushed for more info!
JoeKnowsBest:	You would use your poor sick cat as a ploy to get more gossip?
DebbieDoesGossip:	Uuummm . . .
JoeKnowsBest:	Never mind. Don't answer that.

DebbieDoesGossip—logged off at 8:24 p.m.

Unraveling of a She-Shepherd

Just got out of a marathon session with the Chief. He was grilling me about a surgery I was scrubbed in to earlier—a surgery with Addison Shepherd.

As a scrub nurse, one of my jobs is to log my account of the surgeries I participate in—I note everything—from how many sponges were used to what procedures were performed and under what circumstances. My notes are often more detailed than the surgeons' own notes—that's my job. To record the most detailed account of the surgery possible. So anyone reading the notes will know exactly what happened in the operating room.

And in this case—something very unusual happened.

Or at least, it seemed unusual to me. Now, I really can't get into the details—for legal reasons—you understand. But it's enough to say that what happened in that surgery has created a rivalry between Alex Karev and Addison Shepherd that—quite frankly—I'm really looking forward to watching unfold . . .

Joe, of course, seems to have some crazy idea that these two are destined to become MORE than just adversaries. He thinks they'd make more sense as LOVERS or some such nonsense . . . Whatever. He wasn't in that surgery with me today. He doesn't see these two every day the way I do . . . And he definitely didn't see the evil eye Karev gave Addison after she lit into him on the stairwell . . .

Mark my words. That woman is beginning to unravel. And from the looks of it, she plans to take Alex Karev with her. I heard she's permanently assigned him to the Vagina Squad.

Heh . . . Like any woman in her right mind would want Alex Karev up her skirt!

Instant Message Conversation

DebbieDoesGossip—logged on at 4:32 p.m.

DebbieDoesGossip: Well. Izzie managed to convince Denny to get the LVAD.

JoeKnowsBest: Isn't that another name for Dracula or something?

DebbieDoesGossip: Not Vlad. LVAD. It's a battery-run heart pumping device.

JoeKnowsBest: And that's a bad thing?

DebbieDoesGossip:	I don't know. It's probably fine. But it means he won't be up for leaving the hospital for a while . . .
JoeKnowsBest:	Be still his battery operated heart.
DebbieDoesGossip:	I'm sure Izzie will be glad to have him around longer, but . . .
JoeKnowsBest:	You think he'll get tired of living in the hospital.
DebbieDoesGossip:	Wouldn't you?
JoeKnowsBest:	R U Kidding? I was squirmy to leave after just a few hours. Hospitals smell funny.
DebbieDoesGossip:	No they don't.
JoeKnowsBest:	Yes. They do. Like . . . I dunno. Stale micro-waved french fries or something.
DebbieDoesGossip:	You think hospitals smell like french fries?
JoeKnowsBest:	Not good fries. Not waffle-cut crispers or anything. I'm talking gross fries. Like soggy-make-you-nauseous fries. Undercooked fries.
DebbieDoesGossip:	Sometimes I really worry about you.
JoeKnowsBest:	Aw shucks.
DebbieDoesGossip:	No, seriously. I really worry.

DebbieDoesGossip—logged off at 4:47 p.m.

You Didn't Hear It from Me, But . . .

Rumor has it that Dr. Callie Torres . . . doesn't wash her hands. I know, right? Gross. And totally implausible—I mean. She's a surgeon. A doctor. She treats patients. Of course she must wash her hands, only . . . all I'm saying is—that's what I heard.

I've heard a few other things, too, today. Seems the grapevine is up and running, full speed ahead. Which is always fun . . . I love good gossip days. So here's the rundown on what all I've heard . . .

Addison and Derek have been having some . . . sex problems. As in weeks and weeks of bad to lukewarm to really really sad and very boring SEX problems. We're talking—awkward head-bumping. Overcompensation. Lack of coordination—you know. Sex problems.

Until . . . the other night. When, out of the blue, Derek apparently came home to his trailer and—for lack of a better phrase—jumped Addison's sexually frustrated bones. In the shower. Hot & steamy soapy shower sex.

I mean—HELLO. All this, of course, is according to Addison, who couldn't contain her gleeful morning-after-really-good-sex glow the next day. She's amazingly talkative before her first cup of coffee. Catch her on the right morning, and she'll spill all sorts of details about her and McDreamy. We're talking up-close and personal . . .

But I'm a lady. I won't get into THOSE details. (wink.)

Next rumor: Burke is really mad at Cristina.

Actually, it's less of a rumor and more of an observation— I was passing by them in the hall earlier, when I overheard the end of what sounded like a VERY interesting conversation . . .

Sounded like Cristina and Burke are having a few sex problems themselves; Burke was accusing Cristina of falling asleep—DURING sex!

Now—first of all, I know how many hours Cristina has been working. I'm surprised she hasn't fallen asleep on rounds, let alone during sex, but . . . for her to fall asleep on Burke?

I'll just say this. One afternoon, last year, after a particularly grueling night shift in the Pit—I decided to roll my chair to the back corner of the reception desk, and shut my eyes. Just for a moment. I was just sooooo sleepy . . . Know who nearly bit my head off when he noticed me taking a snooze? That's right. Dr. Burke.

Given his reaction then—I can only IMAGINE what his reaction must have been to Cristina!

Another juicy tidbit: I had a follow-up appointment at the vet's office (for my cat)—and this time, I used the opportunity to get a few details from Dr. Dandridge about his LOVE life . . .

As soon as I started talking—his whole face lit up! He told me all about "this amazing girl" he's met . . . (You and I know he meant Meredith Grey, but I didn't let on that I knew her . . .) He talked about her with such . . . reverence. He clearly thinks the world of her. I get the feeling he's a little bit in awe of her—and of his growing feelings toward her. He said his feelings are catching him by surprise . . . in a really good way.

It was actually very sweet—listening to him gush. He told me all about the dinner he was planning to cook for her that night, right down to the type of wine he'd chosen (something white and dry) . . . And then he asked me if I thought it was too soon for him to tell her about . . . his past.

I've known Dr. Dandridge a long time. I know all about his wife—how she died. How it's haunted him over the years . . . I also know how important it is for him to move forward . . .

So I simply assured him that if the time were right, he'd know what to say. And that I had a gut feeling this amazing new woman in his life? She probably had a few things from her past that she could share, too.

I don't know if it made him feel any better, but he did thank me for my advice. And then refused to charge me for the appointment. Sent me home with some fancy cat food for Skittles, and that was that.

Meanwhile—I also heard some disheartening news—about Denny Duquette. Word around the floor is that he's been getting progressively more and more depressed. The longer he stays in bed on this LVAD—the more listless he becomes.

It's a bad sign, because that kind of emotional stress can cause serious health problems down the line . . . And I can only imagine what Izzie Stevens must be feeling. She practically convinced him to get the LVAD in the first place—and now, if he's resenting her for that . . .

I still say she's getting dangerously close to him. He's a patient. HER patient. Everyone knows Izzie is falling for Denny—but it's as though no one is willing to do anything about it. Dr. Burke, Dr. Bailey—the other interns. They all just look the other way and continue to let it happen. I just don't get it . . .

Meanwhile—where IS Izzie? I've been paging her about one of her patients, and she's nowhere to be found.

Whatever. I'm on break in two minutes. If she wants to ignore her job to flirt with her patient, then so be it. I'm just going to gather up my stash of new trashy tabloids, my favorite dark chocolate candy bar, and take my break. Somewhere nice—like maybe out on a bench or something . . .

OK—Wait. My stash of magazines is gone. As is my candy. Seriously. WHO keeps pilfering from my stash of goodies????

PS—As I typed the line above, I also yelled it aloud. And a moment later, Nurse Olivia leaned over to say: "You didn't hear it from me, but it's Izzie. She's the one who gets into your stash of goodies, usually to share them with Denny."

That's it. Izzie Stevens? I'm watching you.

Instant Message Conversation

DebbieDoesGossip—logged on at 12:04 p.m.

DebbieDoesGossip: U there?

JoeKnowsBest: I thought we weren't speaking.

DebbieDoesGossip: You're the one who logged off in a huff. Over McDreamy.

JoeKnowsBest: Whatever. The dude saved my life. If I wanna side with him, I'll side with him.

DebbieDoesGossip: All I'm saying is—he's not as good of a match for Grey as McVet. That's all I'm saying.

JoeKnowsBest: I thought we agreed to disagree on this point.

DebbieDoesGossip: We did.

JoeKnowsBest: Okay then.

DebbieDoesGossip: I just wanted to let you know that I've come up with a pros and cons list—and I'm posting it on my blog.

JoeKnowsBest: Oh sure. I have a blog, too, you know. I can post things on MY blog if I want.

DebbieDoesGossip: Wanna hear my first Pro-Vet Item?

JoeKnowsBest: He doesn't have fleas?

DebbieDoesGossip: He's NOT MARRIED.

JoeKnowsBest: Yeah, yeah.

DebbieDoesGossip: I'm not kidding. Since when do you root for a married man to get together with another woman? How would you feel if Walter cheated on YOU?

JoeKnowsBest: But Walter wouldn't.

DebbieDoesGossip: What if he did?

JoeKnowsBest: But he never would.

DebbieDoesGossip: So what kind of guy DOES? That's all I'm saying. McVet is amazing AND available. I don't care how dreamy McDreamy seems— bottom line is—

JoeKnowsBest:	He's married. Yeah. I get it. You're missing my point.
DebbieDoesGossip:	Which is?
JoeKnowsBest:	That you can't choose who you fall in love with. You just can't. Doesn't make you evil or anything . . . it just makes you human.
DebbieDoesGossip:	Nothing McDreamy about a McCheater.
JoeKnowsBest:	Why are we even discussing this? We're talking hypotheticals here. It's not like Derek and Meredith are ACTUALLY hooking up or anything.
DebbieDoesGossip:	You're right. It's silly.
JoeKnowsBest:	Totally silly.
DebbieDoesGossip:	OK.
JoeKnowsBest:	OK . . . You're still putting up the pros & cons list on your blog, aren't you?
DebbieDoesGossip:	You bet I am.

DebbieDoesGossip—logged off at 12:26 p.m.

McVet vs. McDreamy

My buddy Joe and I have a little debate going. Over who WE'D pick if we had the chance to choose between McVet and McDreamy. I mean—if there were a contest, if we stood these two dashing men next to each other . . . Who'd land on top?

Joe's all about McDreamy—"He saved my life, this . . ."— "He's my super duper hero, that . . ." Blah blah blah. I'm a McVet fan, all the way.

From 10 to 1, here are the Pros & Cons as I see them:

#10

McVet: Loves saving animals. All animals. Equally.

McDreamy: Loves catching animals (OK, fish) and frying 'em up in a pan before breakfast.

#9

McVet: First date includes birthing a pony, a home cooked meal, and a steamy hot shower. Hello. Birthing a PONY, people.

McDreamy: First date? Does getting drunk and going home with the first stranger he meets in Seattle count? How about finally going out for a drink at the bar across the street and "accidentally" dropping unsigned divorce papers onto the floor? Anyone?

#8

McVet: Which brings us to—totally single. Single McSingle.

McDreamy: Oh—right. Forgot to mention he had a wife . . . then decided to stay with his estranged wife once she came to town. But—hey. What's that got to do with anything, right?

#7

McVet: Owns his own business AND the building he works in—which just so happens to be painted a beautiful, soothing shade of blue—with an amazing apartment right upstairs.

McDreamy:	Yeah, dude. Nice TRAILER.

#6

McVet:	Amazing head of hair, with just the right touch of McScruffiness.
McDreamy:	OK—never mind. Let's call it even on the hair.

#5

McVet:	Fixes eggs, bacon, hash browns, coffee, and fresh juice for breakfast—enough for two.
McDreamy:	Helps himself to his own bowl of Icky-McHealth-Nut cereal in the morning. Then mocks Meredith for eating leftover grilled cheese.

#4

McVet:	Scary and damaged and willing to admit it.
McDreamy:	Again. Couldn't even admit he was married.

#3

McVet:	Takes things slow. Doesn't try to hurry Meredith into anything . . .
McDreamy:	Again—with the jumping into bed the first time they meet thing . . .

#2

McVet:	Accepts Meredith just the way she is.
McDreamy:	Yells at Meredith in the stairwell. And the CT scanning room. And the scrub room. And the OR . . . Practically calls her a whore—I mean, seriously?

#1

McVet:	Oh, right—and because it's still worth mentioning. He's TOTALLY available.
McDreamy:	And he's TOTALLY married. Just saying.

Going Postal

OK, all hell is breaking loose today—things are really out of control. It feels like everyone is going postal, which is why . . . the only thing I can think of to do right now . . . is blog.

Strange as it sounds, blogging's become . . . sort of a safe place for me these days. It's something I can control. And something I can use to deal—in some small way—with the craziness all around me right now . . .

And to hide. Because, in my experience, when things begin to spin THIS far out of control—there's no stopping them until something even BIGGER and BADDER happens, so . . .

I'm going to sit here. And type.

Here's the thing. I know something. OK—I don't KNOW know, but I have a very strong suspicion. And I feel I should be doing something about it. I know I should be doing something about it, but—I don't know what. Or how. Or—even why I should be the one to step up, when it doesn't actually involve me . . . And me stepping up might very well wind up really HURTING someone else—one (or maybe even some) of our interns . . . and . . .

. . . So I'm blogging.

I'll start with the obvious. We have a lot of patients today. Gunshot wounds—because there was a shooting. A restaurant employee—he really DID go postal. Shot up the restaurant . . . hurt—even killed—a bunch of people. Not fun.

But it's not just that—the patients, I can handle that kind of craziness. It's the rest of my co-workers that . . . are one by one beginning to lose it.

Take Addison Shepherd. She lost it with McDreamy earlier—
I only caught the end of their argument, but that was enough.
They were standing right above our main nurse's station, so
everyone heard her—as she yelled at Derek about not being able
to compete for his affections because (as she put it) "I'm NOT
Meredith Grey!!"

Bad enough people were within earshot—even worse when
Addison and Derek looked down to see Meredith standing right
there, as well. I can't even imagine what could have pushed Addison far enough to lose it like that. She's usually so composed, so
polished, but . . .

Like I've been saying, though. She's beginning to crack. And
it's showing.

Then—well, then there's Callie. MAN. Is SHE on a tear
today—Seems Meredith Grey really set her off, something about
her dog and its bone cancer. All I know is that Callie won't stop
grumbling about Meredith and "being part of that stinking, dys-
functional family." Let me just tell you, Dr. Torres is a little scary
when she's angry. I mean—I wouldn't want to mess with her on
the wrong day is all. Have you SEEN how forceful she is when
she's re-setting bones?

Oh. And you should have seen Cristina Yang today after Burke
didn't let her go with him to get a transplant heart. She was livid.
Can't say that I blame her, actually—turns out Karev weaseled
his way off the Vagina Squad and onto the transplant—right under her nose . . .

But still. She's reacting like a girlfriend—not a surgical intern. Which is unusual for her. She's not one to LET her emotions take control . . . In fact, of anyone, she's the intern who's
best at separating her personal life from her professional
life . . .

Speaking of the transplant case—it's a heart. And it's for
Denny. That's right, Denny Duquette is finally getting his long
awaited heart . . . So you'd think that Izzie Stevens would be ec-
static. She should be beside herself—especially after Dr. Bailey

(in a severe lapse of judgment, if you ask me) agreed to let Izzie help prep Denny for the surgery . . .

But instead? I saw Izzie wandering around—looking so lost, so forlorn . . . I don't know. It was bizarre—her face was so . . . hollow. Worried. And, frankly, a little bit frightening.

What's strange is that, one of the gunshot victims I was treating earlier today? He described this guy—Petey—the guy who came in with the gun and shot up the restaurant? He described Petey in exactly the same way . . . said he had this distant, hollow look in his eyes . . . like he was scared, and worried, but resolved. Resolved to do something drastic.

He said Petey looked just like that the moment before he pulled out his gun and began to shoot.

Which brings me back to why all I can do right now is blog.

I just saw Izzie pull George O'Malley out of the locker room. I saw her hurry him down the hall—I have a pretty good feeling they were heading in the direction of Denny's room.

And my gut—my gut says something terribly terribly wrong is about to unfold . . .

But I can't move. I can't do anything about it, because I don't ACTUALLY know anything. I'm not covering that part of the floor. I'm down here—in the Pit. I have patients here to monitor. It isn't my place to just up and leave, but—

WHAT WAS THAT? Holy crap. Was that—Were those gunshots????

Instant Message Conversation:

DebbieDoesGossip—logged on at 11:37 p.m.

DebbieDoesGossip:	Joe.
JoeKnowsBest:	I'm here. What's the update?
DebbieDoesGossip:	Burke's alive. He suffered a GSW to the shoulder.

He's stable, but he's lost a lot of blood. And . . . his hand. He can't move his hand properly.

JoeKnowsBest: Jeez.

DebbieDoesGossip: I know.

JoeKnowsBest: But—he's going to be OK, right?

DebbieDoesGossip: The Chief and McDreamy are in with him now . . .

JoeKnowsBest: He HAS to be OK.

DebbieDoesGossip: Too early to tell.

JoeKnowsBest: Wow. Deb—Wow. OK. Tell me—what can I do? Are you going to be there all night? Want me to stop by your place and feed Skittles?

DebbieDoesGossip: There's something else.

JoeKnowsBest: More than Burke getting shot?

DebbieDoesGossip: Afraid so . . . Denny's supposed to be getting a new heart tonight.

JoeKnowsBest: That's great—wait. Oh. OH. Oh no. And Burke's been shot. Oh Jeez—Burke's been SHOT.

DebbieDoesGossip: And—

JoeKnowsBest: And? There's more??

DebbieDoesGossip: I think so. It's just—this gut feeling I keep having.

JoeKnowsBest: What's your gut feeling saying?

DebbieDoesGossip: I just . . . I'm getting worried about Izzie.

JoeKnowsBest: And when you say worried . . . ?

DebbieDoesGossip: Crap—Burke's in trouble—Joe. I have to go—

JoeKnowsBest: But—?

DebbieDoesGossip—logged off at 11:49 p.m.

Where Are All the Suck-Ups?

There's something to the phrase: "It's quiet. Too quiet."
Because that's what it is right now. Too quiet.

Everyone's tense. The Chief's wife, Adele, is here—along with his niece. Sweet girl. Had to cut her prom short because—well—it looks like her cancer, which had been in remission, is back again. Poor thing. All she wanted to do was have a wonderful prom night. And now she's stuck in a hospital, listening to her aunt and uncle argue . . .

And Burke. Wow. Dr. Burke. I can't believe he's been shot—and that there's major damage to the nerves in his arm. In his hand. I can't imagine this hospital without Dr. Burke as one of its surgeons—but I'm getting ahead of things. Burke says Shepherd will operate, and everything will be fine. So—it will just have to be fine.

Only . . . I've been watching Shepherd today. He's not himself. He keeps double and triple checking all of Burke's charts . . . I think he's nervous. About operating on Burke. About the responsibility involved with possibly keeping Burke from ever being able to operate again . . .

And Bailey—I can tell she's shaken up by all of this. By seeing Burke in that hospital bed. It's always hard when it's one of your own, and—

Hold on a second. Bailey's started ranting something about—"Where are all of my SUCK-UPS??" She's right. Where ARE all of her suck-ups? Where are all of the interns??

Why isn't Cristina down here looking after Burke? She was running Trauma 2 earlier, but that was ages ago . . . And Meredith?

I can't remember the last time I saw Meredith—or George and Izzie for that matter. Not since—Oh jeez. Not since . . .

Not since I saw them running down the hall—not long before Burke was shot . . .

Oh no. Oh no no no—this could be bad.

Interrogation Station

I was right. It was bad. It was very bad.

Somebody cut Denny's LVAD wire. So his heart would get worse. So he would move up the transplant list—and be sure to get his NEW heart . . . which he did. But at what cost? I can't believe ANYONE would do such a thing—It's—it's unforgivable.

And I think we all have a pretty good idea of who did it. But no one can prove anything for sure, it seems . . .

The good news is—Denny's operation was a success. He has his new heart, he's doing well . . .

But—I am not exaggerating when I tell you—there will be hell to pay.

None of the interns involved—Yang, Grey, Stevens, O'Malley—even Karev—are giving up anything about what happened. None of them will talk. So the Chief has set aside his day to speak to each of them individually. See which one of them he'll be able to crack.

I'm stationed not far from the interrogation room now.

First intern up was Karev. He's been in there a little while—not too terribly long, and—OH! Here he comes. He seems to be leaving in a hurry. He looks a little flustered, a little red in the face . . . but also too smug to have actually buckled. I don't think the Chief got anything out of him—Wait. Here comes the Chief now. He's shaking his head. Looks unhappy.

Nope. Doesn't look like he managed to intimidate Karev.

The Chief's saying something to Patricia. Sounds like he's asking for Cristina Yang.

Later . . .

Yang's been in with the Chief a little while now. About as long as Karev when he finally left. It's been very quiet in there—with the exception of just a moment ago, when it sounded like Cristina might have raised her voice a bit—

The door's cracking. Cristina's in the doorway—What's she saying? She keeps saying—almost insisting—"I'll tell you. I will. If you just tell me how you keep your edge, Chief. How do you do it??" Yikes. The Chief just shooed Cristina out—and she looks . . .

Well, frankly, she looks more upset than I've ever seen her. Even when she was a patient she had more of an edge than this and—Oh my. I think . . . she's crying.

Later than That . . .

Wow. Izzie just darted out of that interrogation room—like she was on a mission or something—The Chief followed her out, but she was already gone. Wonder what that was about? Because— let me tell you—she looked entirely too happy to have actually admitted to anything incriminating . . .

I've never seen her that giddy. When she threw open the door, she blurted out (as though suddenly realizing something), "It's my turn. It's MY turn!"

Then she dashed down the hall toward—where else? Denny's room.

Boy—the Chief looks tired. And a little confused. Perplexed. But mostly, just worn down. Like HE'S ready to crack. I don't envy him his position right now. There's nothing fun for him about any of this . . .

Even Later.

OK. George has been in that room a LONG long time now . . . Almost double the time of anyone else. I'm half inclined to think George is in there, just spilling his guts to the Chief, only . . .

Everyone who passes by the room insists there is no talking going on inside whatsoever. That there are literally NO voices. But I know those two are still in there. There isn't another entrance to the room. We'd have seen it if either of them left, so . . .

What on earth's going on in there?

Ah! The door's opening. Here comes George, and . . . Yeah. He's just trotting away, almost as though he doesn't have a care in the world. It would seem the Chief was unsuccessful in cracking O'Malley as well. Interesting.

Meredith, meanwhile, has been sitting out here, close to me. Just waiting.

The Chief just poked out his head—and asked for Meredith.

You should have heard the sigh she let out before walking in. Man—to be a fly on the wall in that room . . .

And Later Still . . .

Meredith's been in there the longest. And I can TELL she's in there talking. The tone of her voice sounds very insistent. Almost confrontational . . .

I have a feeling they aren't actually talking about Denny. Or the LVAD wires. Seems to me Meredith had too much time out here to herself—to mull over all sorts of things that must have been bubbling under the surface already . . .

For instance—I know she's upset about her dog. Her and Mc-Dreamy's dog, I should say. The dog that Finn's going to have to put to sleep.

Forget all the Denny stuff—that's enough to make a girl sigh heavily right there . . .

Anyway, the fact is—

Woah. Now, that's a first. The CHIEF just left the room—before Meredith. He seems to be in a hurry—Wow. I wonder why he just left like that? I wonder what she just said to him??

Here's Meredith, pausing in the doorway. Watching him leave.

Well—I guess that puts an end to the interrogations, now, doesn't it?

Once upon a Prom

So—here we all are. In our place of business. Trying to attend to a hospital full of sickies, and . . . our second floor nurse's station has been commandeered to host a fricking PROM.

Look, I GET that the Chief is having some issues with his wife. I do. I even get that because of those issues, he pretty much has no choice but to do whatever she insists on him doing. And if that means throwing a prom for his sick niece, it means throwing a prom for his sick niece.

But for the love of all things sacred, does the prom have to shut down my regular NURSE'S STATION?

So, now I'm crammed over here at the station by the elevators—with a bird's eye view of all the glittery stars and helium balloon arches and flashing photography lights off in the distance. Actually, the swirling disco ball DOES look pretty cool from down here . . . BUT STILL.

I'm convinced the whole glittery mess, echoing across the entire hospital foyer, is just trying to taunt me as I sit here, crammed into my makeshift nurse's station, pretending to do actual work.

And to top it all off, I'm wearing panty hose. Because—I have two hours to kill between shifts tonight and that means—I'm going to the prom. I'm wearing sequins. And a push-up bra. And these damned panty hose, which—btw—are totally giving me a wedgie.

At any rate, as I've been sitting here all day, waiting to go guzzle punch and wow my colleagues with some snazzy dance moves, I've taken it upon myself to collect a few stories about some of their proms.

Plus—the other nurses and I have come up with our own prom-night superlatives. What can I say? It's a slow day, and this is way more fun than updating the charts . . .

I remember my prom, for instance. I was a vision in daffodil yellow. I had a daisy corsage. My date's name was Peter . . . or—wait. Was it Stanley? At any rate—he looked just like a young Robert Redford (if you're too young to know what that means, then take my word for it, Redford was HOT). It was perfect . . .

Well, perfect until my date—was it Mike?—decided Prom Night was the perfect night to come out of the closet. So he ditched me for the DJ. Which would have been fine, actually—except that they took the limo and left me stranded alone at the prom in my daffodil dress. Had to call a cab to get home from my own prom.

Yeah—now that I think about it, prom kinda sucked.

Seattle Grace Prom Stories:

Izzie Stevens

"Most Comfortable in a Floor-Sweeping Ball Gown"
Oh wow. I loved prom. My date was the quarterback of the football team and, well, our school didn't have a ton of money, so we just converted our gym. Lots of balloons and streamers. Very "Pretty in Pink." Had such an amazing time. Really. It was great. It was almost as perfect as tonight's going to be—did I tell you that Denny proposed? He asked me to marry him. Hear that? MARRY HIM. I'm so excited. Bailey totally just kicked me out of his room because—well—I have to come back during visiting hours but, that's OK. Because I am going home, right now, and trying on every dress in my closet until I find the PERFECT dress to come show my new—Oh wow. My fiancé. To show my fiancé, Denny. OK—I have to go. Have to go home and change this MINUTE!

Cristina Yang

"Most Likely to Surprise You with Her Dance Moves at Prom"

Yeah. Mine was a pity–prom date. My mom made me go. With her best friend's dorky-ass son who—I swear—to this day has never been on another real date in his life. But that's not the bad part. I was actually pretty OK with providing the kid with a date to prom. I mean, let's face it—I'm hot. I'm a hot date. I'm a hottie-hot prom date. But once we got to the party, this uber-dork turned into creepy-molester-guy. Totally tried to feel me up— right there! By the punch bowl! In front of the entire school!!! Then he threw up. All over my dress—not because he'd been drinking. NO! But because he was nervous. He'd never been so close to touching a female breast in his life. It was great. Really. Stellar prom. Totally rockin'.

Alex Karev

"Most Likely to Spike the Punch"

I didn't make it to my prom. I had a prom date. I even picked her out one of those flower wrist things. It was in the fridge. The guy at the flower shop said to keep it in the fridge . . . I mean, I wasn't so into the prom thing, but my date was. And I liked the girl, so . . . But I never made it to my prom. My old man—he showed up about the time I was supposed to leave to pick up my date. He hadn't been home in a while—a long while—he looked like crap. Smelled like booze. Wanted to know where my ma was. Wouldn't take my word she was still at work—she had the night shift—so my old man—he started busting things up around the house, and . . . Anyway. I stayed home that night. I never made it to my prom. Never picked up my girl. Never spoke to her again, actually. I guess she just figured I stood her up, and after that, she wanted nothing to do with me. Probably just as well, really. Like I said. I wasn't so into the whole prom thing anyway.

George O'Malley

"Most Likely to Obey Curfew on Prom Night"
I had a nice time at my prom. Well—until the end. See, my date? She was cooler than I was—in fact, I was a little surprised when I asked her and she said yes. But she did, so I was psyched. Went all out—got my dad's car for the night; I even rented the most expensive tux I could afford. It was going to be a wonderful night. And it was, like I said. Until the end . . . Because, well. There was this after-party we were supposed to go to—at the school. A lock-in. It was going to be a blast—and it meant I'd get to spend the WHOLE night hanging out with this really cool girl that I really really liked, only . . . As we were driving to the lock-in, she asked me to swing by the local college instead. Turns out, she wanted me to drop her off—at her college BOYFRIEND'S dorm room!!! On Prom Night. OUR Prom NIGHT!!! So . . . I did. I dropped her off. I even waited to make sure she got in the door OK because—well, just because. That's what I did. And I don't really want to talk about it anymore right now, OK?

Callie Torres

"Most Likely Wouldn't Be Caught Dead at Prom"
What are you talking about? I totally went to prom. Stag. Screw the whole wait for some stupid boy to ask you just to have him try and cop a feel first chance he gets crap. No way. I went to prom solo, on purpose. Picked out the sexiest dress I could find. Fire engine red. Got to the party. Made a fashionably late entrance. Stepped out onto the dance floor, and—I danced. Danced like there was no tomorrow—and let me just say. It was seriously fun. Especially when everybody ELSE'S dates kept trying to hit on me—yeah, that part was great. But let's face it—even when you're IN high school—high school boys are boring. And short. Not that I mind short guys—I kinda like them, actually, but . . . Anyway. That was my prom. Only—now I have another prom to

go to, don't I? Again. By myself. Because stupid George is acting
like a stupid boy—wow. I guess they never DO outgrow it, do
they? Well, the good news is, I have an equally sexy dress to wear
to this prom. Plus—now that I'm older, I have cleavage to help fill
it out. That's a happy thing. Yay cleavage, that's what I say!

Meredith Grey

"Most Likely Asked Out Her Own Date to Prom"
Please. I wouldn't have gone to my prom if you'd paid me. I was
not the prom-going type. If anything, I was the anti-prom type.
Couldn't be bothered. By the time prom rolled around, I had one
foot out the door—SO ready to graduate and move away, go to
college, get started on my REAL life. Stuff like—prom? It just
wasn't something I was interested in . . . You have to understand.
My mom was always working—working hard. She was very demanding. She had very high expectations for me, her only daughter . . . So I went out of my way to thwart those expectations,
whenever possible. I had pink hair. I listened to REALLY loud
music. I stayed out past curfew. I was kinda a mess . . . and—
well—proms aren't messy. They're sparkly and hopeful and full of
happy people. I don't do so well with . . . happy people. I'm not
sure I trust them, really. Especially people who were happy
enough in high school to be going to prom. I mean—seriously. I
can't even believe I'm going to prom tonight. And with a former
Prom King, no less? I'm going to prom with THAT guy. Wow. I've
come a long way. A long way from my angry pink hair days . . .
only . . . why is it things still feel so messy? Because they do. My
entire world feels extraordinarily messy right now. Why IS that?

Miranda Bailey

"Most Likely Ran the Prom Committee"
Not only did I run the Prom Committee, but I was part of the official Royal Prom Court my senior year. That's right—I wore a
tiara. Don't look at me that way, Debbie. Like you're about to fall

outta your roll-y nurse's station chair. I was INVOLVED in my high school's activities. I gave it my ALL. Because that's what I do. I give things my ALL. My dress was lavender. Beaded. My hair was pulled back in a loosely pinned up-do. My date was tall. I had a good time, and—I mean it. Stop looking at me like that. I was a prom GURU. So shut your mouth and get me the chart for my patient in 2446. NOW!

Preston Burke

"Most Likely to Own His Own Tux"
I do own a tux, actually. In fact I own two tuxes—both are freshly dry-cleaned, hanging in my closet . . . Not that I'll get to wear them tonight. Wish I could. It would be a nice distraction . . . And I would enjoy having the chance to dance with Cristina . . . But you want to know about my high school prom? I don't re-member that much of it—a pretty typical prom, I guess. I just re-member how nervous I was, leading up to the big night. I was worried because—I didn't know how to dance. So, I enlisted the help of my uncle. He had rhythm. And . . . he taught me a few dance moves. Nothing complicated—just a few simple steps. I stayed up nights before the prom, just practicing. Because I wanted to impress my date. I didn't want her to think I was some clumsy idiot or anything, so . . . Anyway, it all worked out. I didn't step on her feet—and she thought I was a wonderful dancer, so . . . Debbie? Thanks, by the way. For stopping by—to visit. I know you're busy with other patients and—well, just wanted you to know I appreciate it. Very much.

Derek Shepherd

"Most Likely a High School Prom King"
Actually—no. I wasn't a Prom King. I did go to several proms—I think I went to one every year—even as a freshman . . . I guess I always knew a lot of senior girls or something? Anyway—I always enjoyed prom. The thing is—I enjoy wearing a tux. I know—most

guys hate them. Think they're uncomfortable, the dress shoes are tight, feel they look too much like a penguin . . . But as for me? I enjoy the tux. Especially now, when I basically live in scrubs, it's nice to have a chance to put on something nice. Something crisp. Something—classic. Anyway, my proms were all very nice. I went with very nice girls, and had a very nice time with each and every one of them. And, no Debbie. I'm not going to get more detailed than that. I'm not going to tell you about getting drunk or getting laid on Prom Night. You want to know why? Because I'm a gentleman. And a gentleman never kisses and tells.

Addison Shepherd

"Most Likely Got Laid on Prom Night"
Ha! I so did NOT get laid on my Prom Night. Oh my—no. Not even close. I was such a band geek back then . . . Went to prom with this skinny kid who couldn't dance to save his life. It was a disaster—you should have seen my dress . . . layer after layer of ruffles . . . Oh yeah. Definitely no sex for me on prom night. I didn't come into my own until well after high school. And well after prom. You know how some girls in high school look 25— and some look their age? Some just look—like kids? Well, that was me. I had braces. The big chunky metal kind. With rubber bands. Colored rubber bands. I wore bands to match my prom dress. THAT'S the kid I was in high school. I mean—seriously. Who'd want to get busy with that?

Instant Message Conversation

DebbieDoesGossip—logged on at 1:55 a.m.

DebbieDoesGossip:	Kill me. Kill me now. I may never walk on these poor tired toes again . . .
JoeKnowsBest:	Enjoyed the prom, I take it?

DebbieDoesGossip:	Prom's still going on! Tell me, who invented high heels? What moron ever decided high heels were the way to go?
JoeKnowsBest:	I'm a little bitter you didn't think to ask ME to the prom, btw . . .
DebbieDoesGossip:	Oh, please. I didn't even plan to stay at the thing—but then I got there . . .
JoeKnowsBest:	And you had a good time.
DebbieDoesGossip:	I did, actually.
JoeKnowsBest:	What's your dress look like?
DebbieDoesGossip:	Silvery and shimmery.
JoeKnowsBest:	Sassy. Tell me you got a prom pic?
DebbieDoesGossip:	Duh—Oh man. It feels GOOD to sit down again. Nice of Olivia to cover my shift for me tonight . . .
JoeKnowsBest:	You've been working hard. You deserved a night off . . .
DebbieDoesGossip:	I did, didn't I? So, did I tell you—Oh. Oh man.
JoeKnowsBest:	What? You can't just "Oh man" me, then quit chatting.
DebbieDoesGossip:	There's bit of a congregation forming, over by the elevators . . .
JoeKnowsBest:	Congregation of what? Handsome men in their tuxes?
DebbieDoesGossip:	Well—yes, actually. McDreamy. McVet—and the Chief. Along with Bailey, and Addison . . .
JoeKnowsBest:	Sounds like a gaggle of very attractive people . . .

DebbieDoesGossip:　It looks serious.

JoeKnowsBest:　Serious how? Oh—speaking of serious . . . did you hear about Denny?

DebbieDoesGossip:　Huh? How would you know anything about— Oh my god.

JoeKnowsBest:　What?

DebbieDoesGossip:　Denny died.

JoeKnowsBest:　So you did hear?

DebbieDoesGossip:　No! I've been at the prom all night, but . . . I'm watching Izzie Stevens, right this moment, sweeping toward me in the most unbelievably beautiful gown with . . . an expression she'd only have if—

JoeKnowsBest:　I'm sorry, Deb. I know he was close to everyone there . . .

DebbieDoesGossip:　I wish you could see her—she looks so . . . Oh no. Oh no no.

JoeKnowsBest:　What?

DebbieDoesGossip:　She just admitted it. She just admitted that she was the one who cut Denny's LVAD wires.

JoeKnowsBest:　Oh, Izzie . . .

DebbieDoesGossip:　And—no. I couldn't have heard her right.

JoeKnowsBest:　Heard her what?

DebbieDoesGossip:　Heard her quit. Joe, she quit. Izzie Stevens just . . . quit the surgical program.

DebbieDoesGossip—logged out at 2:15 a.m.

Beginning of the End . . .

You know those nights when you just can't sleep because your mind is buzzing and buzzing and buzzing? So much buzzing, that eventually you just give up, get out of bed, and fix yourself something to drink?

This is one of those nights.

Plus, I'm nursing my swollen, blistered, post-prom damaged feet. As cute as my silver sling-backs are, they are definitely NOT designed for dancing.

But that's not what my mind's on tonight. I got home from the hospital HOURS ago, and I still can't get over EVERYTHING that's happened.

Burke was shot. Shepherd performed nerve surgery—and there's no guarantee Burke will be able to operate again . . . It's nuts. How can you go from being a powerhouse surgeon to a patient with questionable hand function, practically—overnight?

I stopped by Burke's room tonight, before heading home, and noticed Cristina was there—in her prom dress. Just standing by his bed. Holding his hand . . . They weren't speaking. They were just . . . there.

It was lovely and sad all at the same time. I hope Cristina is able to stand by Burke through this. Because something tells me . . . there will be a lot more for him to overcome . . .

Joe tells me there's something going on with Callie Torres. Apparently she opened up to George, spilled her heart to him, and . . . he hasn't been able to reciprocate. Which always stings.

But that's not the only thing . . . According to Joe, Callie witnessed something tonight. Walked in on two—unnamed—individuals getting busy in one of the exam rooms during prom.

Now, it couldn't have been just ANYONE—or else, who cares, right? Certainly, there's no reason Callie would pay any attention, unless . . . Joe's convinced it must have been Meredith and Derek, but I don't know. Surely they wouldn't be willing to take that kind of step—after all they've been through this year? They really want to go there? Like that?

Then again—there was definitely something going on between them when I was paged away tonight. Paged away to—and this is the really heartbreaking part—to help Olivia prep Denny's body for transport to the morgue.

That's the image that's really been haunting me tonight. The one I can't quit seeing when I close my eyes. And what's funny is that, it's not even something I witnessed in person. It's what Olivia described to me—about Izzie, sprawled in her beautiful rose-colored prom dress, across Denny's bed.

Izzie wouldn't leave him. He was dead, and she was there, and—she just wouldn't leave. She COULDN'T leave. Until Alex—that's right—Alex was able, finally, to coax her away. He scooped her—petticoats and all—into his arms, and lifted her away from the bed. And then he just held her there. While she cried. In his arms.

Oh wow. Now I'm crying again. And I thought I'd managed to cry myself out hours ago.

So Izzie quit the program tonight. She took responsibility for the Denny situation, and then . . . she quit. Just like that. Said she isn't a surgeon. That she CAN'T be a surgeon.

And then she walked out. Her skirts rustled down the steps as she left, with Alex and George in tow . . . Which brings me right back to . . .

Meredith. Caught between Finn—who stepped up—immediately sensing she needed to go home and be with Izzie. He wanted to help Meredith, to take her home, and—

Then there was Derek. Standing beside her—with eyes, not for Izzie. Not for his wife. But—for Meredith. I saw the whole thing. He didn't move. He just tilted his head, in that signature McDreamy way, and—quietly said Meredith's name.

It was so subtle, I almost didn't hear it at all, but . . .

It was clear. She was definitely torn between those two men, standing there in their tuxes.

So maybe something DID happen between Meredith and Mc-Dreamy tonight? Maybe Meredith DOES have a choice to make here . . . Maybe . . .

Like I said, my head is buzzing. With all sorts of questions and no easy answers. Most of all, I know I should sleep, as I've got the early shift in the morning, and I know I'll be regretting this late-night blogging the minute my alarm goes off in just a few hours . . .

So, this is Nurse Debbie. Signing off for now, sure to be back very soon with more of your very favorite, very juicy Seattle Grace Gossip.

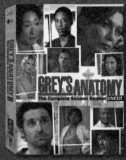
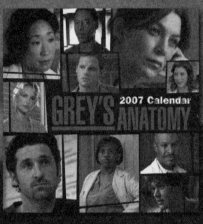